An Artless Murder

by

Sydney Abrams

An Arts and Crafts Mystery

An Artless Murder

Cover Art by *Tina Lynn Stout*

The Wild Rose Press, Inc.
PO Box 708
Adams Basin, NY 14410-0708
Visit us at www.thewildrosepress.com

Publishing History
First Edition, 2025
Trade Paperback ISBN 978-1-5092-6258-8
Digital ISBN 978-1-5092-6259-5

An Arts and Crafts Mystery
Published in the United States of America

Dedication

I'm just a small cog in the wheel that makes all of this possible—starting with my husband, who still encourages me to spend my time living in my imagination. I'm also incredibly grateful to Eilidh, my editor, who's been with me from book to book and yet she still returns my emails. And then there's Charlie, our big, scruffy dog, who keeps me company and provides a soundtrack of soft snores as I write—unless I read aloud during editing, in which case he leaves in a huff.

Please note that while I did delve into some research to ensure that certain parts of the story were treated with the care they deserved, *Flat Rock Falls*, its characters, and everything within the pages of this book are entirely fictional and a result of my imagination run amok. Any blunders in procedure are mine and mine alone.

Chapter 1

Friday

I arrived at the Main Street Café early, before the local rush, and easily slid into a parking spot. The happy jingle of the bell on the door welcomed me, and I was immediately enveloped in the intoxicating aroma of bacon, eggs, hashbrowns, and toast, the staple diner breakfast my aunt Claudia had been serving for almost forty years. I spotted my cousin Jack hunched over his plate at the end of the counter and hopped onto the stool next to him.

"Morning! What brings you here so early?"

He took a bite of toast and answered while chewing. "Since I'm going to be volunteering for you at the Workshop later, I'm heading to the precinct early. I didn't want to wake Annie, so I'm grabbing breakfast here. How about you?"

"I'm picking up a tray of goodies for all you volunteers."

Aunt Claudia swung through the kitchen door and called over to me, "We're not quite ready for you yet, Alex."

"No worries, I'm early," I said. "Maybe I'll have a little something while waiting."

She grabbed an order pad. "What'll it be?"

Aunt Claudia didn't have to wait on customers anymore, but she said it kept her young to be busy and bustling around, so within minutes she deposited a plate with a bacon biscuit sandwich in front of me. A little later, Jack and I were joking around about who could shovel their food faster, and I noticed her staring at us.

"What?" I asked, looking down at my shirt. "Did I dribble?"

"No," she said. "I'm just looking at you two. Peas in a pod, just like when you were kids."

My mom and I had spent many holidays here, so Jack and I grew up together and were close, like siblings. Since losing my mom, Aunt Claudia had effortlessly taken on the mantle of a mother figure, which warmed me to my core.

"Are you getting sentimental in your old age?" I teased.

I couldn't believe it, but her eyes grew misty behind her old-fashioned bifocal glasses. "Maybe. I'm just very proud of both of you."

"Aw, Mom," Jack said, grinning at her.

"Hey, I'm allowed. You followed in your father's footsteps, and Alex, you picked up and left a big-time career. That takes guts."

"Well, I sort of fled my old life," I said, with a laugh.

"Yeah, you did." Jack guffawed.

I left the chaotic life of a political strategist and moved to Flat Rock Falls to open the Creative Workshop, a collective for artists. Three years later, the Workshop now housed over a dozen artist studios, a gift shop, a gallery, and we had also become a community hub for classes in every art form imaginable. I had minored in art history in college, so this wasn't as much of a leap as it seemed, although it was a night and day lifestyle change.

Aunt Claudia was growing impatient with our smart-aleck reaction to her sudden onset of emotion. "Geez, try and give a compliment," she said as an aside.

I held up my crossed fingers. "Hopefully your compliments are well-placed, and everything will go off without a hitch for our grand opening of the sculpture garden."

She gave my hand a quick slap. "This is stuff you can do in your sleep, and you know it."

Janice, one of the Café's long-time waitresses, emerged from the kitchen holding a large tray with a lid. "Here ya go, Alex. Brownie bites, macaroons, peanut butter and chocolate chip cookies, grapes, bananas, and strawberries."

"Gee, you got all of your favorites," Jack said, sarcastically.

I slid off the stool and hoisted my bag onto my shoulder before grabbing the tray. "And why not? There might be leftovers."

Aunt Claudia had moved on to another customer, so Jack lowered his voice and asked, "Any more issues in the building?"

"Nothing else so far, and even the social media snarks have gone silent."

The Workshop had recently become the target of some petty pranks and a negative social media campaign.

"Okay. Just keep me posted."

"You know I will, but I'm thinking, or I should say, hoping, whoever's behind it has grown bored and moved on."

"Perhaps, but I wouldn't count those chickens yet."

"Bwrak, bwrak," I squawked as I walked toward the door. Aunt Claudia heard my chicken impersonation and simply cocked an eyebrow before returning to her customer.

Back at the Workshop, I dropped the bakery box in the small kitchen off the lounge and went through the double doors out to the courtyard. A verbal tug of war was going on between my two part-time staffers, Maggie and Ryan, who were working on the craft tent setup. I lingered a moment to see if they could work this out on their own or if they would need my intervention.

"Yeah, but if we start the line there, we'll end up too close to the garden," Maggie insisted, putting her hand on her hip. Her small stature was no match for her spunky personality, and anyone who thought her multicolored hair and funky glasses indicated a flighty mind would be sorely mistaken. Plus, being a professional photographer, she had an eye for detail, so I rarely questioned her opinion on such matters.

"I see what you're saying, but we have to leave enough lawn space for the Movie on the Green," Ryan countered, brushing his sandy hair from his forehead in frustration. Ryan's tall, lanky physique hid the finely honed muscles of a sculptor, and his boyish good looks and affable personality made him a joy to be around, usually. Occasionally, he could be like an overly rambunctious puppy.

"What do you think, Alex?" Maggie called over to me.

As I walked toward them, the dew from the grass created dark stains on the toes of my work boots. Nothing made me crankier than heat plus humidity, and I hoped the morning sun would lead us into a dry, breezy summer day. I would need all the bonhomie I could muster as we approached the grand opening.

"Here's what we're going to do," I said, swinging out my hands to point like an airline stewardess. "Let's mark off two arcs for the arts and crafts booths. This will leave a wider open area in the center, and the arc will give each booth a little breathing room." I grabbed the can of spray chalk and walked to a spot ten feet in from the boundary line and marked it with an X.

"We need about six feet between booths, so let's mark the other side at around eighty-five feet." Ryan took the can from me, used his stride to count off the space, and then marked another X on the opposite side.

Maggie nodded in approval. "I think if we start putting up the canopies, we can gauge how far back to make the arc."

"Good idea." I walked over to the piles of canopies Ryan had brought down from the storage room and said, "I'll help distribute these, and then I'll leave you guys to it."

"Thanks, Mom," Maggie said, in the mocking tone of a moody teenager.

Ryan laughed, and I shot them both a look, then broke into a grin as I made my way to the courtyard doors. The truth was, I loved being surrounded by their youthful exuberance, even if I often felt like a den mother.

On the way to the front desk, I looked up and down both hallways. The building now felt lived in, and a creative energy mingled with the scents of paint, clay, stone, textiles, and photography chemicals. If I could, I would bottle that aroma and wear it as a perfume.

Our new glass-enclosed gift shop was tucked to the left of the central staircase. It was dark now, but later, when open for business, the track lighting would reflect off all the surfaces like a beacon drawing you in to a world of artistry.

I didn't feel like being cooped up in the office, so I decided I would go mobile and take my laptop outside. But first, I needed another cup of coffee. It was my third, but who was counting? I jogged up the stairs and took a left to enter my apartment, a private sanctuary I had carved out during the renovations of the old two-story brick school building.

Baxter, my big, scruffy dog, jumped down off the couch and greeted me with enthusiasm as we walked in tandem to the kitchen.

When my coffee finished brewing, I asked, "Do you want to come down with me?"

He responded by bounding over to the door.

Back in the courtyard, I let him pick the table and then we settled in. I worked while he kept a watchful eye on the Workshop grounds. He was on high alert for rogue chipmunks and squirrels.

Later, Maggie came over and plopped herself down across from me. "The canopies are set, so you can check them and let us know if you want anything shifted one way or another."

As I finished typing, I said, "It's looking pretty good to me. I think you guys did a great job."

"Thanks. I'm worried, though, that we won't get everything done in time for the patron and volunteer reception on Wednesday." Maggie's eyes scanned the garden and her face scrunched up. "There's still so much to do!"

"Relax, it all feels a bit chaotic right now, but actually, everything is well in hand, and we're right on schedule."

"I know you're right because you know what you're doing with this stuff, but it still just looks like a mess to me. Do we know if the path lights are working now?"

"We'll check them out tonight." I shifted in my chair to face her head on. "You're being a nervous Nelly about this, which is not like you. What's really going on?"

Maggie pursed her lips. "I think it's the uncertainty with the recent harassment. Have you looked at our socials today?"

"I'm not sure I would call it harassment. That's a bit extreme. And no, I haven't. I don't want to look," I said, and picked up my coffee as a means of procrastination.

"You're going to have to at some point, so you might as well get it over with."

"Might I remind you, I don't like social media on a good day. Why don't you check it?" I suggested.

"Oh, all right. Give me your laptop, it'll be easier on there," she said, reaching across the table.

Over the last month, the social media smears and the odd things happening in and around our building, such as someone pulling out all the garden lights, were mostly just an aggravation. However, there was the underlying question of *why* we had become a target, but I hadn't voiced that concern to Maggie yet.

"They've struck again," she said with a sigh.

I steeled myself. "Let's hear it."

"Okay, here goes. It says, 'The Creative Workshop is a sham. The art is mass-produced and overpriced. You can't just cover the *Made in China* label and claim it's a one-of-a-kind piece of art. Buyer beware.' "

"You are kidding me! Let me see that."

Maggie slid the computer over to me. "Alex, you know responding to this kind of stuff doesn't help matters."

"Well, this one is easy," I snapped. After pulling my reading glasses down from the top of my head, my fingers tapped out a quick response. Before posting it, I read it aloud to Maggie. "Our artists have impeccable reputations, and as always, the public is welcome to visit the Creative Workshop to see them in action."

"That sounds fine. But what are we going to do to stop this?"

I clicked the button to post the response. "I don't think there's anything we can do. I'm sure this is a made-up username, but I'll dig into it anyway."

"Who has this much time on their hands? I mean, don't people have better things to do than anonymously mess with people online?"

"You'd be surprised, which is kind of depressing to think about. Anyway, I'm keeping Jack in the loop, and I'll go over it at the garden meeting later. Otherwise, it's out of our control, so we can't let it take over our head space." I closed the laptop and stood up. "Come on, let's go walk the garden before the volunteer crew gets here."

Maggie, Baxter, and I left the courtyard and strolled into the garden, where the stunning sculptures by our artists Elliott and Ryan would take center stage. We had immersed ourselves in the research on the varieties of trees, shrubs, and flowers that would provide the canvas for each sculpture and were finally able to enjoy the fruits of our labor.

Maggie stopped to smell a fragrant rose. "This is just idyllic. I can't believe how great everything has turned out."

"And we don't have to rely on our thumbs being green!"

Since this would be a community garden, we already had a lengthy volunteer list of avid gardeners ready to help keep it maintained.

"No kidding. I like to photograph them, but I am not into weeding and pruning."

I looked at her long fingernails, each painted a different color to match the streaks of colors in her hair, and laughed. "I would imagine not. I actually like grubbing around in the dirt every once in a while."

She looked at my paint-stained jeans, work boots, and haphazard ponytail. "I would imagine so."

We continued on in a companiable silence. Even though Maggie was young—early thirties compared to my late forties—we just clicked, and our bond had deepened this past winter when we narrowly escaped the hand of a killer. This shared experience, and the subsequent time coming to terms with it, gave us a unique soul friendship.

The slamming of car doors caught my attention. "Sounds like they're here. I'll wrangle the volunteers, and you can go on and get some of your own work done."

"Okey doke, thanks. I'll take Baxter over to his fenced area. His doggy door is open, right?"

"It is."

Maggie called Baxter, then wound around the path to open the fence gate, and I retraced my steps and took the sidewalk to the parking lot.

"Good morning!" I called out.

Bert, from the Garden Gate Nursery, closed the doors of his van and rolled a cart full of annuals onto the sidewalk. "Hi, Alex. It's a beautiful morning to do some gardening, isn't it?"

"It sure is. Thanks again for all your help. I could

not have planned this garden without you."

Bert was tall and sinewy, with weather-worn skin on his face and forearms from his many years working outside, and his eyes crinkled as he smiled. "Oh, it's my pleasure. I'm looking forward to bringing my lunch and unwinding on one of your benches."

"I plan to take a coffee break out here now and then, too," Penny said, walking up to us.

Penny had recently been appointed manager of the Bennet House Mansion at Bennet Park, which was a short walk from the Workshop.

"I can't imagine you'll have much free time on your hands since you're now running the Bennet House," I said.

"Oh, I'll be able to sneak away now and then. That's the joy of being the boss, " she said with a wink.

Tucker approached, looking more like he was ready to board a yacht than work in the garden, with a polo shirt over cream-colored khakis and boat shoes with no socks. "Good morning, ladies, Bert," he said, tipping his straw hat.

"Hi, Tucker," I said. "Do you need some coveralls and wellies? I'd hate for you to get dirt on those duds."

"I'm afraid I can't stay long. I have a meeting I must attend, but I thought I'd drop by to go over the layout again."

"Okay, sure. We'll let Bert have the final word, though, since he's the expert."

I had only recently met Tucker when the volunteers started working on the garden. He had proven to be an enthusiastic helper, but he was also very opinionated about where things should go and tended to assert those opinions with some tenacity.

"Yes, of course. Come on, Bert, I'll show you what I'm thinking." He started toward the garden path, leaving Bert no choice but to follow.

I waited as more of the crew arrived: Daisy, the high school senior who worked in our gift shop, her friend Luke, and Jack and Diego.

Diego, a textile artist who had already made a name for himself with his exquisite wall hangings, was our newest addition to the Workshop. He started out a little shy, but was already showing a willingness to throw himself into whatever was going on at the Workshop, and via the softball league, he and Jack had become fast friend.

The next to arrive was Winifred. She owned the Celebration Emporium on Main Street, a shop that sold everything from party supplies and greeting cards to ornaments and candles. Winifred had lived in Flat Rock Falls her whole life, so she was the one to ask if you wanted to know something about Flat Rock or anyone who lived in it. However, she was also known as the town's busybody. She loved to gossip and would often ask nosy questions, which often bordered on inappropriate.

She considered herself an artist in her own right, and I had to let her down gently when she wanted to put some of her things in our new shop. Fortunately, I was able to honestly say that our gift shop was only for Workshop artists.

I wasn't being snobby. I fully supported amateur artists; heck, I considered myself to be one most of the time, especially compared to the professionals at the Workshop. But people who made claims of grandeur and shamelessly self-promoted could be a bit exhausting.

She had enthusiastically volunteered to help in the garden, though, so I made an effort to make her feel welcome.

"Hi, Winifred, I'm so glad you could come out today," I said.

"Sorry I'm late! I got sidetracked with my latest masterpiece. It's part of a series I'm doing, and it has many secret layers to it," she said theatrically. Her stacked hairstyle with a trendy lavender rinse reflected the sunlight like a halo, creating an interesting contrast to her personality.

"That sounds intriguing. You must tell me all about it," Diego interjected. He led her away from the parking lot, looking over his shoulder to give me a quick smile.

As the group drifted toward the garden, I tugged Jack's sleeve. "Hold up a sec."

"What's up?"

I waited until everyone was out of earshot. "We got another one."

"Sabotage or social media?"

"Social media."

"Have you tried to trace who it is?"

"Not yet. Just saw it before you guys arrived."

"Hmm." The muscle in his jaw tensed as he stared off in the distance. "Let's go sit down."

I checked to make sure the volunteer crew was well in hand, then we moved to the courtyard. "I kind of hoped whoever was behind this had moved on, but I guess they're not done yet. I just can't figure out why someone would be targeting us."

"I know I've asked you this already, but have you had any interactions that would qualify as contentious? You know you can sometimes be a bull in a china shop."

He winked at me to confirm this was a gentle ribbing.

I didn't even bother to feign indignance. "No! That's the crazy thing about this. We are fully immersed in the community, and the artists are all happy. I keep racking my brain, but I can't think of anyone I've had problems with."

"Well, clearly someone is not happy. What about the building? Has anything else happened?"

"Only what I've already told you. The rag stuffed in the sink drain with the water left running, pulling out the path lights, some of the garden pots turned over, and similar minor stuff. The sink thing could have been costly, but we caught it quickly, so no damage was done."

"It mostly sounds like pranks, but coupled with the social media campaign, this is leaning toward a more calculated effort."

"I know. That's becoming a concern."

Jack leaned back in the chair. "Look, as you also know, there's nothing we can do when there's no evidence to identify who's doing this. Plus, the rag in the sink could have been an accident, and the stuff in the garden doesn't really meet the threshold for misdemeanor vandalism. The lights were pulled out, but not cut or damaged, and the pots weren't broken. So step up your security, talk to everyone, and keep your eyes open."

"That's the plan."

"You've talked this over with Walter, right?"

Walter had started out as a friend and benefactor of the Workshop. Recently, our friendship had grown in a new direction and we'd become something of an item, although it was a long-distance relationship, which suited us both just fine. I had already been married once, and while the split had been amicable, I wasn't eager to jump into a full-time relationship just yet.

"Of course," I answered. "Walter says the front and back door cameras aren't enough, and he wants me to get security cameras to cover more of the building and grounds. But I'm just not comfortable with the message that sends, like, 'If you come to the Workshop, you will be watched.' It's just creepy. I came here to get away from the gritty realities of life."

"Sorry, but I'm siding with Walter on this one. Why wait until something bigger happens? So please give it a good think. When is he coming back to town?"

"He's in London right now, but he'll be here for the grand opening."

Jack stood up. "Okay. In the meantime, keep mulling over if someone could be reacting to something you didn't think was a big deal. With these kinds of things, it could be a student, so think through everyone who comes into this building."

"I will. My gut is telling me it's just kids with too much time on their hands."

"Let's hope so. I'm keeping my eye out for any new reports about this kind of stuff happening elsewhere in town, but so far, you seem to be it. In the meantime, I'm going to go help get those benches set."

"Okay, thanks. I'll come join you guys in a minute."

I watched Jack saunter over to where Diego was working on a bench. The more I thought about it, the more I was sure there was nothing to worry about. We read every day about cyberbullying and minor vandalism, so it shouldn't be surprising it would strike here, even in our quaint little hamlet. No one was immune, and it was only a matter of time before whoever was doing this would grow bored and move on to their next target. At least that's what I told myself.

Chapter 2

Before returning to the garden, I rolled the cooler with drinks from the kitchen to the courtyard and put the tray of treats on one of the nearby tables. Out of the corner of my eye, I caught Bert and Tucker having an animated conversation at the edge of the property.

"How's it going over here?" I asked, approaching them.

Bert looked exasperated, but he kept an even tone as he said, "We're just discussing how far toward the tree line we should go with the benches and potted plants."

"I think it would be lovely for people to be able to sit under the trees, looking at the garden and building from this side, don't you?" I asked.

"I do, and it's natural shade, too, but Tucker doesn't agree."

"What don't you like about it?" I asked Tucker.

"I just think the stand of trees should be preserved as is. And it adds to the maintenance in general. I strongly feel we should just focus on the sculpture garden and not do anything over here."

From my past life in politics, I found when people dug their heels in for no significant reason, it usually meant there was something else behind it. I scanned the landscape and landed on what I thought might be the cause of his resistance. Tucker's house was behind the tree line.

"Are you concerned people might wander onto your property, or that we could do something which would change the outlook from your house?" I asked.

Tucker hemmed and hawed. "Um, well—"

I quickly added, "Yours is not the only house bordering the Workshop's property, so if you have an issue, we should talk about it." I refrained from saying I wished he had voiced his concerns sooner. I did not like last-minute problems.

Tucker looked embarrassed. "If I'm being honest, you're right. Sasha and I want to maintain our privacy, and she's worried people might wander around in the woods and even onto our property. I'm not as concerned, but I do have to admit she has a point."

"Fair enough. Bert, what do you think?"

He pushed his cap back and scratched his forehead. "Well, for one thing, we don't need to clearcut anything. You won't lose any of your privacy or view anyway, because your houses are too far away. We can put a few benches in front of the tree line and just do a bed of mulch to protect the ground, which is low maintenance. People wandering around onto private property is more in your area of responsibility, Alex. The Workshop land goes beyond the tree line, so what do you propose?"

My wheels were spinning, trying to come up with a viable solution to a problem we should have anticipated, or at least my insurance company should have mentioned when I added the garden to our policy.

"Whether we put the benches back here or not, we need to make sure no one trespasses onto the adjacent properties. A fence isn't the answer. There's an aesthetic issue, particularly if it's chain-link. Plus, it would be cost prohibitive to do something substantial enough to be effective. A four-foot fence can easily be climbed."

Bert added, "And you don't really want metal signs nailed to the trees that say No Trespassing."

I had an idea. "You know what? Let me talk to Ryan. He and Elliott work with power tools all the time, so maybe they can make some artsy signs we can stake into the ground."

Bert nodded. "That could work. What do you think?" he asked, looking at Tucker.

"I guess so," he agreed, reluctantly. "And you'll not disturb the woods?"

"Nope. They'll remain untouched," Bert answered.

"Okay then, we have a plan," I said, with a calculated enthusiasm to end the discussion. With that crisis averted, I moved on to check the progress of everyone else.

Daisy and her friend Luke were talking in hushed voices while they dug holes for the annuals, and I saw the telltale signs of a budding romance as they kept sneaking looks at each other.

"This is coming along quickly!" I cheered.

Daisy shifted on her heel to face me from her squat. "It is. And it's easier than I thought it would be."

Luke added, "Yeah, we're digging the holes, and then they come behind and fill them with the flowers." He pointed toward Penny and Winifred.

"No wonder you're making fast progress; you have an assembly line going. And Luke, thank you for joining us today."

"Sure! I would be bored just sitting around the house."

"Miss Alex?" Daisy asked, shyly. "Would it be okay if Luke hangs out with me when I open the gift shop this afternoon?"

"I don't see why not. As long as you're attentive if a customer comes in."

"I promise," she said earnestly, before she and Luke looked at each other and giggled.

Oh my gosh, these two were so adorable. I envied their youth and innocence, and the wonder that came with it. But then again, would I want to relive my high school days? No way.

I meandered down the path to where Penny and Winifred were putting the annuals in the newly dug holes.

Penny stood up and stretched her back. "It's coming along! We should be done with the bulk of it by the end of the weekend, don't you think?"

"I believe you're right," I said. "Do you guys need any water? I've got some on ice in a cooler."

"Oh yes, thank you," Winifred said.

I went and grabbed a couple bottles of ice-cold water and brough them back. Winifred was now upright and doing some stretches.

"All the squatting gets harder as you get older," she lamented.

"No joke," I agreed. "Stop whenever you need to. We can get the young'uns to do this if need be." I gestured toward Daisy and Luke.

"Oh, it's good for us," Penny said, with conviction.

Winifred looked at Luke and said, in a stage whisper, "Let's just hope he doesn't turn out like his father."

I raised my eyebrows.

"Luke Sr. was a troublemaker when he was young, and I heard from Fran down at the bank that he's been overdrawn a number of times. He's a mechanic over in Pine Brook, you know. Probably rips everyone off."

Penny was aghast. "Winifred!"

I didn't hold back. "I really don't care for this kind of gossip. Luke has been nothing but nice and respectful, and I like him. And making unsubstantiated claims against his father is inappropriate. Frankly, Fran could, and should, be fired for relaying people's banking details, so you should not be repeating it."

"Oh, all right, no harm intended," she said, without remorse. "When you grow up in a small town, you get accustomed to everyone knowing your business, but you wouldn't know that because you're not from here."

"Geez, Winifred. Are you intending to sound offensive?" Penny asked, crossing her arms.

"Not at all! Alex has done wonderful things here, and of course, she has family here. Claudia is a beloved fixture in this town, and Jack serves and protects, so no slight intended."

"Thank you," I said, with uncertainty.

She reached out to pat my hand. "And don't you worry about not having my artwork in your shop. Eva Beaumont and I are hatching a plan to open a small art gallery with artist studios in Pine Brook. She's going to call it *Le Bon Artiste.* That's French."

"Well, isn't that something. I wish you both every success," I said nicely, although in my head I was thinking something very different. I guessed she was telling me I might have some competition.

Penny gave me a look that said a thousand words, but only said, "We better get back to work or we'll never get this done. Thanks for the water, Alex."

I reached out and took their empty bottles. On my

way to the recycle bin, I saw Bitsy and JJ had arrived and were busy raking some mulch on the courtyard side of the garden. Along with Annie, these two were my closest gal pals in Flat Rock. They were both Workshop artists and had recently transitioned to full-time professionals.

JJ, a retired musician, was a free spirit, and her art reflected it. Her painting style was bold. She said after living the disciplined life of a symphony musician, she now liked to break all the rules. She managed to do this in an intelligent and cohesive way, though, which meant her pieces were big sellers.

Bitsy was a painter and watercolorist, but basically, whatever she touched turned into art. Her style was more rooted in nature and centered around birds and whimsical animals. This love of nature inspired her to develop a line of elaborate hats and fascinators. Most of these were also avian-themed. It didn't take long to feel it was perfectly normal for her to have a bird perched somewhere on her head. Her work had developed a following, particularly in the avant-garde circles, and she now had rather robust online sales.

These two friends also made exquisite jewelry, and today, Bitsy had swapped her fancy headgear for a ballcap with an enameled pin of three birds in flight.

"Hey! I didn't know you guys were coming," I said, walking up to them.

Bitsy turned toward me. "We figured we'd pitch in and help before the garden meeting."

"We thought Annie might be out here, too," JJ added.

The lounge door clanged open, catching my attention. "Speak of the devil, here she comes."

"We hoped you might join us," Bitsy called to her.

"I saw y'all through my studio window and thought I'd come say hi," Annie said, with a tinge of the Southern accent that lingered from childhood.

"You're not going to stay and join the fun?" JJ asked.

I laughed, looking at Annie. "I wouldn't count on it. I've known her since college, and she does *not* like to get dirty." Annie also happened to be married to Jack, so I guess that made her my cousin-in-law.

"I should have realized," Bitsy said, scrutinizing her. "She manages to never get even a speck of paint on her hands or clothes."

Annie was a highly regarded photorealism painter, which required a meticulous eye and an unwavering patience. She was also a bit of a germaphobe, so digging in the dirt was definitely not her thing, but in the rest of her life she was a lovable twirl of chaos.

"All right!" Annie said, with good humor. "I can't help it if I don't like to get in the muck. Plus, my shoes are so cute, and they go perfectly with my outfit!" She held out a foot clad in a bright green wedge sandal.

"Those are cute," JJ concurred.

"How's everything going with the garden prep?" she asked.

"It's really coming together," I said. "I've only had to put out a couple of fires, and other than Winifred testing my patience, everyone has been great."

"What's she done now?" Annie asked.

"She was gossiping, as usual, and then, get this, she told me she's partnering with Eva Beaumont to open an art gallery with studios in Pine Brook. I think she told me about it just to rub my nose in it—sort of a retaliation for not including her pieces in our gift shop."

"You're kidding!" Annie exclaimed.

"Nope. But if I'm being mature about it, this whole region is full of artists, so good for them. I imagine Eva will run a great gallery." Eva came from money, and she was an avid collector.

JJ and Bitsy looked at each other as if transmitting a secret message.

"What?" I asked.

JJ answered, "We were going to talk to you about this at another time, when you weren't so busy, but Winifred actually approached us about moving our studio to Pine Brook."

"She's trying to poach you?" I hissed.

Bitsy patted the air with her palm. "Calm down. We, of course, told her we were happy here and had no intention of leaving."

"She didn't ask me," Annie said, disconcerted at being left out.

JJ said, "Well, she's not going to ask you. You and Alex are family. She wouldn't dare approach you."

"It still would have been nice to be asked," Annie said. When I crossed my arms and scowled at her, she hastily added, "I mean, of course I would shoot her down immediately. You don't think she's gone after anyone else, do you?"

I broke into a cold sweat thinking about the prospect of losing my artists. "I have no idea. This is the first I'm hearing about it."

"Well, don't worry. No one is going to be interested. Everyone loves it here," Bitsy said.

Don't worry. Yeah, right. My list of things to worry about seemed to be growing.

****

Later, when I left the office behind the front desk to go to the lounge for the garden meeting, I was greeted by a cacophony of voices from halfway down the hall. The old school cafeteria was renovated to create a large lounge, with a small galley kitchen at the back for our artists to use and for catering events.

"Hi, everyone! Let's get this ball rolling," I said, walking to the front of the room. "I'll be as quick as possible so you can get back to work."

After we went through the logistics of who was doing what for the garden, the craft booths, the load-in of the sculptures, and the volunteer/patron reception, I tackled the sabotage. "Okay, as you guys are aware, we've been the target of some unpleasant social media smears and on-site pranks. Does anyone have anything new to report, suggestions, or any questions or concerns?"

Spencer, a professional painter, and part of my circle of friends, piped up first. "Do you know where the social media campaign is coming from?"

"Not yet. I'm working on it, though."

"I think we should keep our studios locked," he added.

Grumbles of displeasure reached my ears, and I said, "Look, I know we've become accustomed to the carefree atmosphere here at the Workshop, but I agree with Spencer. Even though the so-called pranks have mostly been outside in the garden area, there was the issue with the kitchen sink, which means someone was in the building. Has anyone had anything happen in their studios?"

When no one spoke up, I said, "Good. Let's keep it that way. Keep an eye out, and if you see anything suspicious, let me know right away. And please, try not to engage with whomever this is on social media. If we just ignore them, I'm sure they will grow bored and move on."

Many of the artists lingered after the meeting to continue chatting, but eventually, the room cleared out, and after I straightened the chairs, I went upstairs to my apartment. It was time to track down the social media bandit.

From my days in the political world, I still had access to some hefty software for doing background and research. Previous posters used made-up names and they had no images or personal information listed, and I assumed the one from today would be the same. Since I didn't think this was a professional troll, I hoped the culprit didn't know there was software to help find the IP address where the computer was used. My search might not give a name, but it could narrow down the location.

I made another cup of coffee and grabbed a bag of miniature peanut butter cups before settling in at the kitchen counter. This was my go-to brainpower combo. Baxter stretched out on the couch and his doggy snores provided a soothing soundtrack as my fingers tip-tapped on the laptop keyboard.

Later, he woke with a start when I hissed, "Gotcha!"

The IP address was from the public library in Bennet Park. And even though the posts had different fake names, each time the location was the library. I picked up my phone to call Jack.

Have I mentioned that Jack is the top cop in our little hamlet? Or that after I moved to Flat Rock, Jack cleared me to be a consultant? Believe me, it's not as glamorous as it sounds. Mostly, it was to put my computer skills to good use by lending a hand with mundane office work when he was short-staffed. But we also had battled—my word, not his—a couple of serious crimes, and my problem-solving mind, coupled with his investigative skills, made us a good team. Did I go too far at times? Maybe, but I preferred to think of it as taking initiative. And considering I always volunteered my time, I figured I was allowed some leeway.

When Jack answered, I said, "Hey, so I found out the social media stuff is coming from the library."

"That narrows it down, but from there it's going to be tricky to find out who's behind it," he said, matter-of-factly.

"On Facebook, you can see how long since the person was on, so I got a rough estimate for when the posts were written. I'm going to head over there and see what I can find out, like how many computers they have, who uses them frequently, and if they have cameras."

"Now hold on. You're not going to like this, but you have to tread lightly. These posts don't constitute harassment or threats. There is nothing illegal about posting negative comments, and you can't go in there asking to see video surveillance."

"Oooo, I really hate it when you're right. But if I could find out who's doing it, I could figure out why and what to do about it."

"I understand your frustration, but it doesn't change the facts. Have they all been posted around the same time?"

I looked over the list. "Generally, most are in the morning, like today."

"Okay, look for any patterns, and if you find one,

then you can go and scope out who comes in to use the computers. You might be able to narrow it down."

"That could work," I said, reluctantly.

"Just don't blow this out of proportion and go off half-cocked. I gotta go, but keep me updated."

I sat for a moment after he hung up, indignant at his half-cocked comment. In Jack's absence, I spoke to Baxter. "I'm methodical, a problem-solver. I don't go off half-cocked."

Baxter stared at me as if thinking, *Methinks she doth protest too much.* Or maybe I was just projecting, and his expression actually said, *How long must I wait for a treat?*

Either way, being an impatient person by nature, I really didn't want to wait, so I grabbed my keys and headed to my car.

****

The library, perched on the hill overlooking Bennet Park, offered a bird's-eye view. As I walked from the parking lot toward the building, I couldn't help but take a detour to the patio, which had a great vantage point. At this time of year, the park was scattered with sun-seekers, frisbee throwers, picnickers, and strollers—both the walking and baby kind. The Bennet House mansion sat regally at the end of the pond, which glistened in the sunlight as the ducks glided effortlessly.

In its summer splendor, the park bore no resemblance to the wonders of winter. It seemed bigger without the snow and ice. I still preferred the snow, but I had to admit, with the light summer breeze and the carefree scene below, it was pretty nice.

I entered the library and inhaled deeply. I loved the smell of books, and the memories associated with it of going to the library with my mom. We would eagerly open the book jackets to read the blurbs, accumulating an armload of mystery books to take home. I wanted to scour the shelves for a series I hadn't yet read, but I was on a mission. I looked around for my friend, Lena, the author in residence and head of the children's programming, and spotted her tidying up the lounge area in the children's section.

"Hi, Alex! What brings you in?" she asked cheerily, with her blonde curls bouncing as she walked toward me. Lena's eyes sparkled, like she was always on the brink of laughter, and her infectious personality made her seem younger than her actual age, which happened to change, depending on the situation and who was asking.

"I need to pick your brain. Do you have a minute?"

"Sure, I have story time soon, but until then I'm free. Let's sit down."

I looked around and, not seeing any adult-sized chairs, made the mistake of choosing one of the small beanbag chairs. After toppling over and then righting myself, I clasped my knees and tried to look nonchalant. Lena merely chuckled as she pulled over a pint-sized chair.

"What's up?"

I lowered my voice, and said, "We've been getting hit with some cyber snarkiness, and I traced the IP address to one of the computers here."

Lena's eyes grew wide. "You're kidding, right?"

"I wish I was."

"Wow. I know better than to even ask how you know that, but how can I help?"

I remembered Jack cautioned I couldn't just barrel in and ask to see surveillance tapes, if they even had any, so I kept it casual. "Most of the posts were written in the morning, and I thought maybe you could help me, on the down-low, to figure out who comes in regularly to use the computers, and who might stand out as not a regular. Someone you might not expect. A post actually came in this morning."

Lena's face grew pensive. "I wasn't really paying attention this morning to who was here. Plus, I was out of pocket during the morning kid's group."

I tried not to sound disappointed. "Oh well, it was a long shot."

"Wait, let me think. We have the computer skills class a couple mornings a week, including this morning. We also have a few regular older folks who don't own computers. They like to come in and email when they exchange books. Then there are the moms bringing little ones in, and the students who come in to do research."

"All kids these days have computers, right?"

She nodded. "There's the handful who might not have good internet service and they come to use ours, but most just bring their laptops and study here."

This wasn't going to be as simple as I had hoped. "That means it doesn't necessarily have to be someone using the library computers. It could be someone on a laptop, or even someone sitting in their car in the parking lot using the library Wi-Fi." I felt defeated.

"What timeframe are you looking at?"

"It's been happening over the last month or so. A few have been in the afternoon, but like I said, most have been posted in the morning." An unpleasant thought struck me. "What about anyone from the Workshop? Have you seen any of our gang here?"

"I see a lot of them here checking out books. But I'm

not sure about the computers. I mean, none of them would need ours, would they? And you have good Wi-Fi at the Workshop."

I blew out a sigh. "Well, this was a big waste of your time." I started the flailing struggle, like an upturned crab, to get out of the beanbag. Lena once again chuckled and lent me a hand.

"Geez," I said, "I really need to do some squats."

"Don't we all," she mused. She was walking me out when she stopped short. "Oh, hey, can I ask you a massive favor?"

"Sure!"

"I have to go out of town tomorrow for a seminar. My usual dog sitter just bailed on me. Is there any way Poppy could have a sleepover at your place? It would be for two nights, though, so feel free to say no."

I brightened. "Absolutely. Baxter would love to have a playdate with Poppy."

"Oh, you're the best. Thank you! If it's okay, I'll bring her over tomorrow morning."

"I'll be there. This will be fun!"

Little did I know Poppy's sleepover would set a series of events in motion that would rock my world.

Chapter 3

Saturday

The next morning, Lena arrived with a colorful overnight bag stuffed with Poppy's food and bowl, plus toys, treats, and her favorite blanket. Poppy, a Border collie mix, had pranced into the apartment with great anticipation, and Lena barely had time to unhook her leash before she and Baxter started chasing and playing. They had met each other before at the park, so no introductions were needed.

"Oh," Lena said, as the two tussled on the big leather couch. "I sure hope you don't regret agreeing to do this."

I smiled at their antics. "I'm not concerned. They can go outside and play, and Baxter will really enjoy the company since I'm going to have my hands full with the sculpture garden."

Lena looked hesitant but then gathered her purse and keys and walked toward the door. "Well, okay. Poppy?" she called out. "You be a good girl for Aunt Alex."

Poppy, completely engrossed with Baxter, barely looked up.

After Lena left, I showed Poppy the doggy door, and she and Baxter bounded down the stairs to the fenced-in yard. I then made a cup of coffee to take with me and headed down the central staircase to the front desk, where I found Maggie checking messages.

"Anything important?" I asked.

"Nope. Just inquiries about the fall schedule, and a couple of people letting us know they can't attend class this week."

We had at least two classes each day over the summer, which kept the building hopping. I was worried the social media smear campaign might affect our attendance. "Did it sound like the cancellations were made-up excuses?"

"What do you mean?"

"Like people might be believing the social media stuff."

"Oh, no. I really don't think so. One had a summer cold, and they sounded like it. The other forgot to tell us they were going out of town."

"Okay. Let's keep an eye on this, though. If you notice classes aren't filling for the fall or people are dropping out more, we'll have to come up with a game plan."

Maggie's brow furrowed. "If this affects our business, then it's really going too far. Surely the community knows we're on the up and up."

"Let's hope so." I took my coffee to the office behind the front desk but left the door open so we could talk. "Have you looked at the socials yet this morning?" I asked.

"Yes. Nothing so far."

I sat for a moment, drumming my fingers on the desk. "Maybe I should go over to the library and see who comes in to work on the computers this morning."

Maggie turned to me with a theatrically raised eyebrow. "Do you have a disguise? Maybe a Sherlock Holmes hat and pipe?" She mimicked puffing on a pipe.

"I don't think I need to go that far. I can be

invisible."

"Yeah, right."

I ignored her sarcasm and grabbed my keys. "I'll be back. Please keep an eye out for Bert, okay? He's bringing more plants this morning."

"Will do," she answered. "Happy hunting."

****

I scanned the library to see where I would have a good vantage point of the comings and goings without being too obvious. I chose an armchair in the reading nook with the rack of newspapers and magazines. I had grabbed a magazine and was halfway through the salacious news of various stars when I started feeling like this was a silly escapade. I would occasionally look over the top of the magazine when someone entered, but so far, no one noteworthy had gone to a computer or pulled out a laptop.

Just as I was ready to give up, Daisy entered. No, it couldn't be Daisy. She was too sweet to mess with this kind of thing, but I watched her progress nonetheless. She went to the front desk, and the librarian pointed her to the reference section. A few minutes later, she was back at the front desk checking out a book. As I thought, a purely innocent use of the library.

A tap on my shoulder made me jump clear out of my skin. Ms. Bunkle had used her cane to get my attention.

"What on earth are you up to, Tater Tot?" she asked. Ms. Bunkle had assigned me this moniker soon after we met and had explained she picked the nickname for me because I was small, a little crusty on the outside, but soft on the inside. I didn't even double take anymore when she used it.

"Ms. Bunkle, you startled me! I didn't see you come

in," I hoarsely whispered.

She pulled a chair over and leaned close to me. "I'm not surprised. You look absurd peering over that magazine. And you were fixated on that young girl, Daisy, I think her name is. Now, what are you up to?"

Ms. Bunkle was sharp as a tack. She could be prickly and incredibly forthright, but I liked her a lot, and I kind of wanted to be like her when I reached her age.

I put the magazine down on my lap. "Nothing. I'm just doing a little light reading, and I'm easily distracted," I sing-songed, innocently.

She snorted. "Don't be ridiculous. A gossip magazine? I think not. And you looked like the worst kind of spy peering over the top of it. Don't make me drag it out of you."

I cocked my eyebrow. "You don't miss a thing, do you?"

"Of course not. Now spill it."

"Oh, okay. We've been getting some ugly social media attacks. I traced them to this location, so I thought maybe I would see someone acting suspicious. Or if I got lucky, maybe a post would come in while I was here."

Ms. Bunkle's piercing eyes stared at me for what felt like an eternity but was likely only a few seconds. "I've seen a few of those posts."

"You have? You're on social media?"

"Of course, I am. What do you think? Older people can't be on social media?"

I put my hands up in surrender. "No, you know I don't think like that! I just wouldn't think you'd have the patience for it."

She started ticking off on her fingers. "I'm on group pages for the Bennet House, Bennet Park, the Library, our local Humane Society, the Flat Rock Falls community page and the official city page, and then I have a page dedicated solely for family and close friends, which I keep totally private, so don't even try to friend me. And I'm on your Creative Workshop page. Social media is a great tool to keep up with local news and events. And you'd be surprised how much you can learn about people based on the kinds of things they post."

"You are so clever. See, I have an aversion to social media. I hate it and rarely go on."

"Probably because in your old line of work it was an obligation. You had to monitor it for political business, and for the most part, I would imagine it was simply awful having to read what people posted."

I thought about it. "You're right. It's like an anxiety trigger for me."

"Perhaps in time, the small-town life will fully run through your veins, and you will be able to embrace it."

"Maybe. In the meantime, do you have any thoughts on this smear campaign? Have you seen anyone skulking while using the computers?"

"Skulking? You sure are in cartoon mode this morning. My thoughts? I think like many instances of this kind, the person will get bored and move on to their next target. Unhappy people tend to spread their negativity. As to who I have seen here? There are loads of people. Mostly folks from the senior center and, of course, I've seen a couple of your Workshop people here, including the new fellow, Diego. He has started coming in more frequently. Shelby is often here getting craft books. JJ and Bitsy, of course. They do their story time duo. Daisy comes in with that boy who is clearly in love with her. What's his name?"

"Luke," I said, absentmindedly.

"Yes, that's him."

I thought about the timing, which coincided with the work in the garden. "What about other people from town?" I tried to think of all the garden volunteers and rattled off as many as I could, including Penny, even though I knew she wouldn't be involved in this.

Ms. Bunkle knew most of them and was giving me a rundown on each. She finished with, "Bert is too busy with the garden center, and I doubt he spends his idle time on the computer." Then her face twisted in distaste. "Winifred, though, is an odious creature."

I reared back in surprise. "Ms. Bunkle! That's not very nice."

She tapped her cane. "The truth is the truth, and I tell it like it is. And I don't say anything I wouldn't say to her face. I've known Winifred since she was a child, and she was always what they call a mean girl. She's an information gatherer who loves to gossip, and it's usually mean-spirited. Although, she mellowed a little when she opened her shop on Main Street. She had to be nice to people or her business would suffer. Now she just talks about them behind their backs. Like I said, odious."

"I heard some of her gossip yesterday and told her it was unacceptable."

"Good for you. I've always believed if one keeps silent, they are complicit."

I looked at her with admiration. "I couldn't agree more. What about Tucker? I only met him when we started the final work on the garden."

"He handles some of my investments. Nice enough man. Has a whiff of new money—you know, the ostentatious kind. Big house, and all that. To each his own. His earlier years were tough, so maybe he finds solace in material things." When I cocked my head, she added, "You're aware his wife walked out on him, right?"

This was news to me. "Sasha's his second wife?"

She tilted her head. "Yes, although I'm not even sure they ever got married. It was years ago that his first wife, Eleanor, walked out one day and never came back."

"Oh, how awful! Poor Tucker. What was she like?"

"I always thought she was nice. You'll have to ask your aunt Claudia about her. They were friends. I don't know what happened to make her leave, but it proves the old adage—you don't always know what goes on behind closed doors."

Ms. Bunkle looked up when her friend, Alma, approached us with an armload of books. Alma was the polar opposite of Ms. Bunkle. She had a halo of white hair, delicate features, and a lightly powdered face. She was also a soft-talker, and as I got up to greet her, I had to lean in to hear her as she said, "So good to see you, Alex. How is the garden coming along?"

"Great! I think we'll be ready for opening day. You and Ms. Bunkle will be joining us for the patron reception, right?"

"Yes, yes, we're looking forward to it," she whispered.

Ms. Bunkle spoke with decorum since we were in the library, but her voice sounded harsh by comparison. "Come on, Alma, let's shake a leg. I've got things to do and people to see. See ya later, Tater."

****

It was early evening, and the buzz of activity in the garden was winding down. The non-Workshop volunteers had left, and Ryan was blowing off the paths while the rest of us gathered the garden tools and organized all the supplies for tomorrow's work. Once finished, the gang grabbed bottles of water and congregated at the courtyard tables. Baxter and Poppy were racing back and forth in the grass on the other side of the garden.

"So, what's on the agenda for tomorrow?" Spencer asked.

"We'll place the sculptures and Hank and Twila's glass pieces first thing in the morning, and then the volunteer crew will finish the annual planting and the benches. Once those are done, other than the reception Wednesday, we're in a holding pattern until the end of the week when we put the tables in the craft booths and do all the final touches."

"Hank and Twila's pieces are already here, right? Will you need help with those?" Maggie asked. Hank and Twila lived a couple of hours away and had been part of the winter arts and crafts festival. When they offered to loan some of their glassworks to the garden, I eagerly accepted.

"I've got them in my studio for safe keeping. I'll defer to you guys," I said, indicating Ryan and Elliott, "for the placement of them after the sculptures are in."

In my mind, I equated Elliott with a gentle giant. He was a big guy, with a perpetual five o'clock shadow, and a thick blanket of hair on his strong forearms, but he was quiet and mild-mannered. He and Ryan made quite a contrasting pair, like two animated cartoon figures—a bounding, bouncing puppy with a slow, methodical bear exhibiting much patience.

Elliott nodded. "Sounds good. And Ryan and I

already have some ideas for the signs at the tree line."

"Yeah! We've got some cool options," Ryan said, eagerly. "Aside from the homemade wooden signs, we have some large stone scraps, and we can place them on the ground for one of our painters to write 'no trespassing' or something."

Annie chimed in. "Ugh, I hate painting letters."

"That's because you're too much of a perfectionist," Spencer teased. "I'll do it."

"But I'm happy to decorate them in some way," Annie offered, eagerly. "I could paint flowers or little animals. Something to make it seem like less of a command."

"Great, but there's not much time. I want to move those stones tomorrow, while we have the machinery here to do the heavy lifting. Otherwise, I think we're done for now, except I need to go over things with Aunt Claudia for the reception, so who wants to go to the Café to grab some dinner?"

****

Our group pulled a few tables together, and Aunt Claudia talked with each of us as she took our orders. When she got to me, she said, "Let me guess—grilled cheese and fries."

"Nailed it," I said, and smiled. "And mayo on the side for dipping the fries."

"Yeah, yeah, I know," she said, shaking her head.

"Oh, and when we're done here, I'll chat with you about the week ahead."

"Sounds good."

I was only partly focusing on the chatter going on around the table. Half of my brain was distracted, thinking about who would have used the library internet to post snarky comments. Looking at this group of incredible artists and good friends, I couldn't fathom someone from the Workshop had a hand in any of it. Bitsy and JJ laughed with Annie and Spencer over some anecdote, which was a common occurrence. Diego and Maggie were listening intently as Elliott and Ryan talked about the sculptures they made for the garden. Diego was the only newcomer. Would he do this? He'd been at the library with more frequency, from what Ms. Bunkle said.

I watched his body language, which was tapping a skill from my old job. You could learn a lot about a person, or read a situation, just by interpreting body language. In this case, Diego's facial features were relaxed, one arm was casually draped on the back of the chair next to him and the other rested on the table. His body was turned toward them, and his movements were fluid. These indicated open, trusting, and comfortable.

Granted, sociopaths can fool you, but most people are not clinically sociopathic, and I chose to believe Diego couldn't act so natural while also sabotaging the Workshop, which would harm the very people he was developing friendships with. I might, however, ask him if he saw anything of note while at the library.

I got my opportunity later, when Maggie vacated her seat to talk to Bitsy. I moved next to Diego and started with pleasantries. "Thanks so much, again, for helping us get the garden ready."

He looked at me with bright eyes. "It's been fun! And it's a great way to get to know everyone better."

"Yeah, physical labor is a great bonding experience," I said with sarcasm.

"Oh, it's good for us. We spend so much time sitting in our studios we forget to use all our muscles."

There was my opening. "So, I was over at the library this morning and heard you've been there more frequently. It's a nice walk from the Workshop, and as you say, a great way to combat sitting too much in the studio. But I just want to check, are you having computer issues or is there a problem with the Wi-Fi in your studio?"

Diego suddenly looked uncomfortable. He shifted slightly in his chair and drew his arms close to his body. "No, my computer's fine. I've, uh, just been doing some research for my next art piece and thought it would be easier to do it right there where the resources are."

"Oh, sure," I said, trying to sound casual. His body language was changing as he became more guarded. He had crossed his arms and turned slightly away from me. This piqued my interest, so I took another approach and leaned in so I could speak quietly. "Maybe you can help me, though. You know, these social media slams are a bit concerning. I have reason to believe that whoever is doing it is posting from the library. You haven't noticed anything when you've been there, have you?"

He wouldn't look me in the eye. "No, I haven't. I'm just busy doing my own thing and haven't noticed anyone else." He got up from his chair. "Sorry to run, but I really need to get going. I have some work to do."

"Of course. I'll see you tomorrow." Wow, he either had something to hide, or I had really overstepped and trampled on his privacy.

I was mulling over our exchange, chewing on my fingernail, when I heard Maggie calling, "Hey, Alex, earth to Alex!"

"Oh, sorry, what?"

"We're taking off. Are you coming?"

I was the last one sitting at the table. "Sorry! I checked out for a minute. You guys go on. I've still got to talk to Aunt Claudia."

I helped return our tables to their proper position, then I slipped into the last booth by the kitchen swing door, where Aunt Claudia was sorting order slips.

She pulled out her notebook. "We're all set for Wednesday. Burger sliders, salmon sliders, veggie pinwheels, chips and salsa, devilled eggs, grapes and strawberries, and desserts. As you wanted, all casual and all finger foods. Nothing needs utensils."

"I knew you'd have it locked down. You'll have ample gallons of your famous tea punch?"

"Of course. We'll bring everything Wednesday morning, and then Jeff will return to work the reception." She tucked her pen into her hair bun, signaling our business was done. "Now, what's going on? I saw you over there chewing on your nail. I thought you were trying to kick that habit."

I waved my hand in dismissal. "Oh, it's nothing. Just some social media pranking."

"Oh yeah, I've heard."

"You have?" Man, the older generation was so much more up on things than I was.

"A few customers have mentioned it, so I went on to see what the hoo-ha was about."

"You never said anything! What do you think?"

"It's a bunch of hoo-ha," she said, matter-of-factly.

"Are people buying it? Do they think it's true?"

"Of course not! From what I've heard, people think you must be doing something right, and it's just jealousy, which is why I didn't even think to mention it."

I hadn't thought of the jealousy angle before. "Huh,"

I uttered, my mind turning this over. I sat up straight when a thought struck me. "What about Winifred. Could it be Winifred?" I then relayed the interaction I had with her and her news of opening a similar venue with Eva Beaumont in Pine Brook.

"It wouldn't surprise me if she was somehow involved," Aunt Claudia said, with distaste.

I couldn't help but laugh. "Your face looks just like Ms. Bunkle's did today when Winifred's name came up. How could I have not known about this woman's reputation? I am so out of the loop! Oh, that reminds me, Ms. Bunkle said to ask you about Tucker's first wife, Eleanor."

Aunt Claudia furrowed her brow. "Sad business, that."

"What happened? She said Eleanor just walked out one day and never came back."

"Wow, this is really going back down memory lane. Yes. Tucker said she left a note saying she was leaving him. He said her suitcase was gone, along with some of her clothes."

"That's pretty drastic. Were they having problems? I don't remember hearing anything about this."

"You were just a kid and only here in the summers or on school holidays, so you wouldn't have noticed if your mom and I talked about it, which I'm not even sure we did."

"So what happened?"

"They were no different than many married couples. They got married too young, and even in the seventies and eighties, women were expected to put up with more than they should, but a few were starting to stand up and say 'enough!' "

"Interesting. I'm always startled when I see the depiction of women in movies from that era, considering some of it was within my own lifetime."

"Previous decades were even worse. But anyway, she would complain that everything had to be his way, and he wanted the house just so and expected her to keep it looking like a magazine. He didn't want her working and only doled out a meager allowance. He wanted her to dress a certain way and be the perfect hostess but didn't want her to have her own life. That sort of thing."

"I wouldn't have been happy in that situation, either, but I don't think I'd just leave town over it. You don't think he was abusive, do you?"

Aunt Claudia spoke with confidence. "I honestly don't. I would have known if that was the case. Tucker may not have been the most sensitive husband, but he was not an abusive type. You have to remember, it's a small town, and she didn't have any family left here. She might have felt it was easier to cut ties and start fresh somewhere else."

"Have you heard from her since? Ms. Bunkle said you guys were friends."

"We were. I got a couple postcards from her after she left, but they had no return address, and then I never heard from her again. And I seem to remember that Tucker received some letters, but I don't know what happened after that. I can understand leaving him. They weren't a good match—he was a climber, and she was more down to earth. And at that age, it's not unusual to move on, get caught up in your new life, and then lose touch with people from your past."

I reached over to grab her hand. "I'm sorry. What about Tucker? He must have been devastated, even if he was a jerk of a husband."

"Yes, he was out of sorts for a while, and then he and Sasha got together. She was his secretary." Aunt Claudia gave me a knowing look.

"Interesting."

"Well, it was a long time ago. Water under the bridge. Tucker and Sasha are happy and have been together a long time, and I hope Eleanor's happy. Maybe one day she'll walk through the door."

"I hope so."

****

Upon returning to the Workshop, I sat at one of the courtyard tables while Baxter and Poppy romped in the yard. The crickets played their summer song, and the moon cast its beam over the grounds. It should have been a peaceful moment, but my brain wouldn't stop reviewing the negative comments about the Workshop. So I was actually grateful for the interruption when the door off the lobby clanged open, and I turned to see Diego walking toward me.

"Sorry to interrupt your evening, but can I talk to you for a moment?" he asked.

"Sure, take a seat."

Diego sat heavily in the chair. "I've made an ass of myself, and I must apologize. I panicked when you asked about the library, and it's because I was embarrassed."

"What would you have to be embarrassed about?" I asked, incredulously.

"Well, you see, I'm still new to town, and you all have been great here at the Workshop, but meeting, um, dating prospects is not so easy in a small town. So, I went on a dating site. I didn't want to put the app on my phone or computer, so I used the library computers to log in."

I couldn't help but laugh. "Oh Diego, you're too funny."

He shook his head. "I'm utterly ridiculous. I've never used a dating site before, and it kind of made me cringe."

"Sooo, any prospects?"

"No, I just can't bring myself to swipe left or right or whichever way. It just feels smarmy."

"Listen, I know a lot of people who have used dating sites. Sometimes it works and it can be magic. But personally, I'm with you. I couldn't do it."

"Yeah, I guess I'll just have to do it the old-fashioned way."

I looked at him fondly. "You just keep doing what you're doing, and you'll meet someone. You're quite a catch, so I know it will happen."

"Thanks, Alex. I'm going to delete my account." He looked at me with a gleam in his eye and added, "But I'll probably find a reason to continue hanging out at the library."

"Oh?"

"Lena works there."

"Aha! You see? Lena's awesome, and I don't think you need a ruse to get to know her." Lena was a little older than Diego, but I could totally see them together.

"Well, she's so vivacious and everyone loves her. I get a little tongue-tied around her."

"Just be yourself and take your time. But at some point, take the plunge and ask her out."

"I will. I'm thinking about asking her to join me at the grand opening. Anyway, I've told you all of this because I didn't want you to think I was behind any of the social media business going on."

"Well, thank you for clarifying. So, have you seen anything when you've been at the library?"

"I've been thinking about it since you asked, and no, not really. I'm still relatively new here, so I don't know everyone, but I've seen a few of the Workshop people, and occasionally Penny or Winifred. But they're all harmless. And I just don't see any of the senior center folks doing such a thing, either. Of course, you do know it could be someone out in the parking lot using the library's Wi-Fi, right?"

I grimaced. "Yes, and that's the likeliest scenario. So, I'm just spinning my wheels for nothing. But thanks for thinking it through for me."

Diego got up and said, "You're welcome, but I wish I could have helped more. I'll let you get back to your peace and quiet. See you tomorrow."

"G'night," I returned.

I pondered the futility of trying to figure out who was behind these stunts, then remembered Aunt Claudia mentioned jealousy as a motive. Was Winifred as harmless as Diego indicated? I wasn't so sure. Did I think she had it in her to pull this off? Yes, I did.

Chapter 4

Sunday

Early morning was usually my time to read the news, kickstart my brain playing word games, plan my day, take a walk with Baxter, and drink multiple cups of coffee. This morning, the only similarity was the multiple cups of coffee. Ryan and Elliott arrived before seven a.m. to coordinate the placement of the sculptures, and by eight, the machine Elliott would use to lift each sculpture had been driven onto the path. They rolled the sculptures outside on heavy duty dollies, and then each was roped and lifted into place.

By late morning, the garden was showing the first signs of transformation. Ryan and Elliott both worked with stone, but each had their own style, and they incorporated other materials, like wood or metal, into their pieces.

Maggie and I were discussing options for Hank and Twila's glass pieces. "Since they won't be here until the grand opening, will you take some photos to send them so they can sign off on the installation?" I asked.

"I'd be happy to."

"Hey, Alex!" Ryan shouted, from the other end of the garden. "You better come check this out."

"Uh-oh," Maggie said.

"What is it?" I called back. "And where is Elliott going?" Elliott was jogging to the far end of the building.

"He's turning off the hose, which was running full blast. It's made a mess of the lawn and the far edge of the garden."

The sodden earth squished under my boots as I walked out onto the lawn. "Damn it! I was sure everything was put away last night."

"Well, I know the hose wasn't running when we left because I wound it up on the hose trolley," Ryan said. "Somebody has been messing around again."

"This is going too far," Maggie said, tersely.

"It sure is. There's no way we can finish the bench placement today. It will be a muddy mess if people tromp around out here."

"Luckily we've got a few more days before the patron party," Maggie said.

I sighed with resignation. "I guess Jack and Walter are right. It's time for security cameras."

Maggie muttered under her breath, "I really don't like the idea of being watched all the time."

"I don't either, so I'm thinking I'll only turn them on at night when no one is here. That way, if someone tries anything again, we'll catch them in the act."

"Okay, fair enough."

"You guys continue on here. I'll be back shortly."

I went to the office and pulled out my phone. "Hey, Jack," I said, by way of greeting. "The saboteur struck again last night. The hose was turned on, and it flooded the lawn."

"Any damage?" he asked officiously.

"Not really. Just the far edge of the garden will need a little clean up. Mostly it's the lawn, which slows down our progress of the bench placement. But it was a huge waste of water, which is upsetting, and our water bill will be high. So, I'm crying uncle. I agree we need additional security cameras."

"Good. Do you want my help?"

"Yeah. I don't know what to get, and I'll also need help with where to put them."

"You got it. I'll give you some options later when I'm over there. Although, I'm guessing we won't be installing the benches today, right?"

"Right. But come on over anyway. I'm sure I can find something for you to do."

"I'm sure you can," he said, before disconnecting the call.

I grabbed a dolly and went down the hall to my art studio, which was more of a glorified arts and crafts room. Growing up, my mom had included me in her art adventures, and we dabbled in a variety of art mediums. I had vivid memories of doing silk screening, developing our own film, coming home and finding looms set up in the living room, or the dining table covered with a wood board for making stained glass. Therefore, my studio was chock full of shelves and cabinets holding canvases, paints, bits for jewelry making, stained glass supplies, papers for multi-medium crafts, bits of wood—really anything that caught my fancy. My mom would have loved this place, and I always thought about her as I started a new project.

I had stored the carefully packed crates from Hank and Twila in the corner, and I loaded the dolly and slowly rolled it out to the garden path. Maggie eagerly helped me unpack the glass beauties they had chosen for our garden. There were eight installations in total, including colorful glass agave plants, gorgeous pieces that looked like scarves billowing in the wind, a few orbs with blown glass inside, and some Chihuly-inspired blown glass spirals. As with Ryan and Elliott's sculptures, each had its own marker with the title of the piece, and in this case, the designation of being on loan from Allegheny Glassworks.

The four of us worked in efficient harmony and had just completed our tasks when the sound of cars in the parking lot announced the arrival of the volunteers.

Everyone oohed and aahed as they looked at each sculpture, and then they got to work and filled in the remaining open spots from the cart of plants Bert had delivered.

When Jack arrived, he pulled me aside. "Got your laptop? I have some options for you."

"We can go to the office. No, better yet, let's go upstairs so I can get another cup of coffee."

Jack couldn't help but needle me as we climbed the central staircase. "So what number are you on? Wait, let me guess. Four?"

"I'm not counting, but I think my fourth was a couple of hours ago."

"Geez, I'm amazed it's not rotting your gut."

"The frothy milk foam helps, and so does chocolate. Coats the stomach, you know," I said breezily, choosing to ignore his jibe.

"You are never going to grow up, are you?"

"Not if I can help it. I had enough years having to be sophisticated."

When we opened the door, Baxter and Poppy rushed over to greet us.

"You have a guest!" Jack noted.

"Yeah, Lena needed last minute doggy help. She'll be back tomorrow."

"Baxter seems to be enjoying the play date."

"He is, although they do tend to go on a tear when they're outside. I'll have to watch them closely now since the garden is done."

As I made coffee for us and pulled out some snacks, Jack opened my laptop and pulled up a site for security cameras. I put a bag of chips and the chocolates on the counter alongside our steaming cups and looked over his shoulder.

"Okay," he said, "so you will want to go wireless. And if you're wireless, then you'll need cloud-based storage for video. Range is variable, as is the night vision quality—"

"Argh!" I interrupted, scrubbing my face with my hands. "This is the kind of thing that makes my head explode. It's something I don't really want, and there are too many options. Just tell me what you think I should get."

"Geez. I thought you'd want to micromanage this, like you do everything else."

"Ha-ha. Look, I loathe the thought of Big Brother watching, so I'm practicing avoidance."

Jack tapped the keyboard and turned the laptop toward me. "I'd get these. We can get them delivered tomorrow, and Ryan or Diego can help me set them up."

"Sounds good."

Jack grabbed the bag of chips. "So, have you been thinking? Have you come up with ideas for who might be pulling these pranks?" he asked, between crunches.

"Well, I have a nagging feeling about Winifred." I explained my reasoning, then said, "So, on the one hand she ticks quite a few boxes, but on the other, I don't see her tromping around here at night to turn on the hose, which feels more juvenile."

"You could discreetly try and find out where she was last night."

"Good idea. The real problem is it could be someone using the library's Wi-Fi on a laptop or phone, so this is an uphill battle."

"Anyone else you can think of?"

"Not yet."

Jack's eyes flashed with mischief. "Well, keep thinking. You've managed to tick someone off pretty bad."

He scrunched sideways, but I still managed to land a punch on his shoulder.

****

Back outside, Jack joined Ryan and Elliott, and I wandered around to check in with everyone and played the role of gopher. My last stop was where Penny and Tucker were working. Tucker was wearing gardening clothes today, including fancy knee pads so he could kneel on the path while tucking plants around the sculptures.

Penny was working next to him, filling a garden pot. Shielding her eyes from the sun, she looked up at me and said, "Hi, Alex, I heard about the sabotage. It's a shame the lawn was flooded."

"It's quite aggravating," I said, in exasperation, "but I think everything will dry out in a day or two."

She stood up and ushered me a few feet away. "It feels like someone is trying to stop you from completing the garden, doesn't it?"

I looked at her for a beat and lowered my voice. "I hadn't thought of it that way." Could it be? Surely not. From what I could tell, the social media campaign had nothing to do with the garden.

Penny took my hesitancy to mean she had overstepped, and quickly said, "I'm sure I'm way off base."

"No, no, not necessarily. I can't put my finger on what connects everything, and I just can't fathom why the garden would play a significant role. But you've given me some food for thought."

"Just don't let it detract from what an incredible job you all have done." She swept her arm in an arc. "This looks amazing."

I smiled. "It does, doesn't it?" I noticed Sasha approaching from the parking lot and called over my shoulder. "Hey, Tucker, it looks like your better half is joining us."

Tucker stood up and smiled from ear to ear. "Hello, my love! Have you decided to come out for some garden fun after all?" he asked, jovially.

Sasha crossed her arms. "No, I've just come to remind you not to linger too long. Remember, we have an engagement this evening."

Tucker's face fell. "Oh, it's such a beautiful afternoon to be outside. Can't we put it off for another time?"

"I hardly think so." She walked over to him and leaned in close to speak in his ear.

I couldn't hear what she said, but it was awkward to witness the exchange, nonetheless.

Tucker, however, wasn't fazed and looked at his watch before saying, "Well, there's still plenty of time." He then turned to me. "It looks like working at the tree line is out today because of the water damage, so where would you like me to go next?"

I could feel Sasha's annoyance rising and did not want to get in the middle of a squabble, so I surveyed the garden and said, "You know, I think you can call it a day when this section is done. My crew can handle the rest. There's not much more we can do until the lawn dries out, anyway."

"Are you sure?"

"What about the benches at the tree line?" Penny asked.

Sasha scanned the grounds and suggested, "Maybe you should just stop with the garden. I don't think you even need anything else." And then as if she remembered her manners, she said, "You really have done a beautiful job with this design, Alex. I've enjoyed watching your progress."

"Thank you, but it was a team effort. And we'll see. You may be right about not needing anything else. This might be a good stopping point for now, and we can decide later about those benches."

Sasha was right. Everything looked so good already, and we didn't need the stress of additional work later in the week. As it was, I needed to roll up my sleeves and work on the flooded section of the garden beds. That was enough to contend with.

****

As evening approached, we made a final walkthrough of the garden. Along with the usual crew of Ryan, Elliott, Maggie, and me, a number of workshop artists had come out to help us with the final clean up. The garden lights cast a soft glow on the path, sculptures, and trees, and there was a heady scent of flowers and earth, with a light breeze drying the sheen of sweat from our efforts.

"We did it!" I said to the group.

"I'm so proud of how this came together." Ryan beamed.

"Me, too," Elliott said quietly.

"I put some beer and sodas in the fridge, anybody want one?" Ryan asked.

I answered, "Great idea! I'll go get Baxter and Poppy, and I'll bring down some snacks."

I jogged up the stairs to my apartment and rifled through my cabinets. Fortunately, since I preferred to graze instead of eating three squares a day, I always kept a healthy supply of snack food. I popped a couple bags of popcorn, grabbed the chips, a package of cookies, a can of nuts, hummus, carrots, and pita chips, and a few serving bowls. Having stuffed a tote bag, I looked at Baxter and Poppy and said, "Are you guys ready to go?"

Baxter ran toward the door with Poppy hot on his heels.

After unloading my bounty, Ryan popped open drinks for everyone, and we shuffled tables and chairs around to make a U-shape so we could look at the result of our hard work. Baxter and Poppy went tearing off to romp.

Eventually, only Maggie, Ryan, Annie, and I remained, and we debated if we wanted to go to Fat Daddy's for barbecue or have pizza delivered. We decided on Fat Daddy's, so it was time to get Baxter and Poppy back upstairs. They were barking over at the tree line, and when I called out to them, they ignored me, which was unusual.

"Dang it, they are going to be a muddy mess!" I called again, with no success. "I'm going to have to go get them. Baxter is usually such a good boy, but he's totally distracted having a partner in crime."

"We'll go with you. It'd be nice to look at the garden from the other side," Ryan said.

I looked at Annie's footwear. "Okay, good, you have on boots. Just mind your step, you guys. The lawn is still sopping wet."

We plodded across the mushy grass over to where Baxter and Poppy were focused on something under one of the trees. As we got closer, I could see they had been digging.

"Oh Baxter, what are you guys doing?" I admonished. To the others I said, "I have a feeling I'm going to have some paw cleaning to do before going out. I may have to meet you at Fat Daddy's."

"It's okay," Annie said, "we can order for you."

Baxter came running over with great excitement, and he had something firmly clenched in his jaw.

"What have you found?" I asked him.

He dropped it at my feet, and I reached down to grab it, but reared back like I had seen a snake. "Whoa."

"What is it?" Ryan asked with interest, while Maggie and Annie looked back toward the Workshop, still discussing the garden.

I squatted down to take a closer look. "Oh my gosh. It looks like a bone."

Ryan came over and picked it up. "This is big. I thought they might have dug up somebody's old lunch, but I don't know, Alex, this wasn't anyone's lunch." He pulled out his phone to use the flashlight app. The bone was over a foot in length.

"I don't have a good feeling about this," I said, and walked toward Poppy, who was still pawing at the ground.

"What's going on?" Maggie called over, suddenly aware something unusual was happening.

"You guys stay there. I need to check this out."

I pulled out my own phone and turned on the flashlight, sweeping the ground with it as I approached Poppy. When I got to the spot she was digging in and saw what she was obsessing over, I started to reel.

"Oh my God." I quickly turned around and took deep breaths to keep steady.

"What is it?" Annie asked.

When I didn't answer, Ryan strode over to me. "Alex, what is it?"

I pointed behind me.

"Holy crap! Is that a skeleton?" Ryan screeched.

His loud voice snapped me out of it, and I tapped into my crisis management training. "Everybody, stay back. Ryan, we need to get the dogs out of here. Maggie, can you give him a hand and get them over into the fenced area?"

"Sure. I don't want to get close enough to see anything anyway—Baxter, come!" she commanded sharply.

"Ohhh, I don't want to see anything, either," Annie said, in a quivery voice. "I'm coming with you, Maggie."

Ryan grabbed Poppy, and although she squirmed in his grasp, she was small enough for him to keep hold of, and while they marched the dogs to the fenced yard, I tapped Jack's number on my phone.

When he answered, I didn't bother with pleasantries. "Jack, you need to get back over here. Bring a heavy-duty flashlight."

"What's going on?" he asked, in his official tone of voice.

"I think I know why the sabotage has been happening."

****

Jack and I stood shoulder to shoulder, looking down at the partially dug up skeleton. He let out a breathy whistle and said, "Well, I'll be damned." The atmosphere was made even more eerie when viewed with the light from his flashlight. "Are you all right?" he asked.

"I'm okay now. The initial shock has passed."

"I'm surprised. It's not every day a skeleton is unearthed."

"A skeleton is different than a body. There aren't human features on a skeleton. A body would freak me out."

"Fair enough."

"How old do you think this is?" I asked.

"I'm afraid I'm not qualified to determine that. My knowledge from police training is what protocols to follow. And other than that, it's limited to knowing decomposition can take anywhere from a few weeks to a few years, depending on the climate the body is in. The medical examiner will be able to determine some of it, but for the rest, we'll need a specialist in the field of forensic anthropology."

"Where do we find one of them?"

"Usually at a university. Some major cities carry their own, and of course the FBI has them." Jack pulled out his phone and after a beat, said, "Travis, I need both you and Matt over here at the Workshop, out back by the tree line. Call the medical examiner, bring a crime scene tent, and do a quick check in our database to see if we have a forensic anthropologist on file. If so, text me the contact." Jack disconnected the call, knowing that Travis, his second in command, wouldn't take time to ask questions.

He turned to me. "I can't move anything yet, but I'm going to take a closer look. Do you want to go back and wait with the others?"

Annie, Maggie, and Ryan were huddled in the courtyard. "I think I might. I'm not sure how up close and personal I need to get."

I walked back to the courtyard with my brain spinning a mile a minute. Who was buried, when was this person buried, and why?

"What's the word?" Ryan asked.

"It's definitely a body."

"Eeeew, seriously?" Annie asked, cringing.

"I thought so," Ryan said.

"How long has it been there? Why is it there? Was there ever a cemetery here?" Maggie asked.

"Oh my gosh," Annie gasped. "What if this whole lawn is full of dead people!"

Whenever possible, Annie's imagination liked to create B-list movie scenarios, so I simply said, "I'm sure the original school wasn't built on the grounds of a cemetery."

"I bet it's going to take a while to unearth the remaining bones. It was still partially buried, right?" Ryan asked.

"Yeah," I replied. "Jack will likely have to enlist a forensic anthropologist."

Annie's eyes grew wide. "Does it have to stay there until the specialist comes? I've seen archeology programs where they have to carefully remove the skeleton, and it's slow, tedious work. What are we going to do? How can you sleep here knowing it's out there?" She shuddered and hugged her shoulders.

"Look, it's a skeleton. It doesn't have anything to do with the here and now, so I'm not worried about sleeping here."

Maggie chimed in. "And surely it will be removed before we have the patron event on Wednesday. We can carry on, right, Alex?"

I grew frustrated by the assumption I would know anything at this point, but I kept my cool. "I hope so, but I really don't know. Look, it's going to be a long night, and I'm sure it will be a while before I have any answers, so why don't you guys go on to dinner. Jack might need to talk to you, but I think it can wait until tomorrow."

"You're sure?" Ryan asked, reluctantly.

I had a feeling he wanted in on the action. "I see Travis pulling in now, and we need to let them do their job. I'll find out what I can, and we'll talk tomorrow."

Annie shook her head. "I've lost my appetite, and I doubt I'm going to sleep tonight, but as long as you don't need us for anything, I'd rather leave."

"I'm fine, really."

"Okay. Will you let Jack know I've gone on home?" she asked.

"Sure."

The threesome walked to the parking lot together, and I gathered up the food from the courtyard and went to the kitchen to make a thermal carafe of coffee to take out to the guys. Once the pot had brewed, I grabbed a small folding side table and some paper cups and schlepped it across the lawn to set up on the periphery of the scene. The light inside the crime scene tent created an eerie silhouette of the three men inside. One was kneeling, two were standing. I could tell which was Jack from his telltale hands-on-hips stance.

"Knock, knock," I said, just outside the tent flap. When Jack stuck his head out, I said, "Annie wanted me to let you know she's gone on home, and I told Ryan and Maggie they could take off, too, but you might need to talk to them tomorrow. And I've brought a thermal carafe of coffee. It's over there on a table."

Jack stepped out into the open. "Thanks. I can talk to Annie when I get home tonight or in the morning. And yes, someone will talk to Ryan and Maggie tomorrow, although your statement is probably sufficient."

"What's the status of things?"

Jack walked to the table to get some coffee. "I've called the medical examiner. He'll be here in a while to look at the bones, then we'll have to get a forensic specialist to date them while we sort through any evidence found on site. If the ME feels it's not archeologically significant, we can move forward removing the bones tonight, and I'll have Matt document everything with video and photographs."

"I'm assuming you haven't found something to identify who it is."

"Heck, a good bit of it is still buried, so we don't know anything at this point."

"What do you want me to do?" I asked.

"You might as well go inside. We'll be here a while."

"Okay. Will you come up when you're done?"

"Depends on how late it is. I'll at least text you at some point."

Upstairs in my apartment, I tried a number of things to distract myself. After cleaning Baxter's and Poppy's paws, I threw in a load of laundry, then I watched TV, but my mind kept wandering and I would lose track of the storyline. I even resorted to running the dry mop around the living area. Ultimately, I ended up standing at the kitchen window staring at the crime scene tent while mindlessly snacking on hummus and crackers. There was a lot of activity going on down there, but it was too dark to see what they were doing.

My phone rang, and seeing Tucker's name on the caller ID made me cringe, but I felt obligated to answer.

"Hi, Tucker," I said, neutrally.

"What's going on out there, Alex? We just got home and noticed some bright lights over at the tree line."

How much should I say? I would stick to the facts. "Unfortunately, the dogs got a little wild this evening, and they dug up something just inside the tree line."

"What do you mean? What did they dig up?"

"Well, it appears to be skeletal remains."

"What?" he shouted.

"I'm sorry to say that's all I know at this point."

"Is it on the Workshop's property? You must be spinning."

That was a good way to put it. "It is distressing, and it's too dark to determine whose property it's on. It's possible this could be a burial from a hundred years ago, before the subdivision of the land. We just won't know for a little while."

"I'm going out there," he said.

"Uh, Tucker, please don't. Jack and his team are working the site, and they don't want anyone there, including me."

He was silent for a few seconds, then said, "Well, keep me updated." And as an afterthought, he added,

"Please."

"Of course."

After we hung up, I stewed over how disruptive this was going to be. I really needed to develop a plan for how to get to the bottom of this in order not to have the garden opening collapse.

It was almost eleven p.m., which meant in London it was going on four a.m. This was a significant event, but not an emergency, so calling Walter was not an option. Instead, I decided to pretend I was talking this over with him. I perched on the stool at the kitchen counter, opened my laptop, and started a new file. What did I know so far?

The Workshop had been targeted with social media slams.

We had minor vandalism outside in the garden.

A skeleton was unearthed in the woods just beyond the tree line where we were going to place the benches.

Latest sabotage of flooding the lawn delayed our work at the tree line.

Were these events connected? The sabotage started when we announced needing volunteers and began the final stages of the garden. Was Penny right? Did someone want to stop us from completing the garden so we wouldn't go near the woods? Did they know the body was there? I thought through the timeline, and my gut told me this all had to be connected. My fingers hovered above the keypad as I drew my conclusion. The skeleton buried in the woods must be the victim of a murder.

Chapter 5

"You've got to be kidding me," I muttered to myself. I was jumping to all sorts of conclusions. "But seriously, could the skeleton be a victim of foul play?"

Baxter, who had been dozing next to Poppy on the couch looked at me with mild indignation for waking him.

"Don't look at me that way. You guys dug up the body," I said to him.

I checked my phone, willing Jack to text. It worked, because as soon as I set my phone down, he texted he was on his way up, and a few minutes later, there was a knock on the door.

"It's open," I called out.

Jack came in and went directly to the cabinet to get a glass, then he moved to the sink and filled it with water.

"How's it going out there?" I asked.

After downing the water in one long gulp, he said, "It's a hot mess. Along with the medical examiner, we managed to release the rest of the skeleton. We video-chatted with the forensic specialist, and the ME got the okay to take the bones. We've also bagged everything we could find around and under it."

"Any identification?"

"No."

"What now?"

"The area will remain cordoned off, and Gabe's on

duty tonight. The ME will do what he can and then work in conjunction with the forensic anthropologist to determine how long the body has been buried there."

"So we don't know if this is someone from the nineteenth century or a few years ago?"

"Right. We might be able to determine a date range from some of the items found with the remains. There's not much, and we have to sift through layers of dirt, but maybe there will be something to narrow things down and hopefully help identify who it is."

"Well, at least we know it wasn't during the time I've owned the building. I would have noticed if someone was burying a body out there in the woods."

"Probably, but then again, if it was in the middle of the night, you wouldn't have noticed," Jack pointed out.

"But you'd have to dig a pretty big hole, right? Which would be really hard to do without being seen or heard." I was grasping at anything to make this situation have a less severe impact on the Workshop, but Jack was not making it easy.

"One reason remains are found is because someone didn't bury the body deep enough. And let's face it, the dogs were able to dig this up. But you're right, my guess is it would have been before your time here. How long was the building vacant when you bought it?" he asked.

"I'll find out. Surely no one would have buried a body out there when schoolchildren were here," I said, aghast.

"Let's hope not." Jack put his glass in the sink and walked toward the door.

"Wait, before you go, I started a file on this and made some notes."

He came back and leaned his elbow on the counter.

"Why am I not surprised?"

"Well, you'll be glad I did, because I think this explains all the sabotage."

Now he used his hand to prop up his face. "I know you can't help but overanalyze things, but I think you might be getting ahead of yourself."

"Think about it. The smear campaign and the minor vandalism all started when we announced looking for volunteers and the real work started on the garden. And the last bit with the hose delayed our work at the tree line. Someone did not want us working near the woods. I also think it means this was a murder victim."

"Okay, now you're really jumping the gun. Why don't we see what the ME comes back with first? If this turns out to be someone from a hundred years ago, it's just a coincidence in timing."

"Mmm," I muttered, not pleased at the dismissal.

He started toward the door. "If you don't mind, see what you can dig up about the building occupancy, and then leave it be until we have more information."

Still not pleased, I spoke a little sharply. "Yessir. Will we be able to move forward with the garden opening? How long will the tent be out there?" I asked, pointedly.

Jack turned back toward me, exasperated. "I really can't answer those questions yet. I will touch base at some point tomorrow morning, okay?"

He looked tired, and I regretted being snippy. "Sorry, I'm doing the bull-in-a-china-shop thing, aren't I? I'm just stressed about how this will impact the grand opening, and I'm taking it out on you."

His face softened, and he gave me a smart-aleck grin before responding. "Yes, you are, I know you are, and it's okay. Seriously, try and get some sleep. Hard as it is, think of it as a means to learn patience."

I laughed. "Smart ass."

After the door closed, I returned to my laptop. Jack was right; patience was not my strong suit, so I stared at the list, looking for loopholes that could disprove my theory. I didn't find any, so it was time to put out the SOS to the gang to meet me here in the morning so we could brainstorm about the skeleton.

****

Monday

I was at the Bushel Basket market when the doors opened to make a quick twirl through the aisles. With my tote bag full of fruit, pastries, and OJ, I made haste and got back just as Lena arrived to pick up Poppy. We walked together from the parking lot to the building.

"Sorry to come so early, Alex, but I want to get Poppy settled at home before I head to the library."

"No worries! I'm always up early."

"What's going on with the tent?" she asked, pointing to the crime scene tent.

I grimaced. "Thanks to Baxter and Poppy, we've had some excitement."

"Oh no, what did they do?"

"They dug up a skeleton."

Lena stopped mid-step. "You're joking, right?"

"I'm not. Come on up, and I'll tell you about it."

As I unloaded the groceries, Poppy danced around in a frenzy of glee for Lena's return, and I relayed the events from last night.

"This is unbelievable! I have so many questions, but I'm sure you don't have answers yet to any of them!"

"You're right about that. We don't know who it is,

when it was buried, the age of the skeleton. Nothing yet."

"Wow. If you had some information, like date, age, or gender, you could check NamUs."

"What's NamUs?" I asked.

"It's the National Missing and Unidentified Persons System, a database for missing persons."

"Do you have to be law enforcement to use it?"

"No, anyone can access it for searches or for listing a missing person."

"Wow, once we have a little more information it could prove helpful. Thank you!"

"You're welcome. We librarians aim to please," she said, with a smile.

"Of course! You guys know everything."

Lena laughed. "Not everything, but we know how to find what people want to know. You have some experience in that area, yourself."

"Not to the degree you do. I know how to dig and get answers, but only in a fairly finite scope."

"Well, if I can be of any help, just let me know. And keep me updated! In the meantime, come on, Poppy, let's get a move on," she called out as she gathered Poppy's overnight bag. "And finding a skeleton notwithstanding, thanks again for babysitting Poppy."

"No problem," I said sincerely. It really wasn't their fault their doggy instincts drew them to dig up the body.

I had time to take a quick shower and was just putting out the food when there was a rhythmic tap of knocks followed by JJ sticking her head in the door.

"We're here," she called.

"Come on in," I called back.

JJ, Bitsy, and Spencer filed in, followed by Annie, who was dragging a rolling whiteboard behind her.

"Where'd you find that?" I asked, suppressing a laugh.

"I had it in my studio and brought it up on the elevator. I thought we could use it for plotting clues," she answered, with enthusiasm.

"Well, this is a turnabout from last night when you were pretty freaked out," I said.

"I know. But once I got home and decompressed with a bowl of ice cream, I realized you were right. It's not like finding a dead body. It's a skeleton, and it could be so fascinating to unearth the history of who and why."

Spencer said, "Annie filled us in a little more after your text last night."

"We all agreed not to bother you because we knew you'd be worn out, but how are you? You've had quite a shock," Bitsy said.

"I'm actually fine. It was certainly unexpected, but like Annie said, there's a detachment when it's an old skeleton."

JJ was standing at the kitchen window looking at the crime scene tent. Thus far she had remained mute, which was unusual.

"You okay, JJ?" I asked.

She turned back to us. "Yes, I'm fine, but I think we need to do a smoke cleansing ceremony. It's an important custom."

We were all accustomed to JJ's free-spirit vibe, and we embraced her creativity, although occasionally it was with a discreet eye-roll. "What's involved?" I asked, hesitantly.

"I will gather some spices and greenery to burn as an offering for peace, community, and protection. In silence, we can project our own prayer or wishes for the soul who was left to return to the earth in such an isolated way."

Bitsy said, "What a nice idea."

Annie nodded. "And we could commemorate the site by planting something there."

"I agree," I said. "I just need to talk to Jack to make sure they are done before we do anything."

"Good." JJ breathed deeply through her nose and released a slow breath. "Now let's get to work."

"Right. Help yourself to food, and who wants coffee?" I asked.

With full plates and steaming mugs, we sat in the living room, staring at the whiteboard.

"Where do we start?" Spencer eventually asked.

Bitsy frowned. "We don't know anything, do we?"

"I bet we know more than we think," Annie said.

I got up and grabbed the marker. "Annie's right. We don't have many hard facts, but we aren't totally empty-handed." I started writing the same list I had created on my laptop.

"So you are thinking maybe this is connected to the sabotage?" Spencer asked.

"It could be. I don't like coincidences, and the smear campaign and sabotage began when we started the big garden work. Lena told me about a missing persons database, which got me thinking. What if this skeleton was a victim of foul play, and the killer didn't want us finding the remains? If someone went missing, even decades ago, it would still be an open case."

Bitsy said, "So someone might have gotten nervous when they saw how close we were working to the tree line."

"Right. That database might be a good avenue to

explore."

Spencer raised his hand to stop our conjecture. "I get what you're saying, but you also have to put on the board the simple scenario where the dogs happened to be messing around, caught a whiff, and dug up old bones. And the sabotage is totally unrelated."

JJ nodded in agreement. "Yeah, if the skeleton is a hundred years old, it's not going to have anything to do with anyone who is still living."

"You're right," I conceded. "I'll start another column with that in mind."

There was a knock at the door, and Maggie entered. I found it humorous when none of my friends bothered to wait for me to answer their knock. I actually liked it. It meant we were like one big family.

"Sorry," she said, bustling in, "I wanted to check the machine and get the first classes underway before coming up."

"Were there any questions about what's going on out back?" I asked.

"Nah, with all the work we've been doing out there, I'm sure they think it's related to the garden."

"That reminds me, I need to call Jack and get him to sign off on me putting out an email to the Workshop folks and the garden volunteers. They do need to know what's happening. You guys carry on here and bring Maggie up to speed, and I'll be right back."

I grabbed my phone and stepped into my home office. Jack picked up after the first ring. "Not much to update yet," he said, jumping straight to the point.

"I didn't think so. I'm just calling to confirm with you that it's okay to send out a press-release type of email to the Workshop and garden people, letting them know what's going on."

"Hold on." I could hear him close his office door at the precinct, and the creak of his desk chair as he lowered himself into it. "Okay. Keep it short and simple. Stick to the facts and don't add any filler."

"Um, Jack, it's not like I didn't do this sort of thing a gazillion times in my old job."

"Right, of course. I'm also just talking out loud for myself because I'm going to have to release an official statement in about ten minutes. So wait to do yours until after that."

"Will do. Have you heard anything from the ME? And what about the items you took from the site?"

"They are examining the bones now. As to the items we brought back here, Matt is sifting through soil and documenting everything. If you come by here in a couple of hours, I may be able to give you an update."

I perked up. "Sure, no problem."

A phone rang in the background. "Gotta go," he said, before disconnecting our call.

"Any word?" Annie asked, when I rejoined the group.

"The ME is examining the bones now." Noting more items had been added to the whiteboard, I said, "You guys have been busy."

Spencer used the marker as a pointer. "This side outlines your thoughts on it being connected to the sabotage."

"Which means we have a crazed murderer in our midst," Annie said ominously, hugging her arms.

"This side," he said, pointing to the right side, "lays out that it could be a more historical death. A family burial plot from a hundred years ago, or it could be murder, or depending on the date range, it could be there was no foul play, but the body was placed there for another reason."

"Like what?" I asked.

"If the bones are really old, say, from the nineteenth century, then it could have been before this was even a town. Think old West movies. When someone died while traveling from one place to another, like in a wagon train, the body would be buried, and then they would continue on."

I perched on the arm of the couch. "I hadn't thought of that."

"That's because he watches a lot of Westerns and you don't," Maggie said.

"I think I need to learn about the origins of Flat Rock Falls and the whole area. And maybe take a trip to the library for more back history."

"Don't you want to wait until we know how old the bones are?" Bitsy asked.

"You guys know I can't just sit around and wait. I need to *do* something. And hey, if nothing else, I'll learn more about our town."

JJ got up from the couch. "Well, since I think we've covered everything we can do for now, we'll let you get to it. Should we plan on meeting later?"

"Sure, I'll text you guys. And not to sound like a broken record, but nothing leaves this room, right?"

There were multiple mumbles of "Yeah, yeah."

"We've been down this road before, so we know the drill," Annie said.

Once I was alone and had my professional hat on, I sent out a statement to all Workshop artists and the garden volunteers. I kept it short and simple. I knew I would probably get a number of inquiries, and I came up with a couple of stock lines to keep a lid on things.

Then, before going to the library, I did a little research on our town and the area around it. Spencer was right. In the early days of the colonies, it was very difficult to access parts of the state, including ours, and it could take weeks to do so. So if this was a historical skeleton, it could prove to be the sad loss of someone making the arduous journey across the state.

In the mid-late nineteenth century, the area was known for logging and industrial expansion, and there were a number of settlements and small towns. These communities would have had the means to provide a proper burial. It could have been part of a family burial plot. I would need to find out what homesteads were originally here because there might actually be other remains. I also wanted to see what kind of information was put in newspapers back then. It was time to go to the library.

****

Lena was busy with a children's group, so I asked the librarian at the checkout desk how to access the microfiche. I started with the closest town with a newspaper and chose an issue from the late nineteenth century. It was fascinating, and I quickly became engrossed.

The personals section listed who visited whom, who traveled where, birthday luncheons and who was in attendance. There was even a short notice about someone who went out of town to see a doctor. The politics page had succinct reporting, but in the same column there were blatant opinion pieces or sarcastic tongue-in-cheek blasts. In the midst of these would be a short paragraph about a murder, followed by the town's financial statement. What a jumble of information.

I also loved seeing the ads, including a gold-plated carpet sweeper on offer at a particularly fine establishment, and Pilsner beer was recommended as a cure for a number of ailments.

I scanned a few more editions over four decades before acknowledging I wasn't really accomplishing anything and was just indulging my interest in social and political history.

Lena approached me and asked, "Hi, what are you doing here? Are ya looking for something specific?"

I swiveled in my chair to look at her. "Remember I told you that the pups dug up skeletal remains?"

"Remember? That's not something I'm likely to forget anytime soon," she said, with a grimace.

"Me neither! Anyway, I'm on a quest to find out what I can about why it might have been buried there, and thought I would do a little research on the early years of our area by looking at newspapers."

"Oh! Did you find out the period it's from?"

I let out a laugh. "No. True to form, I'm just spinning my wheels. I thought while waiting, I would dig around to see when this area was developed and if any homesteads would have had a family cemetery on or near my property."

"Ah, that's a good thought. And at least it's fascinating stuff to look at."

"Even though it hasn't helped so far, it is fun. But hey, do you know how I could find out who occupied the Workshop building in the past? I know it was a school, but don't know how long it was unoccupied when I bought it, or if it had been used for something else at some point."

"Since it was a school, which is a government building, I would go to the property assessor or the county deed office. It should be easy for them to trace, and it will take less time than digging around here."

"Of course! Thanks. I'll go there on my way to see Jack. I bet they would have info on the original town layout, too."

"We've got historical maps here. What period do you want?"

I didn't even know what I was looking for, so I guessed. "How about 1900 or thereabouts."

Lena did a search on the computer and then went to the archives. She brought back a roll of paper and unfurled it on the table. Using books to keep it flat, I scrutinized the old map of Flat Rock Falls.

"Well, there's Main Street, and some of the residential lots over where Aunt Claudia lives, but so much of the area was forest."

"Logging was pretty big back then," she said.

I traced my finger along Main Street to find the approximate location of the Workshop. It was all forest, which told me there probably wasn't a family burial plot on the land. "It looks like across from the Bennet House is the next cluster of residences."

"Yeah," she said, leaning over to look. "These smaller plots across Main Street were likely homes for local tradesmen. Later maps would show the development of your part of town after the estate sold off various parcels of land. The school where the Workshop is was built in the twenties, right? Do you want to see something from that timeframe?"

"This is so cool to look at, but no, I better move on.

I'm guessing any later developments would not have had family burial plots on their land, so I don't think I'm dealing with a cemetery on the Workshop's property, which is good to know."

Lena leaned her hip against the table. "Yes, dealing with a cemetery site is certainly complicated. But have you thought about the ramifications if this is a more recent death? In current times, an unmarked grave in the woods is a serious matter, and the reason for it can't be good—" Lena cocked her head in confusion when she realized I was no longer standing next to her.

"Um, are you okay?"

Chapter 6

"Alex, can I get you something?" Lena asked with concern.

I had fallen back with a thunk into the chair and then leaned forward to bury my head in my arms on the table. "No, I'm fine," I said from the crook of my elbow.

"Uh-huh," she uttered, unconvinced.

I shoved myself upright and swiped my hair back from my eyes. "Really, I'm fine. You know, we've been discussing the possibility that this was a victim of foul play, but it was in a theoretical way, and in a more historical way, but what you've brought up made it personal. This skeleton was a person, and that makes it all too real, particularly if it was a violent death."

"Ah, the Nancy Drew façade has slipped away."

I looked at her sideways. "Right. But aside from that, which is bad enough, if this is a more recent death, we are talking a major crime that happened on or near my property. It could have far-reaching implications for me and the Workshop."

Lena squeezed my shoulder. "Well, the way I see it, you're going to brush yourself off and tackle this one step at a time, and Jack will do his job. Between the two of you, you'll find answers."

I pulled myself together and said, "You're right. Together we'll get through this. Thanks so much for your help."

"Anytime."

I sat in my car for a few minutes to organize the swirl of thoughts in my head. It was important to acknowledge finding human remains in this manner meant this was likely a tragic death, and being proactive was a way to help find answers.

The property assessor was just up the block from the police precinct, so I parked at the station and walked it. A bell at the top of the door announced my arrival, and a woman came out of the office to greet me at the counter.

"How can I help you?" she asked. Her voice had a pleasant but professional tone.

"I'm looking for any information you might have on 1715 Main Street."

"Do you have a parcel number?"

"No. I'm the current owner." I pulled out my license. "I'm just interested in the occupancy of the building. I know it was originally a school, but it was vacant when I purchased it."

"Oh, it was a government building. I can look it up over here." She moved down the counter to the computer and used the keyboard like someone with a lot of typing experience. Her keen dark eyes behind gold-rimmed glasses scanned the page, then she smiled and said, "Ah, here we go."

I pulled a notepad and pen from my purse. "Great!"

"It was in use as a school from 1914 until 1976. When the new school complex was completed, it was then used as a regional office space and storage for the education department until 2004, and then it became only records and old equipment storage until it was listed for sale in 2012. It sat vacant until you purchased it. I'll print this out for you." She swiveled to the printer.

"Thank you. So, is it typical to have a number of years with nothing really happening in a building such as mine?"

"It's not uncommon. The education department holds onto properties in case there's a need down the road, otherwise repurchasing land and rebuilding is cost-prohibitive. In larger towns, they often move all the government services to an old school building—tax assessor, county clerk, licenses, etc. But in more rural areas, they can often sit fallow for over a decade."

"I wonder why they decided to sell this one?"

She took off her glasses and carefully folded them, unlike me, who just shoved them on top of my head. "My guess is it became obsolete, and we're not a big enough town to be of any other use. I see here you got a pretty good deal on it."

"I did. Is that unusual?"

"Depends on where it is. If it's in a small town like ours, they will often let it go for pennies on the dollar."

"Which is how I was able to afford to buy and renovate it."

She put her glasses on again and scanned the screen. "Oh yes, you're the Creative Workshop. I came to your gift shop a few weeks ago. That building has so much character, so it's wonderful to see it brought back to life."

"Thank you! And I'm glad you came to our shop. Hopefully you found something."

"I did. Too many things! I'll be back for more gift shopping."

"How nice. Please tell me your name."

"Cora."

"Nice to meet you, Cora, and if you come by again, please stop in and say hi."

"I will."

Back out on the sidewalk, I checked my phone, which I had put on mute while I was in the library. I groaned when I saw fourteen missed calls and texts and scanned them quickly to make sure there was nothing urgent before heading to the precinct.

Walking through the doors was like walking into a time capsule. While the exterior had gotten modest facelifts over the years, the interior held a firm grip on the nineteen sixties. There was a tall counter with a thick scarred wood top, and a well-worn church pew sat against the wall for the waiting public. I had clocked some time here and recognized many of the same adverts on the corkboard affixed to the wall.

Gabe was on desk duty and waved me through the swing door at the end of the counter. "Jack's expecting you."

"Thanks. Weren't you on duty last night?"

"I went home for a few hours of sleep but wanted to come in and man the phones so they can do what they need to."

"You guys really need a secretary out here."

"Maybe someday." He chuckled.

When I entered the precinct room, there was a hum of activity. Jack was in his office on the phone, so I wandered over to the tables with the evidence bags. Matt was using a laptop to document each item into the computer. I didn't want to disturb his progress, so I tried to assess the assortment from about ten feet away.

"There's not much to go on, is there?" I asked.

"Nope," Matt said, while typing. "Jack is on the phone with the ME right now, but from what we found in the site, this is not a recent death. Most of the fabrics have totally decomposed. Which, in itself, helps give us some direction."

"How?"

"Well, synthetic blends take anywhere from twenty to over two hundred years, or never. Cotton usually takes a few months. Denim goes in about a year. Wool is between one and five years. But of course, a lot depends on soil and climate conditions."

"Wow, that's fascinating. And it really makes you think about what you buy, doesn't it?"

"Sure does. We know about all the plastic out there filling the landfills, but we don't think about the clothes we wear."

I mentally went through my wardrobe. Thankfully, my clothing nowadays mostly consisted of jeans and cotton shirts. But I did have a number of yoga pants for lounging, with the good intentions of exercising. I needed to look at those labels.

Jack emerged from his office, and called out, "Gather round, I have some news."

Matt and Travis perched on the edge of a desk near Jack's office, and I asked, "Can I stay?"

He nodded, then read from a piece of paper he had scrawled on. "The remains are of a female, age is between seventeen and early thirties, and height approximately five feet three inches. There were no identifying features, like a surgical plate with a serial number. Dental examination shows composite fillings. While not conclusive, it indicates this death occurred after the early 1960s. And the type of composite was more widely used prior to the late nineties or early 2000s."

"So we have anywhere from a late-teen to full adult.

And the body was buried between twenty and sixty years ago," Matt recapped. "What about ethnicity?"

"Forensic specialists are moving away from the usual methods of determining ethnicity, such as bone structure, and are using DNA to determine genetic ancestry. So it will take more time to get that answer."

"What about cause of death?" Travis asked.

"There was a skull fracture, and the medical examiner is reporting that the death was likely due to blunt force trauma," Jack said.

"Could have been an accident though, right? Like from a fall?" Matt asked.

"The fracture was behind the right ear," Jack answered, pointing to a spot at the base of his head behind the ear. "Most of the time people fall forward, not backwards, but we have to keep an open mind about it."

"And you would report an accident, not bury the body," I said.

"People do strange things in a moment of panic, so you can't rely on what you think would be logical."

"You're right," I said, in agreement.

"Okay, Matt, Travis, you know what to do. Continue to test and research the evidence from the scene. The ME will analyze the skeleton for any further clues. Alex, with me," he said, and turned toward his office.

I took a seat by his desk. "Well, any hopes that this was a historical death is out the window, isn't it?" I pulled out the printout from the assessor's office. "Here's the info on the building occupancy."

He took the sheet and quickly scanned it before putting it on his desk. "Thanks. And yeah, I know it would have been easier if the skeleton was from early nineteen hundreds or something, but it is what it is."

"I know. I had a reckoning at the library, realizing this is not an archeology mystery like on TV, but an actual person whose life was cut short."

Jack paused then said, "You had an important learning moment. In my profession, the minute we forget we are dealing with human beings, it's time to hang it up."

I nodded and let out a breath. "So, can you explain some of the findings in the ME report?"

"There's a lot of medical jargon, but they can tell a lot by the skull shape, how much the bones have fused in the skull, and things like the growth plate in the long bones of the body, and the width of the hip bones. I can only relay, not explain, as some of this is over my head."

I was jotting notes as he spoke. "Thanks, this is good. I don't need to know any of these details, but I find it interesting and may do some research just to learn a little more."

Jack gave me a lopsided grin. "You always did like to know why and how, even when we were kids. If I told you something, you would go and look it up to make sure I was right."

"And if I recall, I often enjoyed telling you when you were wrong," I said, with satisfaction.

"Enjoyed? No, you relished it."

"Guilty as charged," I admitted. "So, were the remains on my property?"

"Travis checked the land survey, and yes, it appears they were. Unless we get a surveyor out there to do an exact measurement, we could be off by a foot, but we're close enough to make the call."

"Oh," I said, feeling the weight of this news. I might not have had any further involvement had it been on someone else's property. I chewed on my thumbnail, then stopped myself and put my hand under my leg. "What do you want me to do?"

"There really isn't anything to do at the moment. This is a twenty-to-sixty-year-old crime. There's nothing to research and no one to talk to yet. We can't even request dental records until we can narrow things down more."

"There must be something I can do."

"Not really. I know you like to be proactive, and believe me, if I had something for you to do, I would gladly accept the help. For now, I need you to lie low and keep quiet about any of these details. If this was murder, and the murderer is still alive and in town, we don't want to spook them. So the best thing you can do is go about your business and not get yourself mixed up in this."

"What about the gang? Surely, I can talk it over with them."

He stared at me. "Official answer is, no. Off the record, I know you will, regardless of what I say, so please stress with them the need for discretion."

"Of course. I trust them one hundred percent."

"I know, but my official answer is still no."

"Now what about the reception on Wednesday and the opening next weekend. Do you think we can move forward?"

"I don't see why you can't. The remains and evidence have been removed, and it has nothing to do with you or the Workshop. So yes, you can move forward."

What a relief. "Great, thank you."

"The tent will come down this afternoon. The forensic specialist sent us a form with a checklist, so we want to take one more look at the site, but otherwise, there is really nothing to preserve out there. Matt even took soil samples from a radius around the burial site."

"You're lucky to have such a good team."

"I am. We may be small in numbers, but these boys are as professional as you can get."

"Hey, if Matt is done, can I look more closely at the evidence you found from the site?"

"Sure. I wanted him to get everything documented before handling things, so let's both take a look."

We approached the table and, while there were lots of bags, there wasn't much inside each. "Matt explained about the degradation of the various fabrics, which I guess is why there's not much here."

Jack scanned the data form Matt had created. "Yup. Tiny fabric scraps, a few threads, a metal button and zipper from jeans. Nothing much to speak of."

"Any labels?" I asked.

"Let me check." After looking at the list, he said, "Three label fragments. Bags seventeen A and B, and eighteen.

I pawed through the bags until I found the label scraps, then pulled out my phone. "I'm going to snap a pic of a few things to look up later."

"I didn't see anything on the labels, like a store or brand name."

"No, but certain codes within the clothing industry might help us narrow the date."

He looked at me, impressed. "I knew I kept you around for some reason."

"I used to spend time trying to figure out if I could machine wash some of my clothes. I hated schlepping to the dry cleaner. Nowadays I don't even have to separate my loads. I just throw it all in the washer together."

Jack moved back to the table. "There weren't any shoes, which is interesting."

"The poor thing was barefoot?"

"Yes, or they were removed after death."

Thinking of someone removing her shoes before burying her made me shiver. "Oh, how awful. What about jewelry?"

After checking the list he said, "There was a pair of silver earrings." He pawed through the pile to find the bag.

I snapped a photo of the earrings. Even after all the years in the ground I could tell they were good quality. The teardrop shape was tasteful, with an intricate but delicate design woven in silver, and even the hook was well crafted. "But no rings?" I asked.

"No. Hmmm," Jack muttered to himself

"Hmmm, what?"

"Well, it seems to me if there were any rings, they were stolen, or taken to delay identification. But why not take the earrings?" He checked the log. "They were found mid-skeleton, like the hip area."

"Oh!" I said in a rush, pleased I could contribute something. "Could be they were in her pocket. When I take off earrings, instead of putting them away, I often stash them in my pocket."

"Maybe that was it."

"Did Matt note if there was a silver mark or anything?"

Jack looked at the evidence log. "No, but he probably hasn't examined them closely yet. He gets everything logged in, first."

"Can I take them out?"

"Yes, but put on gloves. Matt might be able to get prints off these." Jack pulled two pairs of gloves from a box and handed me one. After donning his own, he slipped the teardrop earrings out into his hand, then tipped them into my hand.

"These are nice. Looks like marcasite and silver." I pulled my glasses down from my head and turned them over in my hand to look for a hallmark. "There's a mark, but it's too tiny for me to see."

Jack called over to Matt, "Do we have a jeweler's loupe?"

"Yessir," Matt replied, and rifled through his desk drawer.

I held one of the earrings close to my mouth and exhaled, then examined the hallmark. "Pt950. So it's platinum. But no designer's mark."

"Geez, why did you breathe all over it?" Jack asked, perplexed.

I laughed. "I've been watching a TV show where dealers road trip looking for stuff in antique stores. The experts do this when the piece is not clean or clear enough to read easily. Don't ask me why, but breathing on it makes the hallmark stand out. I've always wanted an excuse to try it, and to use a loupe!"

"Well, I'm happy we could oblige on both counts."

I got back to business, and said, "Okay, so these are platinum earrings. Tasteful, well-made, and not cheap. They would have probably been bought at a jewelry store."

Matt was watching this unfold, took the loupe, and confirmed my findings, then typed it into the laptop.

"Okay, well, I guess my work here is done," I said, then turned to go but stopped myself. "JJ wants to do some kind of cleansing ceremony at the burial site. Is that okay?"

Jack's eyes went squinty. "What kind of cleansing ceremony?"

"Something to do with burning spices while we do a silent prayer or wish for the departed soul."

Jack nodded in approval. "As long as you are on your property, you can do whatever you like. When the tent is gone, we're done with the site."

"Okay, thanks," I said. "You know JJ, she's all into this stuff. But in this case, I think it would be a worthwhile and meaningful gesture for whoever she is."

Once I left the precinct and was walking back to my car, a shroud of darkness descended as I thought about the poor soul whose life was cut short and unceremoniously buried in the woods. I also couldn't shake the feeling that this was only the beginning.

Chapter 7

Monday Afternoon

I wanted to continue investigating the skeleton, but it was time to tend to my duties as director of the Workshop. I went to the office behind the front desk and tackled the texts and voicemails I continued to receive since sending out the announcement. Using the stock line I came up with earlier, I assured people this had nothing to do with the Workshop, the police would release a statement when they had any updates, and at this time, the garden events would continue as scheduled.

Once I finished, I wanted to wander the halls to check in on the classes and make myself visible. The more normal we appeared, the better.

My first stop was the craft room. The door was open, so I stepped inside to observe the knitting class. Shelby, the instructor, was a master of all needlecrafts, and she also led our scrapbooking and card-making groups. People tend to do these crafts as a form of relaxation, so this classroom had a calm, low-key vibe, and there was always friendly banter amongst the participants. Today, the chatter was accompanied by the clicking of knitting needles.

"Hi, Alex, are you going to join us?" Shelby asked, good-naturedly.

"Ha! I wouldn't dare drag down your class. My mom tried to teach me to knit, but my hand always became a tight claw, and it was far from relaxing. Needlepoint was better, but not by much."

Shelby laughed. "One of these days I'll get you in here."

"Good luck with that. But if anyone can successfully teach me, it would be you."

I continued on my way. Spencer was working at his easel, so I knocked lightly before entering. "How's it going?"

He turned toward me with a paintbrush in his hand. "Okay. More importantly, how are you? Is there any news?"

"Jack and his team are almost done with their work here, and he said we can move forward however we want as soon as the tent comes down."

"Good."

"And I have some other news, but let's wait until we're all together later so I only tell it once."

"Oh man, you're going to leave me hanging!" he said, in mock dismay.

I laughed. "Yup." Then I grew serious. "It really is better to keep this discussion contained. Jack doesn't want the details discussed, and only reluctantly agreed, off the record, that I could keep you guys updated." Okay, Jack didn't agree to anything, and I couldn't lie. "Wait, I exaggerated that. He actually doesn't want me talking about it, but I told him I trusted you guys."

"Loose lips sink ships, as they say," Spencer said.

"Right you are," I agreed, walking toward the door.

I had snuck a peek at the incredibly detailed tromp l'oeil painting he was working on. It was so real-looking it felt like I could reach out and grab an object in the painting, and it always amazed me that a big guy with big hands could do such small, delicate work. This one was of a shadow box with a pocket watch, an old portrait photograph of a gentleman, and a vintage ink pen.

"Beautiful painting, by the way."

"Thank you, ma'am."

After a few more studio visits, my last stop was Maggie's photography studio. I wanted to enlist her help, and besides, I loved this room. The smell from the chemicals used to develop traditional film took me back to my childhood, when my mom turned one of our bathrooms into a darkroom.

Maggie was sitting at her computer, deep in concentration. I knocked on the door frame, and she looked up at me with her eyes shining bright behind her deep purple glasses. "Hi! Any news?" she asked.

"A little, but I don't want to interrupt. You look like you're working on something important."

"Nah, just scrutinizing this photo one last time before submitting it for approval from the client." Maggie always had a steady stream of freelance work. "Come on in."

I closed her door and then pulled a stool over to her worktable. "It's been a busy morning, but not necessarily the most productive."

"What'd you find out?"

"I'll fill you in, but first, do you remember I mentioned Lena telling me about a missing persons database?

"Yeah, vaguely. We didn't really talk about it."

I raised my eyebrows. "I thought maybe we could do a little digging on there. I've got a general timeframe from Jack, and it's a big span of years, so it might be pointless. But maybe if we made a list of any missing persons from the information I have, I could start asking some questions or do some research and maybe narrow down the list."

"Let's do it," she said, sliding off her stool.

"Don't you need to finish your job?" I asked, tilting my head toward her computer.

"It's not due until next week, so I'm good."

"Okay, let's go up to my apartment."

****

Maggie and I sat across from each other on the floor with our laptops on the coffee table. I filled her in on what I learned, and we hashed over theories, but as soon as we pulled up the NamUs site, we grew somber.

"This is sobering," Maggie said, scanning the online search form. "Before doing any filters, there are over twenty-four thousand current entries for the US."

"It's overwhelming to see how many people are missing, and to think about what those families must be going through." I breathed deeply, and said, "Okay, let's look at what filters we can use."

After entering the gender and height and date range, the number shrank to forty-six in our state.

"I'm amazed it dropped so much with what little we have to go on."

"Me too, but now I fear it will be an exercise in futility."

"Why?"

"I've started playing with the location filters, and depending on what county, the number could be zero or twelve. We just don't have enough information to make this worthwhile."

Maggie tried her hand at the county filter. "You're right. But there are zero missing persons in our county, which tells us something."

"Being in the mountains, and more rural, our county is not very populated, so I'm not surprised. I mean, Jack would likely have mentioned it right away if the department had an open missing persons case file."

"But now we can assume the skeleton was from a surrounding county or even from another state."

"Perhaps. However, and I hate to say this, but I'm sure not every missing person is entered on this site. Someone has to report them missing in the first place."

Maggie abruptly closed her laptop. "Argh. I don't know how we'll ever be able to do this."

"We might not. At least we know there are no missing persons reported from our town or county. And the investigation is in the early days. Jack and the ME may find something helpful. Speaking of which, a pair of earrings were found at the site." I pulled up the image on my phone and handed it to Maggie while I explained my theory about them being in the pants pocket of the victim.

"These are nice, and you're right. If she was murdered, these probably would have been taken along with rings or any other jewelry. Particularly if this was a robbery turned deadly," she said.

Maggie looked forlorn and I didn't feel all that great myself, so I decided we should do something to lift our spirits. "Come on, let's get out of here for a while."

She got up from the floor in one smooth motion, something I could no longer do, and said, "Good idea. Can we take a walk down Main Street and window shop?"

"Sure, let's mingle with the living."

We took a left out of the Workshop onto Main Street

and walked the few short blocks to the commercial center. Flat Rock Falls was a small town, but both sides of the street were lined with an array of shops and services to meet most every need. Granted, you couldn't find everything, but we still had independently owned stores, and we liked it that way.

We passed the Cut and Curl hair salon, which was next door to Drake's Barber Shop, and stopped to peruse the real estate listings hanging in the window. Then while Maggie lingered in front of the thrift store window, I moved down the way to look at the bookstore's display. Ultimately, we ended up at Sugar Rush, which was what I had anticipated.

This was no ordinary sweet shop. Yes, there were the ubiquitous jars of candy—both current and nostalgic—and ice cream and fudge. But this was also where you could get baked goods, cakes, pastries, breads, and specialty jams and spreads. The owners liked to mix things up, so some items were only available seasonally, and a lot depended on what they felt like making on any given day.

When it comes to ice cream, I'm predictable. Peanut butter and chocolate was my go-to, and I got two scoops in a waffle cup. Maggie went with pistachio. We found a bench in the shade a few doors down, and it was a perfect moment with the summer banners on the old-fashioned lamp posts fluttering in the light breeze. A few cars passed by, but the pace was slow and easy.

"This was a good idea," I said.

"Dang right," Maggie agreed.

Tucker's wife, Sasha, was jogging on the sidewalk across the street, and I indicated with the hand holding my ice cream. "We should really be doing what she's doing."

Maggie watched Sasha's progress. "Nah, that woman is obsessed with exercise. I've run into her a few times at the park, and we both did one of those new year boot-camp exercise programs. She works out all the time. With weights, too. She doesn't look it, but she's strong. To me, it's exhausting to even think about."

"You did a boot camp?" I asked, incredulously.

"Well, I made it through two classes and then stopped going. It's too hard core for me."

I laughed. "That's two more than I could have done. Does Sasha work?"

Maggie had a mouthful of ice cream, so she shook her head.

"That means she probably has a lot of time on her hands, and focusing on exercise is a lot healthier than watching TV while eating cheese doodles, which is what I would do."

"Hey, don't knock the TV and doodles combo," Maggie chastised.

"Agreed. What was I thinking?"

"Oh, look," Maggie said, "there's Daisy and Luke." They were going into the deli across the street.

"Those two are so cute. I think they may be long-haul daters."

"I think you're right."

We continued to people-watch, and I could feel my shoulders relax as we continued chatting about trivial things.

Unfortunately, our moment of serenity was cut short. The bench we chose was near the entrance to the Emporium, and Winifred stuck her head out and said, "I thought I saw you!"

"Hi, Winifred," I said, pleasantly.

She came out of her shop and stood over us. "Well, look at you guys out here as if on holiday."

"Sometimes you just need some ice cream," Maggie said.

"I wish I were so lucky to have leisure time. I'm just too swamped to play hooky. And actually, I'm surprised you can fritter away time after finding a skeleton. I assume that would require some damage control."

I switched to my professional tone and said, "There's really nothing to do. As I explained in my email, the police are working to identify the remains, and the timeline suggests it has nothing to do with us. So once they are done at the site, we'll be back to the prep for the volunteer and patron reception." This was my opening to see if I could find out where she was on Saturday night. "Speaking of, thank you again for your help in the garden. Did all you volunteers go out afterward on Saturday to celebrate being done?

She tilted her head, disconcerted. "I didn't. Did people go out? I didn't hear anything about it. What do you know?"

She was clearly not happy at the prospect of being left out, so I quickly covered my act of subterfuge. "No, I don't know anything. I should have worded that differently. I was just thinking you all *deserved* to reward yourselves for the hard work."

Her face relaxed. "Oh. My reward was to go home, take a hot bath, and then work on my new art project."

"Sounds pretty nice, to me. And we'll celebrate you all at the reception on Wednesday."

Any further discussion was halted when Ben, from the hardware store, barged through his door and stomped over to us.

"Winifred," he barked, "you have really gone too far this time. Why you think you can stick your nose into what I do with my own business is beyond me."

"Oh, simmer down, Ben," Winifred shot back. "What's got your undies all bunched up this time?"

"I heard you were instrumental in getting my permit denied to have my smoker going out front during the sidewalk sale weekend."

Maggie and I watched this exchange like we were at a tennis match.

"You can't believe I wield enough power to single-handedly kill your plan," she said, innocently.

"I know you had a firm hand in it," Ben retorted.

"Surely there were others who didn't want that dirty thing taking up the sidewalk, sending smoke up and down Main Street."

"Oooo, I love the smell of a wood-smoked barbecue," Maggie said to Ben.

"See? It's a signature summer food! And I sell those smokers. It's a live demonstration as part of my sidewalk sale. For crying out loud, woman, the road will be closed off, so there's plenty of room for all of us. You are messing with my business."

"Then you should have been at the meeting. Maybe you can appeal the decision, although there's not much time, is there?" she said, with satisfaction.

Ben glared at her hard. "One of these days you're going to push the wrong person too far, and you'll regret it."

"Oh Ben, let it go. They said you can have your beloved smoker at the end of the block near the parking lot. So it's not like you were denied everything. Stop being such a sourpuss."

At a loss for words, Ben turned on his heel and stormed back to the hardware store.

My mouth was hanging open, so I closed it, then said, "Wow, Winifred, that's not the best way to get along with your fellow shop owners. Did you really get his permit denied?"

"No"—she scowled—"I'm just the one he knew of who didn't want it out on the sidewalk, so he blasted me. He'll cool off eventually."

"I hope so. I like to think of Main Street as this happy family of shop owners."

"We are, for the most part," she said, dismissively. "But back to the original topic, there's no further news on the skeleton?"

"Um, not yet, and it could take a while."

"Well, the answer is probably more obvious than anyone thinks," she said, conspiratorially.

Chapter 8

I looked at Winifred sharply. "What do you mean? Do you know something?"

She checked herself and became tightlipped. "Oh, nothing. I don't really know anything."

I didn't believe her. "If you do know something, you should talk to the police."

She waved her hand as if swatting a gnat. "No, no. You know me, I'm always babbling on about something. I don't know anything." She feigned looking at her watch. "I better get back to work. Time waits for no one!" she crooned.

I watched her retreat, and when the shop door closed behind her, I looked at Maggie and said, "What do you think she meant?"

Maggie seemed unfazed and had returned to her ice cream. "She's all bluster. I mean, look at the exchange with Ben. Anyway, what could she possibly know?"

"I don't trust her," I said.

"Well, I don't trust her either, which means I take everything she says with a grain of salt. We've already determined no one is missing from this county. And she doesn't even know the handful of details Jack has found out."

I shook it off. "You're right. Dang, she gets under my skin."

Maggie laughed. "I think that's the point. She likes

to make people uneasy."

"At least I was able to find out she was on her own Saturday night, which means she could be the culprit who turned on the hose."

"Maybe, although I do find it hard to visualize her sneaking around in the dark. The social media slams? Sure. But the other stuff just doesn't seem to fit her style." She got up from the bench, and said, "I guess we should head back."

I folded up the paper bowl my waffle cup came in and put it in the nearby trashcan. On my way back to the bench, a storefront across the street caught my eye.

"Wait, before we go, let's stop in Smythe Family Jewelry and ask about the earrings."

"Good idea!"

We crossed the street and entered the store. For some reason, I've always felt that sounds are muted in a jewelry store, as if people speak in hushed tones in the presence of gemstones. The clerk was busy with a customer, so we scanned the jewelry cases and pointed out things—in a hushed tone, I might add—that we would or wouldn't wear. Maggie was holding up a pair of dangly earrings for my approval when the clerk approached.

"May I help you?" she asked, pleasantly.

"Hi, my name is Alex Montgomery, and I just have a quick question." Pulling out my phone, I showed her the photo of the earrings. "Do these look like anything you might have sold here?"

She scrutinized the photo, using her fingers to enlarge the image. "Hmmm, these are lovely. Do you know when they were purchased?"

"No, I'm afraid not."

"We haven't sold them while I've worked here, but then again, I just moved back home this summer. My father might recognize them."

"Oh, are you part of the Smythe family?"

"I am," she said, with pride.

"Well, you would have probably been just a toddler when I was a kid running around here with my cousin Jack. And now, look at us, we're all grown up, and you've got quite a legacy here with the family business. As a matter of fact, your father helped Jack with a case last year."

"Yes, of course," she said. "He told me about that. I'm afraid he's not in right now, but if you want to email me the photo, I'll ask him later." She handed me her business card.

"Great, thank you!"

Maggie and I returned to the Workshop with a fresh outlook, and after a quick stop at the front desk, we went out the courtyard doors. The crime scene tent had been removed, which restored a sense of normalcy, and we found Ryan and Elliott placing the last of the description markers in front of the sculptures.

"What do you think?" I asked, as we approached. "Has it come together like you thought it would?"

Ryan's boyish charm had been replaced by a professional demeanor as he scrutinized every detail. "I'm really pleased. I think it came out even better than I'd visualized."

"Same here," Elliott agreed. "The glass sculptures from Hank and Twila have elevated the whole thing."

"Well, let's not downplay the main attraction. You guys have done a brilliant job. You worked together to plan this, and I could not be happier. You should be proud of yourselves."

"Thanks," Ryan said. "And hey, they came to remove the tent. Are we on schedule to move forward with the reception?"

"We are. But I'm thinking we should not finish placing the benches right now. Let's leave it with just the sculpture garden and not have anyone around the tree line."

Elliott stroked his chin. "Yeah, we really don't need to attract any attention over there."

Ryan nodded in agreement. "We could end up having gawkers congregating around the site. I think it's enough we got the signage installed over there for no trespassing."

"Agreed. Let's keep everyone focused on this," I said, opening my arms to indicate the sculpture garden.

Maggie scanned the area. "So what's left to do?"

"I think we're done! We'll put out the tables Wednesday morning, but otherwise, it's just business as usual."

"Cool," Ryan said.

"How many people do you think there will be?" Maggie asked.

"It's open to the Workshop artists, the volunteers, and our patrons, so I'm guessing around forty-five to fifty. Although, I know a few are waiting to come for the grand opening, so I probably ordered too much food."

"But we get to have the leftovers, right?"

I laughed. "You bet we do."

We often had a gaggle of artists who lingered out in the courtyard at the end of the day, and we had a casual system where people would just randomly bring things to leave in the kitchen, like a bag of tortilla chips and a jar of salsa or a wedge of cheese and crackers.

Maggie asked, "Hey, when are we going to do JJ's cleansing ceremony at the burial site, Alex?"

"I think tomorrow morning would be best." I waggled my eyebrows at Ryan and Elliott. "Do you guys want to join us?"

"I'm not sure what's involved, particularly with the look you just gave us, but I'll come along," Ryan answered.

Elliott hesitated, but when Ryan nodded encouragingly, he said, "Sure, why not."

"I'll send out a text chain once I firm things up with JJ."

A movement caught my eye. It was Tucker, milling around at the tree line. "I'll be right back," I said.

I jogged across the lawn and approached Tucker. "Everything all right?" I asked him.

He appeared startled. "Oh, yes. Fine. I'm just looking for the skeleton site to see if it's on our property."

I pointed to the left. "It's down there, about twenty yards or so. Jack checked the survey, and it appears to be on the Workshop's land."

Tucker started walking in the direction I had pointed. "I don't even see where it was."

"They did a really nice job of putting things back so no attention is drawn to it."

I felt a swell of appreciation for Jack and his crew. They had backfilled the burial site and had even covered it with mulch. If I hadn't had the location seared into my mind, I would not have known it was there.

Before we reached the spot, Tucker stopped. "I guess I don't really need to go any farther." He looked uncomfortable. "This has been such a shock, and I wanted to ensure it wasn't on our property. I'm not sure how we'd handle it if that was the case."

I reached out and touched his shoulder. "I know this has been disconcerting. If it's any consolation, I don't think this has any bearing on any of us. And Jack and his team are taking care of everything."

He looked at me sharply. "So you know how old it is?"

I hedged. "No, not exactly. All I know is it's not a recent death."

"I see. I know Sasha will be relieved. And I know she'll be glad things have been cleaned up enough that it won't draw any unwanted attention. She's very security conscious, you know."

"I think it's wise to be aware of what's going on around you. On a brighter note, we've been given the all clear to move ahead, so I'm assuming we will see you and Sasha at the reception tomorrow, right?"

"Um, I'm not sure. Sasha is talking about going out of town. There's some show she wants to see in New York."

"Oh, but it would be a shame not to be here after all the work you did."

"We'll see. When Sasha is determined to do something, there's no changing her mind," he said, then becoming shy, added, "And it's hard for me not to give her what she wants."

"Well, personally, I find it quite sweet you are so smitten with her. We should all be so lucky."

Tucker favored me with a genuine smile. "Well, I better be on my way," he said, turning to leave.

****

Monday Evening

The gang had assembled in my apartment to brainstorm, and the table held the remains of the takeout Spencer had picked up. We were now all in a food coma. Maggie and Ryan were lying on the floor, and Annie, JJ, Spencer, and Bitsy were in a state of repose on the big leather couch and side chairs, with their feet propped on the coffee table.

With a fresh cup of coffee in my hand, I gave the customary caution that what we were discussing had to remain in the room, then I went to the whiteboard, wiped it clean with the eraser, and started from scratch.

"Okay, on the left side, I'm going to lay out what we know." I wrote as I spoke. "The remains are female, anywhere from late teens to early thirties, and approximately five-three in height."

"How'd they determine that?" Spencer asked.

I read from the notes I had taken when doing some research after Jack had given me the details. "The width of the pelvic spread indicates gender, the long bone lengths help with height, and the extent of the growth plate attached to the bone in the clavicle or femur—something called partial union of epiphysis—and the cranial sutures, help with age. The hair had already broken down because of the soil conditions, so we don't know hair color."

"Wow," Ryan said, "that's some technical stuff. You actually sound like you know what you're talking about."

I choked out a laugh. "I wish. I did look up some of this stuff, and I'm summarizing here, so don't take this as textbook accurate. There are a lot of medical terms I don't remember. But it is fascinating, isn't it?"

"Sure is," Spencer agreed.

"What about the date of death?" Bitsy asked.

"That's more complicated," I answered.

"I guess when dealing with older skeletal remains, dating the death is much harder than we might think."

"Right," I said, returning to my notes. "A forensic scientist would have to study the bones to determine date of death. But from some of the dental work and the decomposition of the clothing, we know the range is from the early 1960s to early 2000s."

"That's a wide margin. So what will Jack do?" JJ asked.

"I don't know. Once he sends the bones off for forensic study, it could be a long time. A science magazine article I read states over four thousand unidentified bodies are found around the world each year, and a quarter of those remain unknown after a year."

"Awwgh," JJ groaned. "This is so depressing!"

"I know. These realities hit hard, but let's try and focus on what was found here. There's more we have learned."

"Okay, keep going," she said, forlornly.

"Jack and I looked at the bits and pieces found in the burial site." I took a printout of the photo of the earrings and used a magnet to hold it on the board. "Aside from what looks like a jeans button and zipper, and an array of plastic buttons, probably from her top, these earrings were found under the skeleton, near the hip area."

Maggie said, "Alex thinks maybe the victim put them in her pocket, and the killer didn't know they were there."

Bitsy got up to look more closely. "Those are

pretty."

Annie stood next to her, tilting her head. "These aren't five-and-dime earrings. They would have been bought at a jewelry store."

Spencer asked, "So how much do you think they would have cost? Like a couple hundred bucks?"

"Maybe. It's hard to know. Alex said there's no designer mark, which makes them more affordable, but the quality is really good."

"To that point, Maggie and I stopped in Smythe Family Jewelry, and I got an email from Brenda this afternoon. She said her dad didn't know for sure, but he thinks they might have sold those a long time ago."

Maggie perked up. "Did she say anything else? Could he dig out any old records?"

"She wrote it was probably pre-2000, and unless it's something high end with a serial number on it, they don't hold onto records more than ten years."

Annie said, "Well, at least it wasn't a hard *no*."

I held up another printout. "This is part of a clothing and jeans label found in the site. I'm going to do a little research to see if this narrows things down at all. I know this one's a Woolmark, but I want to see if I can date either of them."

Bitsy got up and said, "I'll do it right now. Can I use your laptop?"

"Sure, it's over on the counter. It also looks like part of the number five, possibly for the size."

We continued hashing things over until Bitsy brought the laptop over to relay her findings. "There are several sites on vintage clothing. The jeans label doesn't help us, but this a Woolmark used after 1971, indicating a sixty-percent wool blend."

I wrote this new information on the board.

"And I found that odd numbers were used into the early 1980s to differentiate petite sizing. In the eighties, odd numbers switched to teen sizes."

"So, her death was likely between 1971 and, in case the clothing was from a vintage shop, maybe the mid-80s."

"Unless she was a teenager, in which case based on the sizing, she died after the mid-80s," Spencer pointed out.

"But what teenager is going to wear those earrings?" Annie asked.

Spencer became exasperated. "Ugh! What's the difference? All this girl stuff is driving me nuts. Petite vs. teen sizes, jewelry with age parameters."

Annie laughed, then said, "Calm down. This is not a hard and fast rule, but typically, teenage girls are going to wear either very distinctive earrings highlighting their individuality, or they will wear small delicate ones, often with a cute theme that makes them happy. Women, on the other hand, often want something tasteful and classic that will never go out of style."

"And," Maggie added, "teens don't usually have the money for expensive earrings. Plus, I can't tell you how many earrings I lost when I was younger. My mom would never have allowed me to get expensive jewelry."

Spencer patted the air. "Okay, I get it now. So while it's not out of the realm of possibility these were a gift to a younger girl, the chances are they were bought for or by an adult."

"Right!" Bitsy said.

JJ stood and looked in awe at the board. "She is starting to take shape! I can see her in my mind's eye."

"You're right!" I enthused. "We have a petite female, she was wearing wool, maybe a button-down sweater with a cotton T-shirt over a pair of jeans, and she was well-heeled enough to have those platinum earrings. And we're going to guess late twenties to early thirties."

"We've brought her to life," JJ said, in a hushed tone.

"This is kind of chilling," Annie said. "It makes me imagine one of us when we were younger—murdered and buried in the woods." She turned to Maggie with wide eyes. "It could be you."

Chapter 9

"Thanks Annie," Maggie said. "Are you trying to give me nightmares?"

"Sorry."

Bitsy attempted to calm Annie's fear. "Humanizing the skeleton just makes it even more gratifying to think maybe we are going to give her some justice."

Annie still looked creeped out but said, "I guess so."

Spencer took the marker and went to the board. "Now we have to figure out if there is any correlation to what's been happening here." He started making a list. "Social media slams. What do we think?"

Annie tilted her head. "I just don't see it. What would be the point?"

"I think those are more about undermining our credibility," Ryan said.

We all agreed, so Spencer put social media in the unrelated column. "The sabotage. What about that?" he asked.

I said, "I feel if there is a living person connected to the skeleton, it would be motive to disrupt the garden."

"But pulling out some lights and knocking over pots isn't going to do anything significant," JJ insisted. "It's not like it would stop us from completing the sculpture garden. It smacks of the same immaturity as the cyber-bullying."

Maggie said, "I'm sorry, but to me, the social media

slams and the stuff in the garden just don't feel related."

Ryan chimed in, "But what are the odds you'd have someone slinging insults on social media, a second person sabotaging our progress in the garden, and then a skeleton happens to be found. It's too many things happening at once."

We seemed to be deadlocked, so I said, "Well, I think it means we don't have enough information yet."

Maggie, sitting cross-legged on the floor, held up her first finger. "One way we will know is if all the sabotage stops now."

I said, "Good point!"

"There were no social media posts today," she added.

"And nothing further has happened in the garden since Saturday night," Ryan said.

"It's early days, but regardless of what it means, it would be nice if both would stop," I said, and moved to the kitchen to clear the table and wrap up leftovers.

JJ called from the living room, "What about the cleansing ceremony? Are we going to do it?"

"Yes," I called back, then returned to the group. "I've got a bit to do to prepare for the reception, but I can block off whatever time you want."

"It should be early morning," JJ said in a tone no one would argue with.

"How early?" Ryan asked, meekly.

"Sunrise would be best, but I know better than to even suggest it. How about eight a.m. at the site?"

Everyone agreed they would be there, and Ryan said he would text Elliott.

After the gang left, I sat on the couch with Baxter and stared at the whiteboard. I looked at the clock and realized another day had gone by, and I hadn't talked to Walter. Granted, the time difference made it hard on both sides to time things just right. But I questioned the significance of not making it a priority to talk this over with him.

Was I pulling back? We had only become an item last February, so it hadn't even been six months. Or maybe it was the fact that this was the third time death had come knocking on my door, and I was getting used to it.

****

Tuesday

The next morning, I arrived at the burial site before everyone else and sat down on the grass. The air was still, and the only sound was the call and response of the birds above me in the trees. Even though the skeleton was gone, and the human form was gone long ago, there was a spiritual presence in the air, as if she knew we were trying to help her.

"I am so sorry for whatever you suffered," I said softly. "What happened to you?"

Okay, I didn't think I would get some kind of cosmic response, and I don't know why I was talking out loud to an empty burial site. Maybe JJ was rubbing off on me. I did believe in spiritual energy, though. Most of us have experienced the "you could feel the tension in the room" scenario, or to put it more simply, good or bad vibes. Well, this was the same thing. And maybe I was just hoping she would somehow know we cared about what happened to her.

My moment of contemplation was interrupted by the bustle of the gang arriving. JJ carried two large tote bags and was talking to the others as they crossed the lawn.

Annie trudged a few feet behind, dragging a small red wagon.

"Morning!" I called out.

Most of my friends were not early risers, and the telltale signs were evident. Ryan still had a pillow crease mark on his cheek, Annie's eyes weren't fully open, Spencer had a jumbo-sized coffee, and Maggie had hastily pulled her hair up into a turban. Elliott and Bitsy, like me, seemed unfazed by the early hour.

JJ pulled out a large metal bowl from one bag and a tied cloth bag from the other. "So, there are many kinds of smoke ceremonies from cultures around the world, and I've curated a selection for our purposes today. This is not only for the departed soul, but also a cleansing for our land and the garden."

"What's in there?" Bitsy asked, curiously.

"Rose petals, sandalwood powder, turmeric, juniper, cedar, and rosemary, and Yerba Santa sage incense."

"Mmm, that's going to make me hungry!" Ryan teased.

JJ looked at him out of the corner of her eye. "You can eat later. Gather in a semicircle," she instructed us.

Once we were in place, she used a long match and lit the items in the bowl. A pleasing scent drifted into the air on the ribbons of smoke.

"We will now take a private moment to send good wishes, a prayer, or meditation, on the life lost here."

Minutes usually ticked by slowly when in silence, but this morning there was a sense we were all in this moment, and we didn't emerge from whatever place we had been in our own heads until JJ gently cleared her throat.

"While this finishes burning, we can look toward the future." She opened her arms wide. "Take a moment to appreciate the trees, the garden, and our beautiful building."

After an appropriate amount of time, Annie said, "I picked up some ground cover at the Garden Gate Nursery. It's called sweet woodruff, and I brought one for each of us to plant. Do you guys like that idea?"

"Absolutely," JJ said.

Ryan ran back to the Workshop to grab a couple of trowels, and then we dug the holes and tucked in the plants.

By the time we finished, the ceremonial bowl had stopped smoking and only ash remained. JJ took the ash and spread it around the new plants.

"How do you all feel?" she asked.

Ryan chimed in first. "Actually, this was really cool, JJ!"

Everyone agreed.

I said, "I think we're now ready to plow ahead with the events of the week."

Maggie asked me, "I was going to go home and take a shower, but do you want to go over the schedule for today and tomorrow, first?"

"Yeah, let's do that. Do you want a coffee? I'll run upstairs and make you a macchiato and then meet you in the courtyard."

"Sounds perfect."

A few minutes later, Maggie and I had settled ourselves at a courtyard table and were checking things off the to-do list. After Maggie talked about the press release and social media announcements she was working on, I said, "I'm heading over to the Café later, so I'll make sure Aunt Claudia doesn't need us to do anything else before they arrive tomorrow."

"And I'll remind Ryan to bring down the tables later today so if he's not around, you and I can get them outside and set up. I'll have him leave them in the lounge."

"Good. And he and Elliott will make sure the paths are blown and that everything looks good in the garden. There's just not much to do for this kind of thing, so I think we're set."

"It feels like there should be loads to do because we have been working on this so long, but we've finally hit the finish line!"

"Cheers to that," I said, raising my coffee mug. "So, have you talked to Preston lately? Is he coming to the opening?" We'd met Preston during the winter festival. He was a woodworker who lived a couple of hours away, and he and Maggie had become friends.

"I have. He's doing good and is still thinking about moving here. He might come this weekend for the opening, but it depends on if he can get someone to cover him at an arts and crafts fair."

"I'm sure his business is doing well, and I would love to have him here. Any sparks flying between you two?" Maggie had a comical history of bad dates, and recently, a not-so-funny bad situation she barely escaped from.

She turned coy. "Oh, I don't know. We've become good friends, and I think it's best we don't take it any further right now, but you never know. Maybe."

"He's awfully nice, and pretty darned cute."

"He is. Now, since you've grilled me, how about Walter?"

117

"Walter's good. He's in London right now."

"You are being expertly evasive," she said.

I propped my feet on the chair across from me. "Oh, I don't know. Long distance isn't easy. I'm stationary, so my daily life keeps rolling along. Walter travels all the time, so each stretch is different for him."

"Do you feel like it's not working?" she asked, with concern in her voice.

"I wouldn't say that." I could feel my brows pinch together. "He hasn't been here in almost two months, so maybe I'm just returning to what my life looked like without him."

"Well, you are fiercely independent, which is why a long-distance thing should work for you. You don't need him to be here underfoot all the time."

"Maybe. But it's one thing to have a long-distance relationship, and another when it's a three-prong long-distance relationship." I ticked off on my fingers. "He travels for work, then he has his corporate apartment in New York, then he makes a few trips here for just a handful of days each time. So I just don't know how this is going to play out."

"You'll know when you set eyes on him the next time. He's coming this weekend, right?"

"Yeah."

"You'll know when you see him. I have no doubt your gut will tell you immediately."

I looked at her in amazement. "How'd you get to be so wise?"

She smiled at me. "I have a good role model. And I've had plenty of disastrous dating experiences, so I know a good thing when I see it," she said, with a laugh.

"I'm not going to argue with that."

"Now, let's check our social media," she suggested, while I was still in good humor.

"Ugh!"

Maggie pulled up our Facebook page on her phone and when she frowned, I knew it wasn't good. "Well, they've struck again."

"Damn. What'd they write?"

"A skeleton found buried on the grounds. You'll need a ghost buster if you go to the Creative Workshop. Are there any skeletons in the closet? What secrets lie within?"

My jaw dropped. "Oh my gosh. This is awful!"

Maggie tossed her phone onto the table. "I'm speechless."

My emotions got the better of me, and my eyes welled up. "This has got to stop."

"I know! I want to write 'STOP IT!' but I know I can't."

A few tears had leaked out of my eyes, and I harshly brushed them from my cheeks, aggravated I had let this get to me.

"I know you're not supposed to, but should I post a comment back?" she asked. "This is particularly bad."

"No, we can't respond in any way. We just have to ride this out."

Then I came up with a solution. The tears had stopped, and now I was ready to combat the problem.

"Here's what we're going to do. We'll do a series of posts, at least one a day, maybe two, highlighting the different classes we're offering in the fall, the current classes, and the opening of the garden. We are going to bombard them with positive and uplifting posts with lots of beautiful photographs. Maybe highlight an artist a few times a week."

"Yeah!" Maggie cheered. "I'll take care of it. I'll stop in some of the classes each day and take some candid photos to post, same with the garden and sculptures. This is a great idea."

"We can't stop whoever is doing this, so all we can do is move forward and not hide from view. Whoever this is, they're a bullying coward, and we will not be victimized."

"Right!"

With a renewed spirit, Maggie went home to get ready for the day, and I manned the front desk with a robust attitude to greet people coming in for the morning classes.

Later, I stopped to see Annie in her studio. "Hey! You look a bit brighter than you did this morning."

She had her magnifying visor on and talked while finishing up tiny strokes on an area of her painting. "You know I don't like getting up early, but I'm glad I did today. I think JJ's ceremony was really impactful."

"Me too."

I went over to her wall of shelves to see if she had any new props for her paintings, which were always full of whimsy. She had an array of balloon dogs she'd been using in her latest series. They were lined up on a shelf alongside some colorful metal toys, and another held everything from vintage Pez dispensers to leather suitcases.

"I stopped in because I'm going over to the Café for lunch. Wanna come?"

"You don't have to ask me twice. Hold on while I prep this stuff so I can leave it for a bit."

Annie went through a few steps so she could come

back and pick up where she had left off, and then we headed out the front doors for the short walk to the Café. The bell above the door jingled merrily as we entered, and the soft kiss of air conditioning was welcome. It wasn't very hot outside, but in the sun, anything above seventy-five was too warm for me unless there was a good stiff breeze.

We shuffled into a booth, and I caught Aunt Claudia's eye when she emerged from the kitchen.

"What'll you girls have?" she asked, order pad at the ready.

We put in our lunch orders, and I asked, "Can you come sit with us and visit while we eat?"

She looked around the room and, since the waitstaff had everything well in hand, said, "Sure, I'd love to."

When Claudia returned with our lunches, she sat down next to me on the booth bench. "Whew, for a weekday, it's been steadily busy."

"It's summer, so the vacationers are in full swing," Annie said.

"I guess so. Well, catch me up. Are we clear to proceed with the reception?"

Before I said too much, I looked around to make sure no one was sitting within earshot. "Yes, all systems go. And you'd never know anything happened. Jack's guys did a great job re-covering the site," I said.

"Good. Any news on the remains?"

Annie said, between mouthfuls, "We've done a whiteboard, like the police do, in Alex's apartment, and we've come up with a general description—Ow!" she exclaimed, when I kicked her under the table to stop her from saying too much about our part of it.

Too late. Aunt Claudia turned toward me with a

scowl. "Are you meddling in something you shouldn't? And now you've dragged Annie into it?"

I put my hands up in surrender. "No, of course not! Jack has determined it doesn't have anything to do with us or the Workshop. The remains are from before my time here. But since they were found on my property, I want to do what I can. And Annie came up with the whiteboard on her own!"

She looked skeptical, but said, "All right. I know you and Jack can be thick as thieves, but I don't want you roping Annie into anything that would make me worry even more than I already do."

I put two fingers up. "Scouts honor."

"That's a peace sign," Annie noted.

Aunt Claudia rolled her eyes. "You're hopeless." She saw a customer enter and said, "I'll be right back."

There was still no one was sitting near us, so Annie and I continued chatting about the case. I pulled out my phone to look at the photo of the earrings and we were mindlessly talking about what kinds of jewelry we wore at various ages, when Aunt Claudia returned and looked over my shoulder.

"What's this? Are you in the market for some jewelry?"

"No, those were found at the site of the remains."

"Oh." A somberness descended on her normally jovial face, and then she tilted her head and leaned closer to the phone.

"What is it? I know looking at this makes it all too real, so I'm sorry, we shouldn't have been talking about it here."

Aunt Claudia set the phone on the table. "No, it's not that. I feel like I recognize those earrings."

"What? You recognize them?" I said, in shock.
"I can't be sure, but they look familiar to me…"
"Where did you see them?" Annie said, urgently.
"I think my friend Eleanor had a pair like this."

Chapter 10

"Eleanor? You mean Tucker's first wife?" I asked, in disbelief.

"Yes." She waved her hand in dismissal. "Of course, anyone could have had the same earrings. They are nice, but they're not bespoke."

Annie and I looked at each other and silently signaled a message to dial it back. "I'm sure you're right. You said Eleanor sent you a postcard. So it couldn't be her."

"Right, she did. A lot of time has passed, so these probably aren't anything like what Eleanor had."

"You don't happen to remember what year she left, do you?" I asked.

"Gosh, it was so long ago. It was after the summer you and your mom came for a visit like usual, but she had to go back for a summer workshop for teachers. You stayed a few weeks longer. I don't remember what year that was."

I remembered the summer she was referring to. Jack and I were finally old enough to be left to our own devices, and we would spend much of the day outside in the woods, and then we'd walk into town for ice cream or candy. We would also walk to the Café for lunch every day so Aunt Claudia could keep tabs on us. I was still young, maybe ten or twelve, but Jack, being a few years older, was expected to make sure we didn't get into any trouble.

I didn't want her dwelling on this, so I breezily said, "I'm not sure what year that was either. Maybe Jack will remember." I looked at Annie for assistance.

"Do you still have the postcard she sent you? It might be nice to look her up. With the internet, it'd be a lot easier now," Annie said, with encouragement.

"I actually got a couple of them, but if I do, they're buried somewhere in a photo album. The first was from Las Vegas of all places," she said with a chuckle. "That's *not* a place I would imagine her settling, so she was probably on her way to wherever she was going. She sent another one from northern California, which would be more her style."

"I like northern California," Annie contributed.

"Me, too," I said, now genuinely distracted. "Redwoods National Park is a favorite of mine."

Aunt Claudia said, "Anyway, it's likely I've linked two unrelated things. When you asked about her the other day, it brought back a flood of memories, so she's fresh on my mind. That's all."

"I'm sure that's it," I said. "If it will make you feel any better, I'll keep you updated as we learn anything further."

"Please do."

"And for now, please don't talk to anyone about what we've discussed," I said, earnestly.

She looked at me and pursed her lips. "After all the years with your uncle, and now Jack, I know enough to keep my mouth shut."

I wrapped my arm around her shoulders and gave her a side hug. "I know you do."

She noticed a group come in, waiting to be seated,

and slid out of the booth. "I gotta get back to work. I'll see you tomorrow."

"Okey doke."

Once Annie and I were back outside, we were quiet, deep in our own thoughts as we walked, and then Annie grabbed my arm and stopped.

"We have to ask ourselves if it's possible. Could she be Tucker's first wife, Eleanor?"

"I don't know. I didn't say anything in there, but the summer she was referring to was around 1980."

"That fits the timeline."

"It does. I can check some things at home and nail down which year she was talking about."

"And can you use some of your tools to see if you can find Eleanor?"

"Yes. I'll see if I can find her."

"I really hope you can. I don't want to jump to any conclusions, but it would be devastating to find out she has been here all along, dead and buried."

"You aren't kidding." Just the thought of it made my stomach queasy.

We quickstepped back to the Workshop where Annie returned to her studio, and I went up to my apartment to dig out an old photo album. As I pored through the pictures, there was a bittersweet pull at my heart looking at image after image of my mom smiling and laughing. I also watched the timeline of Jack and me growing up from toddlers to teenagers. The memories were overwhelming as I worked my way toward the year I was looking for, and it felt like it was only yesterday we spent our holiday breaks here. Plus, small details started to emerge from my memory.

I've always had a thing for shoes—I even slept with

my first pair of patent leather Mary Janes under my pillow when I was about five years old—and I remembered that the summer Aunt Claudia referred to I had gotten some red high-top sneakers. I wore them every day. After flipping through a couple more pages, there I was, in a pair of shorts and those red shoes. I pulled the photo out and looked on the back. It was stamped 1981. That would mean, based on what Aunt Claudia said and the Woolmark label, which indicated she was wearing wool, Eleanor would have left in the fall of 1981 or winter of 1982.

I pulled out my phone and called Jack. "Hey," I said when he picked up. "Can you stop by here later? I need to go over some things with you and tell you about something that came up when we were at the Café."

"Uh, sure. Is Mom okay?"

"She's fine. Really. I'll explain when I see you."

"I should be able to come over around six."

"Great. Thanks."

I decided I needed a head-clearing in order to work with focus. I put on Baxter's leash, and we ambled down the stairs to the lobby. Maggie was at the front desk and had just hung up the phone.

"Where are you guys off to?" she asked.

"We're going for a little walk. Wanna come?"

Maggie checked the class schedule before saying, "Sure, nothing is happening for a little while."

We went out to Main Street and then turned right on Maple, which was the route to Bennet Park. About halfway down Maple, I stopped in front of a cottage with a sold sign in the front.

"I noticed this had sold when we were in town yesterday looking at the flyers in the real estate office window. I just love this house. It's like a quintessential English cottage." Ivy crept up the stone front, and it had a cobblestone walkway to the front door. It was compact, but it looked like everything had been well-maintained, with the vintage charm intact. "You can see the original woodwork through the windows."

"It is a nice house. You aren't itching to move out of the Workshop, are you?" Maggie asked.

"No. I just like to look. Walter and I spotted this house last time he was here. It even looks like there's a shady private garden in the back. I'd love to get a look inside."

"Maybe you'll get to know the new owners."

"Yeah. I should bring them something from the bakery when they move in."

"You are so transparent."

"What do you mean?" I said, indignantly.

"Since when did you become the town welcome wagon? You just want to see inside the house."

"Okay. Busted."

We continued on and reached the path circling the pond. The water glistened in the sun, and voices carried on the breeze from a frisbee game on the opposite side. Baxter was in full-on sniff mode, attempting to trace the path of every chipmunk and squirrel.

Maggie asked, "So, do you have any more thoughts about the case?"

"Possibly. When Annie and I were at the Café earlier, Aunt Claudia thought she recognized the earrings as a pair Eleanor, Tucker's first wife, had."

"Really!"

"Now, keep in mind, it was nearly forty years ago, and Aunt Claudia couldn't be sure. That's a long time to have an accurate memory, particularly for a pair of earrings that are nice, but not terribly distinct. I tried to downplay it with her because I don't want her worrying about Eleanor, but I'm going to do a search when I get back and see if I can track her down."

"Claudia's pretty tough, but even thinking for a minute her old friend might have been dead and buried all this time would be upsetting. So if you can find her, I know she would be relieved to hear she's safe and sound."

"Yes, but you know, I do wonder. I told you Tucker was a little adamant about us not putting the garden benches close to the tree line. And he didn't want people trespassing onto their property."

Maggie slowed her pace and said, "I think we need to be careful not to speculate, particularly about someone we know. It makes sense Tucker and Sasha don't want people trespassing. I wouldn't really want people tromping around my property."

"You're absolutely right. But I just can't help thinking all this stuff is connected, and he's part of the equation."

"One small part. Let's wait to see what comes of your research. Personally, I hope it doesn't have anything to do with anyone who is here now."

"I have all my fingers crossed hoping that's how it works out, too."

We continued on and made a loop around the pond, with a stop at the snow cone vendor, then returned to the Workshop refreshed and ready to carry on.

Even though it was only late afternoon, I turned on the living room lamps and bumped the air conditioner a degree cooler. I needed the room to be bright and fresh to keep me focused.

I started with a public records search for a marriage certificate for Tucker and Eleanor, and found it relatively quickly. Tucker Hawkins and Eleanor Jenkins married on June sixteenth, 1976. She would have been twenty-three. Nowadays, twenty-three is considered a little young to get married, but in the seventies, it was the norm. This supported Aunt Claudia's conclusion that they got married too young and just weren't a good match. At twenty-three, I didn't really know who I was yet, and at that age we often tried to conform to what others wanted us to be.

I was lost in this mental roll around when there was a knock on the door. "Come in," I called out.

Jack entered and wasted no time. "I got out a little early because you worried me a bit thinking something is up with Mom."

I got up from the floor. "I'm so sorry. I really didn't mean to stress you out. Your mom is totally fine! This has to do with the case, and I had too much to go over in a text or call."

He plonked down on the couch. "Thank goodness. Do you have a beer?"

"Maybe, let me check." I went to the fridge and called over my shoulder, "It's your lucky day."

"Perfect."

I opened and wiped the bottle top and grabbed the can of peanuts. "Sit back and I'll fill you in," I said, returning to the couch.

"I see you and your merry band of cohorts have been busy," he said, indicating the whiteboard with the bottle.

"Uh, yeah. It started last night. This morning we had the cleansing ceremony, and then Annie and I went to the diner, and then I called you."

"Okay, start at the beginning."

"Wait, you first. Any new developments?" I asked.

"Matt has dusted everything he could from the site for prints. He found some, but they're not in the system. He's taken a DNA swab from the jeans button and the earring you didn't blow on, and we'll see if we get a hit, but it's unlikely."

"Oops, sorry. I was just really excited to read the hallmark."

"No worries, I knew we had the other earring, which hadn't been compromised. Anyway, during the time period of this death, DNA was not a regular police tool, so unless a familial match happens to be in our system, it's a dead end."

"What about the skeleton? Is it being sent off for further study?" I asked.

"Yes. It will be boxed up and sent to a forensic anthropologist at the state lab."

"I'm guessing we won't know anything for a while."

"Right. It may take weeks or months for them to even get to it."

"So, we're in limbo," I concluded.

"Somewhat. Let me hear what you came up with."

"Okay." I walked to the whiteboard. "Yesterday, Maggie and I stopped in Smythe Family Jewelry, and I showed the owner's daughter a photo of the earrings." I pointed to the printout on the board. "She showed them to her dad and then emailed me that he vaguely remembers selling them but isn't sure. He knows it would have been over twenty years ago."

"Records?"

"No such luck. Unless it's a piece with a serial

number, they don't keep records past ten years."

Jack had pulled out his notebook to jot some notes. "Go on," he said.

"Then yesterday evening, the gang came up and we started going over what little evidence there is. Bitsy looked up the Woolmark label I took the photo of. It was used after 1971 to code a sixty-forty wool blend."

"So theoretically, the death occurred after 1971."

"Right. There was also part of the size label, looks like size five. Now this gets interesting."

"Why?"

"Odd numbered sizes were initially used to identify petite-sized garments. They are cut slightly smaller so petite or shorter women aren't swimming in their clothing."

"Is there a reason I need the lesson in garment labeling?" he asked, somewhat sarcastically.

I answered with a comedic smugness, "Why yes, there is, grasshopper. You see, odd numbered sizes switched to teen sizes in the early-mid 1980s. So, this has further narrowed in the timeframe. Ta-da!"

Jack looked at the whiteboard. "And you don't think the remains are of a teenager because a teenager wouldn't wear those earrings," he said, pointing to the photo.

"Right! So, while it's only a theory at this point, we are guesstimating the death occurred between 1971 and 1983-ish."

Jack beamed at me. "I have to say, this is damn good work. I'm impressed."

"Well, thank you, sir," I said, with a bow.

"Actually, I'm not surprised. This is what you do so well, and it's why I should never doubt your ability to help, even when it seems there is nothing to go on. I'm just going to pretend I didn't hear you say your cohorts were in on this."

"So it helps?"

"Heck, yes. I'll have to corroborate all of this myself, but if we tick the same boxes, this timeframe is small enough I can have the dental x-ray sent to our local dentist, Dr. Wilkins. Granted, it's long enough ago they'll have to dig deep for the records, and the practice has probably changed hands a couple of times. But it's somewhere to start. If we're lucky, she had dental work done here."

My cheeks flushed with pride. "I'm so glad we could help. We came up with a visual image of her—petite, wearing jeans and a cotton top, with a wool sweater. And based on the platinum earrings, she was probably early twenties to early thirties. It gave us an image to visualize when JJ did her cleansing ceremony."

Jack grinned. "How was that?"

"Actually, quite nice. And Annie, as you probably know, brought some ground cover for us to plant. It was a special moment."

"Good. Now, what about Mom?"

I sat cross-legged on the couch facing Jack. "Annie and I were at the Café this afternoon, and Aunt Claudia happened to see the photo of the earrings."

"Okay, not great to be talking about it in front of her, but otherwise, what's the big deal?"

"She said she recognized them. She thought her old friend Eleanor had a pair like them."

Jack tilted his head. "Eleanor?"

"She was Tucker's first wife. I think it was fresh in her mind because she and I were just talking about

Eleanor the other day. Aunt Claudia said she up and left Tucker and never returned to Flat Rock, and she only heard from her a couple of times after she left. Did you know her?"

"When was this? Her name isn't familiar, but then again, let's be honest, I was a kid, and at that age we considered anyone over twenty to be old and not worth paying much attention to."

I grimaced at his fairly accurate assessment. "Aunt Claudia couldn't quite remember the year, but it was after the summer Mom had to leave for a workshop, and I stayed on for a few weeks. I just looked through old photo albums to confirm it. Do you remember? I was eleven."

Jack rubbed his chin. "It's coming back to me. We walked all over town and Flat Rock Falls State Park that summer."

"Yeah! I had those red high-tops." I grabbed the album to show him the old photos.

Jack choked out a laugh. "I remember. You would not take those things off! Look, in this one you're wearing them with a dress. And what's going on with your hair?"

"All right, I was in transition between hairstyles." No matter how hard I tried, I could never accomplish the fashion trends. Eventually, I realized I didn't even want to, and just did my own thing. "Anyway, eh-hem, it would mean Eleanor left in 1981 or 1982."

Jack sobered. "Which fits the timeframe of the remains."

"Yes. But the thing is, Aunt Claudia got postcards from Eleanor a few months after she left. So it's likely to be a coincidence that Eleanor happened to have the same or similar earrings as the victim. And we have to keep in mind Aunt Claudia wasn't even one hundred percent sure about it. It was a long time ago."

"That's true. But you know how I feel about coincidences."

"I know. That's why I've started doing some research to try and find Eleanor."

"Any success?"

"I just started. I found the marriage certificate for Eleanor and Tucker, which has given me her maiden name, Jenkins. From there, I'm going to see what I can dig up. Maggie and I looked on the NamUs website to see if there are any missing persons from our county. There aren't any, which further supports Eleanor is alive and well somewhere, so I should be able to find her."

"Yeah, Matt already searched NamUs." He cocked his head at me. "How'd you know about that site?"

"Lena. But I should have known you would have done it already," I said, somewhat disappointed I hadn't one-upped him.

"Okay. For now, this stays between you and me. And well, Annie, since she was there when this came up. I'll have a chat with Mom. I'd rather her not be imagining her friend dead, but I can't ignore the line of inquiry."

"Could you talk to Tucker and see if he knows her whereabouts?"

"I will, but at this point, it's kind of flimsy to say it's because those earrings looked similar to some Mom saw almost forty years ago, but I can say they were recognized as belonging to her and it would help us with our inquiries if he knows where she moved to. It's also possible she gave them to someone or donated them before she left."

"Right. And maybe I could discreetly bring it up if the opportunity arises."

Jack looked at me sternly. "That is not a good idea."

"Why not?" I asked, like a petulant teen.

"For one thing, you're already dealing with some sabotage. You don't need anyone getting their back up right now. And if, and it's a big IF, the remains should be Eleanor, you do not want to tip your hand. We must first gather evidence, then ask questions."

"I know, I know. You only ask questions you already have the answers to in order to see how the person reacts."

"In this kind of situation, yes."

"Okay."

"Promise?"

"Yessss," I hissed.

"You do your magic with the research, I'll work my end, and we'll see what shakes out. Now, what about the sabotage? The surveillance cameras arrived, and if Ryan's going to be around, we can get them up tomorrow."

"Let me text Ryan," I said, reaching for my phone. "Are you available in the morning? We have the reception in the afternoon. Or we could just wait until later in the week."

"The sooner the better. Have you had any more issues?"

I texted Ryan, then answered him. "Only a social media post. Nothing else in the garden since Saturday night. I honestly don't think the two are connected. My gut is telling me the sabotage was to delay or derail the garden opening."

"Since nothing further has happened, you may be right. But we're getting those cameras up, regardless."

"I know." I didn't say once this all blew over, I wouldn't have to turn them on. My phone dinged with a text from Ryan. "He says he'll be here by nine tomorrow morning, so whenever you want to do it, he'll be around."

"Great. Tell him thanks." He pushed himself up off the couch, and said, "I'm going to go home and have dinner with Annie. I'll see ya in the morning."

****

I woke up in the middle of the night foggy from a strange sequence of dreams. In one of them I was being chased through the woods. In another, I was observing from a distance as someone dug a hole and dumped a body in it. In yet another, I was at the Café with Aunt Claudia, and she was laughing and talking with the woman we had described from the evidence.

In an effort to stop the loop of dreams, I turned on the bedside lamp and pulled over the notepad I had used the night before when looking up Eleanor. There was precious little on it, but I reread my notes anyway.

Social media? Nothing. At least not in her married or maiden name, although she could have remarried. Family? She had an aunt who passed away in the 1990s and an uncle who died in 2010. She had no siblings. Too late to talk to any family.

Records search? Nothing. Not as much as a parking ticket. No arrests. No death certificate. No marriage certificate for a second marriage. No property purchases. No bank loans. No credit cards in either her married or maiden name. Did she change her name? I didn't find a record of that. But people who lived off the grid did things off the grid. Did she use another identity? Unlikely, but not impossible. But why would she?

I tossed the notepad on the floor. Everything was a dead end. I needed to let this sit for a while and come back to it later. And anyway, I had an event tomorrow, and I needed to get some sleep so I could take care of my own business. The remains had been buried for almost forty years, another day or two wouldn't make much difference. Or so I thought.

Chapter 11

Wednesday Morning

While Jack and Ryan installed the security cameras, Maggie and I set up the tables for the reception. It was proving to be a perfect day, with a light breeze, a few puffy clouds in an otherwise brilliantly blue sky, and thankfully, low humidity. But things turned a little stormy when Jack was showing me how to operate the cameras.

"There are way too many steps to these instructions," I said, in frustration.

"Look, you can use an app, the web browser, or you can even use your cell phone."

"I don't want it on my phone," I hissed. We were at the front desk, so I was trying not to telegraph my frustration to the entire building.

"We can install the software to use on your computer," he suggested, with a patience he probably didn't feel.

"Maybe the web browser?"

"Okay. Just remember, you'll have to be able to demonstrate to Maggie and Ryan how to use it in case you're not here and they need to access it."

"Then definitely web browser. That way it can be monitored anywhere." Ryan sauntered up to the desk, and I said, "Oh! Good timing. We're just setting up the system, and it's making my brain explode."

Ryan said, eagerly, "Cool. I'll help."

We went through the painstaking steps to set up the system. There were so many technical terms my head was spinning, but thankfully, Ryan and Jack weren't fazed, and eventually, we created sign-in credentials and were up and running.

Jack said, "Okay, this is the camera over by the lounge."

I could see most of the courtyard and the garden over toward the parking lot.

"And this is the one from the parking lot end of the building," Ryan said, clearly enjoying the technology.

This one covered more of the property over to the small parking lot off the kitchen side of the building. "That's pretty good quality," I said.

"It is. But you've got a perfect day out there," Jack advised. "You'll want to test it out and see how it is at night and during inclement weather."

"Yeah," Ryan said, "and then if we need to adjust them, we can."

I switched the screen back to the first camera and caught Maggie adjusting her shorts after she got up from a bench. "Oh, I really don't like this."

Ryan chuckled. "Maggie wouldn't either."

Jack became exasperated. "You don't have to have them on during the day, and you're not going to be spying on people. This is for at night when no one is around, which is the whole point."

"Right," I conceded.

"You just have to remember to turn them on," he cautioned. "And since you have it set to delete footage from the cloud after one week, if you forget to turn them off during the day, at least nothing will be permanently saved."

"I guess this is necessary, for the time being, so I'll quit being a pain in the butt."

"Thank you," Jack said.

"No, thanks to both of you guys for helping me get this up and running."

"No problem," Ryan said. "I think I hear the sounds of the catering delivery in the kitchen, so I'll take your gratitude in the form of food!"

I laughed. "Deal. Jack, do you want something?"

He looked at the clock. "I don't have time. I need to get back to the office. But I'll see you guys later."

Ryan and I found Jeff, Aunt Claudia's right hand man, bringing in the catering trays through the back door. After he left, we filled the fridge and lined up the nonperishables on the counter.

Ryan grabbed a brownie and swooned after the first bite. "Dang, these are so good."

I couldn't resist and joined him. "It's the fudge frosting. I could eat five of these, but I'm not going to. I can't be a sugar-zombie when everyone arrives."

****

Wednesday Afternoon, Patron and Volunteer Preview Party

The event set up went smoothly, and I was just placing the last tray on the table when people started to arrive.

Penny came up to me and enthused, "You did it! It's all come together perfectly, as I knew it would. You even had a skeleton to deal with and managed to pull this off."

I adjusted a vase of fresh cut flowers before turning toward her. "Well, if not for Jack's quick work we might not have been able to move forward. And as to the finished garden, I couldn't have done it without you guys! I hope you enjoy looking at your handiwork."

Penny joined Bert, who had arrived looking dapper in chinos and a button-down shirt, and I stood at the head of the table to greet people and show my appreciation for their help. Once everyone had arrived and gotten some food, I filled a plate to take over to the courtyard.

I was proud of what we had accomplished, and it felt good to watch everyone meander around the garden and congratulate Ryan and Elliott on their sculptures. Then I noticed Eva Beaumont approaching my table, and my mood faltered.

"Alex, you have accomplished a remarkable thing here. Do you mind if I join you?"

"Please, take a seat," I said, trying not to show my surprise at seeing her here.

Eva was dressed impeccably, and she carefully smoothed her slacks as she crossed her legs. "I hope you don't mind, but Winifred invited me as her plus-one."

"I don't mind at all." I shoved my plate to the side so I could more aptly go toe to toe with her professional manner. "As a matter of fact, I'm glad to see you. I hear congratulations are in order."

She looked at me with a head tilt. "What?"

"Winifred told me you guys are opening a gallery with artist studios in Pine Brook."

Eva pursed her lips. "She really shouldn't have been talking about that. It's not even a done deal."

I wasn't in the mood to be circumspect. "No? She's been approaching some of my artists about moving their studios."

Eva was too well-mannered to let her genteel mask slip, but the muscle in her jaw tightened before she said,

"That is news to me. Please know I would never condone poaching your artists."

While we talked, I kept one eye on the reception to make sure everything was going smoothly. A gaggle of Workshop artists had arrived and were clustered around the sculptures. Winifred was following Tucker across the lawn. He stopped to turn toward her, and she stepped in close to talk to him. I could see from here he looked displeased. Better him than me. How could one woman ruffle so many feathers?

I realized I should respond to Eva. "I am confident you wouldn't overtly try and take my artists, and no harm done. We all know Winifred talks out of turn sometimes."

"Yes, and it is not a quality I admire."

Tucker had successfully untangled himself and Winifred moved on to her next target, waving and calling out to Penny.

"I'm confident with you at the helm, whatever you end up doing will be a success," I said, sincerely, refocusing my attention back to her. "And if any of my people want to leave of their own accord, they're free to do so, but I would rather they are not approached, at least not on my own property."

"Of course. Winifred can be quite persuasive, but I'm leaning in the direction of just a gallery. With the incredible artists in the area, I could have different one-man or group shows going all year."

"You sure could, and I wholly approve of another venue that supports our artists." I decided to be blunt, but kept my voice low and even-keeled. "Do you think Winifred could be behind the social media campaign against the Workshop?"

Eva shifted her eyes to watch people mill around the garden. I sensed this was not to avoid my gaze, but to distance herself from a situation she found distasteful.

"It's possible. After I read the post about the skeleton, I told her I don't do business that way. She vehemently denied doing it, but I'm not sure I believed her." Now, she turned to look at me. "Suffice it to say if it *was* her, she got the message it should stop. And I will talk to her about approaching your artists. So there should be nothing further for you to deal with."

"Thank you, I appreciate that."

Eva and I sat a few moments in companionable silence, then she stood up, and said, "I'll leave you to finish your food. I know all too well when you're in charge you never get to sit down and eat. Besides, I want to go look at those beautiful sculptures and congratulate Ryan and Elliott."

I popped the remaining half a devilled egg in my mouth and savored the velvety texture as I watched her greet Ryan. Maybe one problem was solved and resolved. I didn't need to confront Winifred as long as the social media headache went away. And talking to Eva made me feel better about things. I liked to have a good relationship with other leaders in the arts community, and I now believed I could fully support whatever she ended up doing in Pine Brook.

I put my empty plate in the trash, grabbed a cup of fruit tea, and made my way to the garden, where I found Ms. Bunkle sitting on one of the benches, scrutinizing a sculpture across the path.

"What do you think?" I asked, taking a seat next to her.

"I'm trying to figure out what it is," she said, matter-of-factly.

"I'm not sure it's supposed to be anything in particular. It's more about creating a feeling."

"Well, I guess the combination of the smooth wood and the stone is pleasing."

"I think so, too." I was worried she might not approve. "What do you think of the garden?" I asked, hesitantly.

"Oh Tater, I can tell you're insecure now, thinking I was being critical."

"No, not at all," I sputtered.

"Look, art is meant to provoke thought, right?"

"Right," I answered.

"So, this piece provoked thought. That means it's good, you ninny. If this garden was full of cherubs weeing water into a birdbath, I would disapprove. What you've done here is create harmony, but in a thought-provoking way."

"I take that as a high compliment."

"Good. You gotta put your big girl panties on and own what you've done."

I laughed out loud. "Ha! I love you, Ms. Bunkle."

"Now don't get all sappy on me. Instead, tell me which of these benches will have my Henry's name on it."

Being a patron, Ms. Bunkle would have a plaque on a bench or a specific part of the garden. "So you want a bench?" I asked.

"Yes. I'd like to park my butt, enjoy the surroundings, and talk to Henry now and then." Her husband, Henry, had passed away quite a few years ago, and I found her sentiment incredibly sweet.

"You tell me which one you want, and I'll earmark

it for you."

Ms. Bunkle's voice became tender. "Okay, when I'm done looking at all the sculptures, I'll let you know. I also want it to be near a flowering tree, and maybe some roses."

"You got it," I said, warmly.

She tapped her cane and, with her tender side back in check, said, "Now tell me what's happening with the sabotage."

I smiled at her for a beat, then leaned back on the bench. "There's been no more sabotage since Saturday night. And I think maybe the social media slams will no longer be a problem."

"Both interesting and circumspect. But okay, I don't need details. What about the skeleton?"

"The bones have been sent off to a forensic anthropologist. It's going to be a while before we know anything definitive. But Jack's doing what he can with what little he has to go on." I shifted to face her. "Oh, and by the way, I asked Aunt Claudia about Eleanor, like you suggested. She said pretty much the same as you, Eleanor just walked out one day, but she got a couple postcards from her after she left."

"So she's somewhere out there. Good."

"Yes. I'm trying to find her. I think it would be nice for Aunt Claudia to know where she is and that she's happy."

"Hopefully what you find will be good news. Some people don't want to be found, you know."

"True. So I will tread carefully." I contemplated showing the earrings to Ms. Bunkle, but Jack's cautionary words rang in my ears, and I refrained.

"Oh good Lord, Winifred seems to be making her

way over here. Quick, walk me down to where Alma is. I don't have the patience to deal with her today."

Winifred scanned the crowd, looking for someone to approach, and in the opposite direction, Alma leaned down to smell a rose. "Okay, let's go."

After leaving Ms. Bunkle at Alma's side, I spent an enjoyable few hours talking with the patrons and volunteers. As evening approached, most of the crowd had left, and it was mainly Workshop artists hanging out in small groups throughout the garden. The sound of laughter and lively chatter carried on the breeze, and as I started clearing the food table, I allowed myself to count this as a successfully pulled-off event.

"Here, let me help," Maggie said, taking a tray from me.

"Thanks, I'll start wrapping up the leftovers if you don't mind bringing in the last trays."

"Sure, I'd be glad to."

Once everything was inside, we worked in tandem to fill containers. "We're going to be eating well the rest of the week," I said.

"You're not kidding. These salmon sliders are so danged good. But tonight, we're going over to the Thunderbird Lodge for drinks and dinner. Wanna come?" The Lodge was not just for out-of-towners. It was also a local hang, and with its large patio overlooking the forest, you would often find locals mixed in with summer vacationers.

"I'm kind of beat. I think I'm just going to stay here and relax."

"With everything that's happened the last few days and then pulling off an event, I don't blame you. By the way, the party was a hit. Everyone loved the sculptures,

Hank and Twila's glass, the garden, and the food spread. Congratulations."

"Thanks, but I can't take all the credit. You all did an amazing job. So off you go, have some fun tonight knowing there's nothing to do until Friday."

I walked Maggie back outside, and then as the group went to their cars, I did a final walk of the garden, using the excuse that I wanted to check for stray napkins or cups, but it was really because I wanted to savor a peaceful moment in the garden by myself.

****

I had left my cell phone up in my apartment and could hear it ringing as I unlocked the door. I ran to the kitchen counter and saw Walter's name on the caller ID. "Hey!" I answered, breathing hard.

"Did I catch you at a bad time?" he asked.

"No! Sorry, I was just walking in and had left my phone here in the apartment." I looked at the clock on the kitchen wall. "What are you doing up at this hour?"

"I wanted to see how the patron event went."

"Oh, you are so sweet. It went really well. We were able to extend a special thank you for everyone's hard work, the weather was perfect, the garden and sculptures looked amazing, and the food was fabulous."

"Well, I knew everything would be done to perfection. This is what you do so well."

"Aw, shucks. So, tell me about you! How are things in London?"

"Good. Busy. But I wish I was there."

Simply hearing his voice confirmed I felt the same. "I wish you were, too. But the weekend will be here soon enough. You're still coming, right?"

"Yup. As long as the flight takes off, I'll be there

late Friday night. Oh, and by the way, I have a little surprise for you."

"Ooo, I can't wait!"

"So, catch me up on anything else that has been happening."

Everything came out in a rush. I let it all out, from the latest social media and sabotage to the skeleton. When I finished, I said, "Sorry, I didn't intend to dump it all on you at this hour."

"Don't worry about me. I'm just sorry we haven't been able to connect this week, and you've had to shoulder this on your own."

"It's okay, I've had my cohorts to help me through it." I giggled and added, "Annie even brought up a whiteboard so we could lay everything out like they do on TV."

Walter laughed. "I can totally visualize that."

"And you and Jack convinced me to get better surveillance cameras, and he and Ryan put them up this morning."

"Good. Are they on?"

"Um, not yet. I didn't want to be spying on the patron event."

Walter skipped a beat before saying, "Well, don't forget to turn them on tonight."

"Will do."

After a few more minutes chatting about nothing in particular, we hung up. I sat for a moment holding the phone and acknowledged how much happier I was. I looked over at Baxter, who was lounging next to me on the couch, and said, "I don't know how I could have doubted how I feel about Walter."

He looked at me as if he wished he could say, *Idiot*.

I turned on a baseball game and relaxed for the first time in days. I always felt a bit of a high after an event. I was proud we had completed the garden and sculpture installation on schedule, even with the interruption of finding a skeleton, and everyone seemed to have a good time at the reception. And more importantly, the negative social media posts didn't seem to have any ill affect.

Later, I was tucked in bed, engrossed in a Dorothy Sayers book, when I checked the clock. It was after midnight, which was way past my usual bedtime, but I was so relaxed and comfy I allowed myself to stay up as long as I wanted. I suddenly jolted, remembering I hadn't turned on the cameras.

"Dadgum," I said out loud, throwing back the covers.

I padded to the kitchen counter in my sleep shirt and opened my laptop. After reading the instruction notes Jack had dictated to me, and three failed attempts, the video feed finally showed up on the screen.

"There we go," I said to Baxter, who had followed me to the kitchen. "All set."

A movement caught my eye. A dark form was jogging near the parking lot, coming from my property. Just as quickly, they were out of view. I sat for a moment and stared at the screen, looking for any further movement, when I noticed something. It wasn't clear, but it looked like someone or something was sitting on a bench. I leaned close to the screen, but it still remained a mystery. And there was no movement.

"What is that?" I asked myself.

I looked away, then back at the screen. Yeah, something was there. I knew I had to check it out, so I went into the closet and hastily put on a pair of jeans and slipped my bare feet into my work boots.

"You stay here," I said to Baxter, before grabbing a flashlight and my phone.

I exited the building through the courtyard doors and tried to visualize where I had seen the form. In my mind's eye, it was at the left end of the garden. I slowly made my way to the garden path, where I came across a wheelbarrow. I used the flashlight to look at it more closely. It was bright green, and I recognized it as one of ours. There was also a can of spray paint on the ground next to it. Before going any farther, I called Jack.

He answered in a sleepy voice, "Alex? Do you know what time it is?"

"Yeah, sorry. Something's weird here. Can you come over?"

"What do you mean, weird?"

"I forgot to turn on the cameras when I got in bed, but remembered while I was reading and got up to do it. I saw a figure just before they jogged out of camera view. Then I saw what looked like someone, or something big, on one of the benches. I came down to look, and found our wheelbarrow, which I know was not out here when I closed up for the night. At least I think it's ours. Anyway, I'm afraid to go any farther."

Jack was alert now. "Wait right there. I'm on my way. Five minutes."

I paced back and forth for what felt like an eternity. Eventually, Jack's car entered the parking lot, and the slam of his car door shutting resonated in the quiet night.

As he approached, I apologized. "I'm sorry to drag you out of bed for what is probably a big nothing."

"No problem. I'd rather you call than go roaming around on your own at this time of night."

We reached the wheelbarrow, and I pointed to the can of spray paint lying next to it, and then we headed down the garden path, using our flashlights to sweep left and right.

"I don't see anything," he said.

"I think it was more toward the end of the garden. If someone vandalized one of the sculptures with spray paint, I'm going to lose my mind," I snapped.

We carried on and wound our way until Jack's flashlight illuminated something on one of the benches.

"Stay here."

"Okay," I said, but I followed him anyway. When we got closer, it appeared to be a person sitting on the bench.

"Hello?" I called out.

No answer.

"Hello, can I help you?"

No answer.

When we drew closer to the bench, Jack put his arm back to stop me. "Wait," he dictated.

This time I obeyed his command, although I peered around to see. "What is it?"

Jack pulled out his phone. "Travis, get over here to the Workshop." He leaned over the figure. "And send an ambulance, no need for sirens."

I became impatient and walked up to Jack. "What the heck is…Oh my God."

A person was seated on the bench with their legs crossed at the ankle and their hands clasped on their lap, holding a rose. The figure was painted bronze, like a statue. My knees buckled, and then it was lights out.

Chapter 12

"Alex, wake up," the voice in the distance said. Then I felt light slaps on my cheeks.

"What? Stop slapping me! What happened?" I asked, foggily.

"You passed out. Can you sit?" Jack asked.

I tried to get up, saw the gruesome scene again, and swooned.

"Nope, sit back down, and let me get you turned around." Jack easily manipulated my position so I was facing away from the scene. "Take some deep breaths. In, out, in, out," he said, slowly.

I sat cross legged on the path, with my head in my hands. "What the hell is that, Jack?"

"I think the question is, who is that? Once you've got your sea legs, I need you to take a look."

I took a number of deep breaths, then said, "Okay, I think I'm all right."

"You sure?"

I first got to my knees, then stood up. "Yeah. I'm okay." But I wasn't okay. What if it was one of my friends? I couldn't look. But I also couldn't allow my fear to stop me from helping. I tentatively turned and walked toward the bench, and then Jack switched on his flashlight.

The sight was appalling. It was a woman, grotesquely posed like a statue sitting on a bench. I'd seen ones like this that were sweet and whimsical. This was the opposite. Her face was completely covered in paint, with a drip line on her right cheek and smudges on her neck where Jack had checked for a pulse. The clothing and hands were all bronze, and there was a straw hat adorned with flowers on her head, also spray painted. Only the hair wasn't fully enrobed in paint. I recognized the hair and knew I would always think of this moment whenever I saw the color combination of purple and bronze.

"I think it's Winifred."

"Are you sure?" Jack asked.

"Well, I can't be one hundred percent sure. She's covered in paint," I said, hysterically.

"Okay, come on, let's go sit down." Jack led me to a bench farther away, out of sight of the crime scene. "While I wait for Travis, tell me everything again."

I sucked the night air into my lungs and blew it out. "So, like I said, I was reading in bed when I realized I had forgotten to turn on the cameras. It was after midnight. After a few tries, I got them on. That's when the flash of a figure jogged off to the right of the screen, near the parking lot," I said, pointing.

"Okay, then what?"

"I scanned the camera to see if there was anyone else milling around or any visible sabotage. That's when I saw what looked like someone sitting on the bench."

"I'll look at the footage, but describe it to me."

"I couldn't exactly tell if it was someone or something. It was too dark for detail."

"So you came down to check."

"Right. I found the wheelbarrow and the can of spray paint, and then I called you." I looked down, and a sea of green plaid reminded me I still had on my nightshirt. "Um, I'm not fully dressed. Can I go up and change?" I asked. I unconsciously pawed at my neckline, and I think Jack correctly interpreted this gesture as me trying to get away from the gruesome scene.

"Yes. I'll be up once the body has been removed. Hopefully there will be some identification. Why do you think it's Winifred?"

"She has a stacked haircut with a trendy pale purple rinse. I could see the purple through the paint. And the shape of the face fits." Talking about it made me feel sick. "I'm going upstairs."

I stood inside the door of my apartment, paralyzed. Everything was going so well, and now my world was spiraling. The colors in my apartment suddenly looked muted, which I knew was a sign of extreme stress. After I changed, I paced back and forth in the living room. What was I going to do? This was a heinous crime left on my doorstep. Why? What did that mean? And poor Winifred. She might have had a difficult personality, but she certainly didn't deserve to die. And to be gruesomely displayed in such a way was a level of deranged I couldn't wrap my head around.

Baxter bolted out the doggy door and barked his way down the stairs to the enclosed yard when the police and ambulance vehicles arrived. I opened the back door and attempted to call him in. When he didn't respond to my calls, I grabbed his leash and walked down the stairs to the yard. Beyond the fence, I could see Jack and Travis at the bench.

Before I saw something I didn't want to see, I turned away, clipped Baxter's leash on his collar, and led him back up the stairs. I looked at the clock and didn't even try to calculate what time it was in London; I needed to talk to Walter.

He was up having breakfast in his hotel room and answered with a cheery "Good morning!" When my response was barely audible, he asked, "What's wrong?"

After I told the story of finding Winifred, he said, curtly, "I'm going to cancel my meetings and change my flight."

"No, please don't do that. I'm going to be okay."

"This is getting serious, Alex, and I can be there in about eighteen hours."

"Look, why don't you hold off until we know more, and then if I need you to come, I'll let you know."

"I don't know. I don't like being this far away."

"I would feel more awful if I dragged you back here and then you were just spinning your wheels. I promise, I will call you right away if I need you here."

"Okay. I'm going to leave my phone on in my meetings. You call me anytime."

After a few more minutes hearing his calming voice, we hung up. Talking to Walter, it had been bearable, but now that there were only the voices in my head, I began to spiral again, so I curled up in a ball on the couch. I don't know how much time had passed when there was a knock on the door. Without waiting for an answer, Jack walked in.

"We're done for now," he said. "The body is on the way to the coroner, and we collected the wheelbarrow and can of paint to see if we can pull any prints."

I hadn't moved when he came in, and from my curled-up position I asked, "How did she die?"

"We won't know for sure until the coroner looks at everything, but there was blood on the back of her head.

So my guess is blunt force trauma."

"Why was she staged in such a way? This is just too awful."

Jack sat on the end of the couch and put his hand on my leg. "I don't know," he said, softly. "Travis has gone back to get the crime scene lights, and we'll be scouring the area for evidence the rest of the night. We are going to need to search both the grounds and building. Do you consent to the search?"

"Yeah, of course, whatever you need to do."

"Thank you. Do you want to call Annie and go stay at our house?"

"I don't know," I mumbled.

"You're in a state of shock. I don't want to leave you here alone, and quite honestly, you don't need to be underfoot while we're working. I'll call Annie."

When I didn't respond, he got up and moved to the guest room to make the call—probably so I couldn't hear what he was saying. He came back to the couch. "Come on," he said, taking hold of my elbow to urge me to get up, "I'll have Matt drive you over. Annie will be waiting for you, and she said to bring Baxter if you want."

"What about my car?"

"She'll bring you back in the morning."

****

Matt handed me off to Annie at her front door, and she led me to the couch in the cozy den off the kitchen.

"Sit. Do you want something to drink? Iced tea? A shot of brandy?"

"No, just some water, if you don't mind."

She brought a glass of ice water over and sat across from me on the opposite couch. "Do you want to talk about it?" she asked, tentatively.

"I don't even know what to say. I know I'm in shock, but even if I wasn't, there's no way to rationally explain what I saw out there tonight."

"Jack told me what, and who, you found."

I nodded. "Yeah. Her hair is pretty unmistakable. It's her trademark." I shook my head, disconcerted. "It *was* her trademark."

"Why would someone do that to her?"

"And why leave her at the Workshop?"

"Somehow, this is all connected, Alex. Winifred, the skeleton, the sabotage."

I used my fist to pound my forehead. "It must be. But I can't see it."

Annie got up from the couch. "Look, don't try and think tonight. The guest room is all made up, and you can go get some sleep."

"I don't know if I can sleep."

"If you don't, you won't be good for anything tomorrow, so try."

I gave in and followed Annie down the hall to the guest room, where I crawled into bed fully clothed. Baxter circled a few times, then plonked down next to me.

****

Thursday

I don't remember falling asleep, but I woke up to light streaming through the windows and a low rumble of voices, probably coming from the kitchen because the coffee bean grinder whirred simultaneously. The sound of the latter was what lured me out of bed.

I quietly opened the door, and the voices became clearer.

"Jack, are you crazy? You can't haul her down to

the station like some common criminal," Annie said, in an urgent, but hushed, voice.

"Look, I've got to do this by the book. You know that. I have to bring her down for questioning like I would anyone else."

"Well, I think this is just absurd," she retorted.

"What's absurd?" I asked, walking into the kitchen.

Annie crossed her arms and glared at Jack.

Jack let out a sigh and said, "Alex, I need you to come down to the station with me to answer some questions."

I cocked my head. "Sure. I'm assuming you need a formal statement from me. What are you so miffed about, Annie?"

"You aren't listening carefully, Alex. He is taking you in for questioning, not to give a statement."

"Jack?" I asked.

"Look, a few things have come up and you have to be questioned. Do I think you need to be concerned? No. But it's a murder, and questions have to be answered."

"Does she need an attorney?" Annie demanded.

"That's up to her," Jack said, with hands on hips.

"Okay, you guys, simmer down. Annie, I appreciate the guard dog protection, but I'm fine to go answer some questions. And Jack, don't blame Annie for being upset. This is your home, and she wasn't expecting you to come in all official-like," I said, gesturing with my hands.

"Well, I still don't like it," Annie complained.

"Come on, I'll drive you and then drop you off at the Workshop when you're done," Jack said.

"What about Baxter?"

"Annie?" Jack asked, giving her his own puppy dog look.

"Oh, all right. You guys go have your chat. I'll take Baxter."

"You've got the spare key, right?" I asked. "Baxter will need breakfast and his doggy door opened, and I gave my whole set of keys to Matt last night."

"Yes, yes, I'll take good care of him. It's Jack who may need a doghouse," Annie snapped.

He pulled her in close and kissed the top of her head. "Don't worry, everything's going to be fine."

When we got in the car, I looked at my phone. It was after ten o'clock. "Holy cow. I didn't realize it was so late!" I also had quite a few missed messages from Maggie and Ryan.

Jack let out a noncommunicative grunt. "Mmm."

I pulled the visor down to check my face and let out a gasp. "Why didn't you tell me my hair looks like this?" I rooted around in my bag to see if I had a brush. Of course I didn't, I never carry a brush, so I used my fingers to try and untangle the mess. I licked my fingertip to get the sleep dirt out of my eyes, and scrubbed my face with my hands, then dug in my bag again and pulled out a no-water mini toothbrush I always kept on hand, scrubbed it around inside my mouth, then swigged some water from my day-old water bottle and swallowed it.

Jack was unusually quiet, so I turned toward him. "What? No smart-aleck comment? Now you're worrying me."

"Let's just get through this interview."

"Fine." I turned back to stare out the windshield for the remaining five-minute journey.

When we arrived at the station, Jack walked me back to one of the interview rooms. I had observed other people being interviewed in these rooms but had not been on this end of things before. It felt inhospitable, which I assumed was the point.

The door opened, and Travis walked in. He turned on the tape recorder, identified himself, and said, "Hi Alex, how are you?"

"Not great, if I'm honest."

"That's understandable." He opened his notepad and flipped pages.

I knew from a recent experience they don't have to read Miranda rights unless they are going to bring about charges, but I felt compelled to ask, "Do I need an attorney?"

"You can absolutely call an attorney. It will delay the process, but you have the right to do so. You are not being charged with anything and you aren't being held. This is a voluntary interview, which you can stop at any point."

"Okay, go ahead."

"Can you give me an outline of last night from eight p.m. until you called Jack?" Travis asked.

"Sure, but it's pretty boring. After the garden reception clean up, I went upstairs to my apartment. Walter called me just as I walked in the door, so you can check the time on my phone."

Travis reached across for my phone, checked the call log, then jotted a note in his pad. "Go on."

"Then I kicked back and watched a baseball game until about eleven o'clock when I got in bed to read."

"Did you see or talk to anyone during that time?"

"No. It was a quiet night. Sometime after midnight, I realized I hadn't turned on the cameras. It took me a few minutes because I don't really know how to use them yet. But eventually they came on. That's when I saw the figure running toward the parking lot and what looked like someone sitting on the bench."

"Can you give any further description?" he asked.

"No. It was too dark, and the person running was wearing dark clothing from head to toe. You guys can look at the footage." I took my phone back so I could look up the sign-in access, which I kept in my contacts, with the custom label, *Big Brother*.

Travis grinned when he read the label. "George Orwell reference—nice." Then he returned to business. "So then you went outside to check."

"Yes. When I saw the wheelbarrow, I knew someone had been doing something on the property. We've experienced some minor vandalism, as you know, so I decided to call Jack instead of exploring any further."

"Your prints were found on the wheelbarrow. Can you explain that?"

I looked at him in surprise. "It belongs to the Workshop, so of course it would have my prints on it."

"What about the paint. Do you have bronze spray paint?"

I shook my head. "I don't, and I don't know anyone who does, so my prints couldn't have been on it."

"It was wiped clean."

"If you're implying I had something to do with this, why would I leave my prints on the wheelbarrow but then wipe the can of spray paint?"

Travis held up his hands. "I'm not saying you had anything to do with this. I'm just getting some details."

"Okay, I'll try not to be defensive." My leg had started rapidly bouncing, so I crossed my legs at the ankle to calm the movement.

"We found the victim's handbag in the bushes. As you suggested, she has been identified as Winifred Chambers. Can you tell me about your relationship with her?"

"I wouldn't say I had a relationship with her. She had approached me about putting some of her artwork in our gift shop, and I explained the shop was only for our studio artists. She then volunteered to help with the garden, so I've seen her a number of times over the last weeks during the final work in preparation for the grand opening."

"How recently have you seen her?"

"Yesterday, at the reception for the volunteers and patrons."

"Did you have any issues with her?"

I sat back in the chair and scrutinized Travis. What was he looking for? A motive for me to have killed her? I chose to be forthright. "Winifred's reputation for being a gossip is legendary. She didn't adhere to the normal social boundaries and often asked invasive questions or talked about people in ways she shouldn't. Did she treat me any differently than anyone else? No. Did I find her a bit tiresome? Yes."

"You've been dealing with a negative social media campaign and some sabotage at the Workshop, correct?"

"Yes."

He picked up a sheet of paper from the folder. "We've done a preliminary search of the victim's home, and we found some notes referring to the Creative Workshop on her computer."

"What do you mean, notes?"

He slid the page over to my side of the table. "Do any of these statements look familiar?"

On the page in front of me was a list of posts about the Workshop. I looked back at Travis, and said, "These are the social media smears we've experienced over the last weeks, but the last two are new to me. Perhaps she wrote them all in advance, and then cued them up to copy and paste."

"Did you suspect she had posted them?"

"Well, that's an interesting question. I had been trying to figure out if the sabotage and the smear campaign were connected. Ultimately, I just didn't feel it was the same person doing both."

"Go on."

"This past weekend, Winifred told me she and Eva Beaumont were going to open a competing gallery with studios in Pine Brook. I got the funny feeling she told me as a not-too-subtle way of letting me know I would have some competition, and it was possibly connected to my not letting her sell her pieces in our shop. So, with opening a competitive business and wanting a little payback, I began to wonder if she was behind the social media campaign, but I didn't have any proof."

"Did this make you angry?"

"Angry? No. I was frustrated by it. Now, I was *not* happy when I found out she was trying to poach some of my artists for their new endeavor in Pine Brook, but I wasn't professionally threatened by it."

"Did you confront her about it?"

"No. As it turns out, I didn't have to. Eva came to the reception yesterday, and she initiated a quiet chat. During our talk she let me know the gallery studio concept was not even a done deal. And then she discreetly indicated I should have no further issues with the social media smear campaign."

"Why do you think she told you this?"

"I don't think she liked what she was seeing and didn't want it to reflect poorly on her. She wanted me to know she said something to Winifred about those kinds of posts being unacceptable. Winifred denied doing it, but Eva believed she got the point across, and it would stop. She also said she was going to talk to Winifred about approaching the Workshop artists. So you see, to me, a weight was lifted. The issue was over and done with."

Travis finished scribbling notes, then put the pen down, and said, "Can you think of anyone who might have wanted to harm Winifred?"

I extended my palms out and said, "Look, she trod on a lot of toes with her gossiping. But she was equal opportunity in her gossip, meaning, she probably talked about everyone at one point or another. Both Ms. Bunkle and my aunt Claudia mentioned Winifred being a gossip since childhood, so if someone was going to kill her over it, it probably would have happened a long time ago." I sat up straight with a jolt. "And I must say, regardless of how much she might have stirred the pot, she did *not* deserve to die. Nothing, and I mean nothing, is so important it warrants taking a life."

He closed the folder. "My last question is can you think of any reason Winifred was staged on your property?"

I bit my lip before replying. "Believe me, that will keep me up at night. It was an awful thing to do to her, and there has to be a reason she was left on my doorstep in such a way. I just don't know what it is."

"Okay, thank you. You are free to go," Travis said, turning off the tape recorder.

"Am I considered a suspect?"

"I'm not at liberty to say. Since you and Jack are related, my job was to ask the questions in order to avoid a conflict of interest."

"Then I guess I'm at liberty to go ask Jack some questions," I said, with more than a touch of snark.

Travis exhibited great restraint and merely extended his arm and said, "After you."

We found Jack in his office. Travis handed him his notes and, once he left, I sat in the chair next to Jack's desk. "Well, that was interesting," I said in a huff. "Would have been nice to have a heads-up about the notes found at Winifred's house."

Jack was looking over Travis's notes from our interview and didn't respond. When finished, he tilted back in his desk chair, and said, "I couldn't tell you anything. You know all too well everything has to be by the book because of our relationship."

"I know. But seriously, am I a suspect?"

"Everyone's a suspect at this point, and you have no alibi."

"Aw, come off it."

"And I must notify you, as a matter of protocol, even though you gave consent last night, I got a warrant in the early hours this morning to cover the search of the building. I sent Matt and Gabe over to do the search." Jack handed me a copy of the search warrant.

I scanned the document. "What? You searched my apartment, too?"

"Yes. We had to expand the search after we found the notes on Winifred's computer. And don't worry, I had Maggie meet them there. Hopefully they'll be done soon. I can't do the search or even be there because we are related."

I opened my mouth, but words escaped me.

Jack said, "Pretend for a second this happened somewhere else. You know the first thing we would need to do is search the grounds and building for any evidence."

I knew he was right, but I was still gobsmacked. "No wonder Annie was so mad at you this morning. What in the hell are you looking for?"

"An indication of a struggle, a weapon, or any sign of blood."

"You have got to be kidding me. Jack, I turned on the security camera, which will have a time stamp, and it caught someone jogging off screen. I couldn't have been in two places at once, could I?" I said, smugly. "And it's not like I was part of a team, where we finished the deed and then I said, 'Wait, let me go turn on the cameras, and you time jogging out of view just right so I sort of have an alibi.' "

"Not to make you even angrier, but there's no proof you are the one who turned on the camera. Therefore, we've got to be able to rule you out and do things like dust your laptop for prints."

"Unbelievable." I sounded tougher than I felt. Right now, the only evidence they had pointed toward me, and I had no control over anything. I had to hope the search yielded the necessary results to prove my innocence.

Jack continued his rant. "And I have to clear the building. What if the murder weapon was found in one of the artist studios, but I hadn't looked for it? I would be fired on the spot! So yes, we've been working through the night to do a proper search."

We were interrupted by a light knock on the door. It

was Matt, and Jack put up a finger for me to wait and left the room to talk to him. I felt nauseous and made sure the trashcan was nearby in case the nausea escalated. I not only had to worry about my own innocence but also that of my artists. What if evidence was planted in the Workshop? Everything was spiraling, and there was nothing I could do about it.

The wait was interminable, but eventually Jack returned and sat back down. "All clear."

I got up and put my hands on my hips, infuriated. "Geez! Of course it was! How can you even think otherwise."

"*I* didn't think otherwise. But *we* had to eliminate you from our inquiries. After seeing the notes on her computer, you were an obvious suspect."

I pondered the significance of searching the building. "So she wasn't killed where we found her?"

"No. There was no blood found anywhere except on her body. No weapon was found and no sign of a struggle. So we had to expand the search. I'm sure if you take a step back you can understand that."

Even though I had been cleared, I couldn't think rationally yet. "I'm not ready to admit any of this makes sense. How you could even think for a minute…" I simply shook my head.

"Personally, I knew we wouldn't find blood, paint-smudged or bloody clothing, or evidence of a struggle in your apartment, but officially, we had to look so we could tick that box. And I'm relieved to say we didn't find anything anywhere else in the building."

"No one connected to the Workshop would have done this!" I said, vehemently.

Jack gave me a look like a parent scolding a child.

"Since you forgot to turn on the cameras, if someone had lured her there and the crime scene was in the building, we would not have been able to exclude anyone from our inquiries."

Properly chastised, I sat back down and said, "That would have been awful. I would never in a million years have thought a murder would take place. We were only dealing with minor vandalism."

Jack softened. "I know. Anyway, if *you* had killed her elsewhere, it makes no sense to think you would then bring her back to the Workshop and draw attention to yourself. So, that premise, along with the extensive search, which took quite a few manhours, by the way, is how we've been able to eliminate you."

I couldn't think of a response.

He tapped my knee. "Hey, this is all good news. I know it's been a rough morning, but shake it off. The important thing is you've been cleared, and so has the Workshop."

My shoulders dropped for the first time since I entered Jack and Annie's kitchen this morning, but I was still a little light-headed. "How can I know I had no part of this yet still feel relief you didn't find evidence that I did? All I can say is, at least my involvement in this is done and I can breathe easier."

"Don't relax too much. Someone went to a lot of trouble to move her, and spray paint her to look like a statue in your garden." He sat back and stroked his jaw. "So, why would someone want to drag you into this?"

Chapter 13

I looked at Jack in disbelief as the reality set in. For some reason, someone wanted to bring this to me, specifically. "Oh, this is not good," I said, with dread in my voice. "Okay, it happened at the Workshop for a reason, so we have got to get to the bottom of it and figure out who did it. The grand opening is this weekend! And in truth, this could destroy my business!" My voice had escalated in pitch to the point the last bit came out as a squeak.

"Look, I know this is distressing, but the investigation has only begun. Give me at least forty-eight hours before you start panicking about the grand opening."

I put my head in my hands. "Oh my gosh, what am I going to tell everyone?" I looked at Jack and asked, "What should I say?"

"The bare minimum. You should notify them that a search was carried out, but do not give out any information about the crime scene. We will be holding some details back from the public. You simply state she was found dead on the grounds of the Workshop."

I nodded slowly. "Okay, got it. Now what can I do?"

"You shouldn't do anything."

I pursed my lips. "You know I'm not going to sit around and do nothing, so don't even suggest it."

Jack looked at me long and hard, then reached in his

desk drawer for the official paper I always signed when helping out with anything involving sensitive material. "Sign this." After I obliged, he said, "Come on." He led me out of the office, then called to Travis, "I'll be back in a bit. Call Eva Beaumont and have her come in for an interview at one o'clock."

****

I hopped up into the passenger side of Jack's police vehicle and buckled up. "Where are we going?"

"Over to Winifred's house. I want to look more carefully through it. If she was targeting you, she might have been targeting other people."

"And you want my help? Well, that's more like it," I said, with satisfaction.

"Actually, my guys have their hands full back at the precinct, and having you with me allows me to keep an eye on you."

I feigned mild indignation. "I won't even dignify that with a response. Can we stop at the Workshop first? I really need to change my clothes and freshen up."

He looked me up and down. "Yeah, you do." He pulled up to the front of the Workshop, put on his flashers, and said, "Be quick."

"Will do." I jogged up the stairs and through the front door and found Maggie manning the front desk.

She lunged at me and gave me a bear hug and in a rushed run-on speech said, "Oh my gosh, Alex. I can't believe this has happened. Are you okay? I was so nervous when they came to search the place, so I called Ryan. It went pretty quickly—well, it took hours, but I thought it would have been longer since we had to stop in every studio. And don't worry, I watched like a hawk while they were in your apartment." She finished, slightly out of breath.

"Thanks, Maggie. I'm okay. The Workshop has been given the all clear, and I've been cleared, myself. And I'm sorry, but right now I have to do a quick change and head back out. Jack's waiting for me out front. We'll talk more later."

Maggie's face still registered concern, but she said, "Don't worry, we'll cover everything here. What should I tell people?"

"Nothing. If anyone asks, you don't know anything except a body was found, and we are assisting the police in every way. You can talk to the gang, but not when other people are around."

"Got it." Before I could dash off, she reached behind the desk and said, "Wait, here are your keys."

I ran up to my apartment, but stopped short inside the door to scan the living room and kitchen to see if there were any signs of the search. I noticed a few things had been moved around, but otherwise, they hadn't left a mess. My skin crawled at the thought of them looking through all my stuff, but I didn't have time to dwell on it.

After giving Baxter a treat, I did a quick-change into fresh clothes, threw my hair into a ponytail, washed my face, and brushed my teeth. I paused when I saw my reflection in the mirror. The dark circles were more pronounced this morning, but again, I didn't have time to dwell on it and just applied the shortest of my cosmetic routines. I took an extra two minutes to send a text update to Walter while I powered back a cup of coffee, then scuttled back downstairs.

"So what's the plan?" I asked Jack.

"We were only able to do a basic search last night at

Winifred's to get her laptop and to make sure she wasn't killed there. Now I want to go through things more slowly. I'm thinking you probably weren't the only person she was targeting."

"Could be."

"Obviously, someone had a motive to kill her. But the real question is why they chose to leave her body at the Workshop."

"Was it convenience or something more directed at us?" I mused.

"Or you, specifically."

I scowled at him. "Are you trying to rattle me?"

He kept his eyes on the road. "Nope, just reminding you there is more to this than a puzzle to solve. This was murder, and it could prove dangerous for you."

"Point made."

A few minutes later, we were parked in front of Winifred's bungalow on Cherry Street. As we walked to the front door, I couldn't help but notice the great care she had taken with her flower beds and the cheerful pots on the front porch. It made me sad to think she might have been puttering around out here yesterday morning watering her plants, having no idea that before the end of the night she would be dead.

"You didn't deserve what happened to you," I said, softly.

"What?" Jack said, turning the key in the lock.

"Nothing," I replied.

We entered the small but meticulously maintained house, and Jack pulled out two pairs of gloves. "Take these," he said, handing me a pair. "Just in case we find something, we don't need to contaminate the scene."

"Where do you want to start?" I asked.

"You take the living room, and I'll take the bedrooms."

"Okay." I moved from the entryway to the cozy living room. There was a chintz-covered couch with a matching armchair. Between these was a side table with a lamp and a book with a bookmark sticking out of it. I walked over and picked up the book. Agatha Christie's *13 Clues for Miss Marple*.

A set of bookshelves ran across the opposite wall under the windows. On top were neatly displayed framed photographs. I knelt down to look at some of the book titles, many of which were mysteries. Well, Winifred and I at least had one thing in common. Too bad we never talked about books. It might have proven to be a bonding experience.

A narrow hutch with a drop-down desk was the only other piece of furniture in the room. I opened the glass doors of the top half and found an assortment of knickknacks, mostly figurines. I closed the doors and moved to the drawers below. One held old cards and letters alongside new stationery, and the other had notepads, her well-worn address book, and the clutter that often ends up in drawers.

I hadn't come across her business records yet, so I went back to the entry way. "Jack?" I called out. "Does she have a home office?"

"Off the kitchen," he called back.

A short hall led to the kitchen. Like the living room, this room was also neat and tidy. No dirty dishes in the sink or clutter on the counters. A brightly colored kitchen towel hung on a hook by the sink, and a tea kettle sat on the stove. The walls were painted a soft yellow, with yellow and white valances over the windows.

Jack's heavy footfall came down the hall toward the kitchen. He was a big guy, and his sudden presence in the kitchen made the space feel smaller. "Nothing in the two bedrooms. She has zero clutter—it makes it easy to search."

"Yeah, she was very tidy." I looked around the kitchen and then to a room addition which ran across the length of the back of the house. This was her home office and art studio. All three of the walls of the extension had windows, and there was a door to the back patio, which had a table for four with a bright green umbrella. The patio led to the small but manicured backyard. "I really like her house. It's compact, but it's light and airy."

"Feels a little tight to me."

I elbowed him. "That's because you're a big guy. You'd be bumping into things all the time."

"Yeah, I'm feeling a little claustrophobic, so let's get this done. You take the left side, and I'll take the right."

I went to the shelves first. There were three-ring binders full of paperwork from her business. Just as with her house, she was meticulous, keeping neat records of receipts and expenditures. I only perused the business paperwork enough to note while she wasn't getting rich off her shop, she wasn't losing money, either.

"I could take some lessons from how she keeps her paperwork," I said to Jack.

"I don't know about that. I think you're obsessively organized," he said.

"I am, but she has some cool graphs to show what kinds of items sell well, and at what times of year. That's a smart business mind."

I moved down to the drawers and found more

organization. There were file folders, clearly labeled with all her household bills, and a detailed notebook with repair services and contacts for every conceivable component of home maintenance.

"Nothing of interest here," I said, then wandered over to the art area.

An easel, with a work in progress, was placed where she could take advantage of the natural light. She had a rolling cart to hold her paints and brushes and a small bookshelf where she kept varnish, gesso, magazines she used for her collages, and some art books. I counted twelve finished pieces, which were leaning against the wall, some stacked three deep.

"She was really into the collages," I said to Jack.

"Was she any good?"

"Well, some of them are a bit rudimentary, but others are pretty good." I held one up for him to see. "She has a few like this, where she used cutouts from magazines to create flower shapes."

"I see why you didn't want her things in the Workshop's gift shop," he said.

"They're not all like this. It looks like she was advancing and doing things with more depth. There's a market for ones like this," I said, holding up a different one with a wash of brooding colors and a more abstract design in the pattern of the cutouts. "Complex collages are a pretty big business right now."

"Still not really my thing," he said.

"To each his own," I retorted, putting the canvas back down. "By the way, does she have any family? Did she have a will? I wonder where all this stuff will go?"

"She had an emergency contact in the datebook Travis found in her purse—a sister in Pittsburgh."

"Good. I'm glad there's family." I moved back to the office and, not knowing what else to do, fiddled with the stapler for a bit, then I picked up a glass paperweight and tossed it back and forth between my hands.

Jack had moved to her computer and was sifting through the desktop folders. "Matt only did a perfunctory search on here because she kept her notes on you on her laptop. Plus, her laptop was mobile for using the Wi-Fi at the library. But I want to make sure these folders don't have smoke screen labels."

"What do you mean?" I asked, snapping a rubber band I had found in a little bowl on the desk.

"Like a folder named 'recipes' might not be recipes, but actually, notes on someone else." He looked up at me. "Why don't you take another walkthrough while I do this." That was his nice way of saying my fidgeting was annoying him and to get out of his hair.

"Okey doke." I went back through the kitchen to the part of the house Jack had searched. There was a small guest room, a full bathroom, and the master bedroom with a small attached bath. Back in the hall, I opened a closet that housed the washer and dryer and linens. Sheets and towels were neatly folded and organized by color.

"She must do spring cleaning every month!" I called out to Jack."

"I told you," he called back.

I tried not to feel discouraged and tamped down the uncomfortable feeling that Winifred had disliked me, in particular, enough to target me and only me. Could I really have rankled her so much?

Back in the living room, I sat on the floor in front of the shelves and scanned the book titles. If nothing else, maybe I could find a new book to look for at the library. I used my hand to tilt the books so I could more easily read the titles, and when I got to the *Women's Murder Club* series, one of the books felt heavier than the others. I pulled it from the shelf and opened it.

"What have we here?" I muttered to myself. The pages of the book had been cut and a small hardcover notebook had been inserted. "You wily woman. What was so secret you needed a hidey-hole?"

I opened the notebook and found small, neat handwriting. Flipping through page after page, I knew I had hit the jackpot. It was like a journal, with each entry dated, except instead of daily musings and personal thoughts, she had made notes on people and the details she had learned about them. No names were written, only initials or, in some cases, a code name.

"Jack, I found something." I jumped up and rushed to the kitchen. I pulled out a chair at the table and sat down. "Come look at this."

Jack looked over my shoulder as I flipped through the pages. "This takes busybody to a whole new level," he said.

"It sure does. I knew she was a gossip, but this is a bit over the top. It reminds me of the first *Midsomer Murders* episode, where the town busybody watched everything, kept notebooks, and blackmailed people. Except I don't see Winifred as a blackmailer. This mostly looks like accumulating info purely for gossip, you know, who was seen doing what and with whom. But there are some other more cryptic entries."

"We're going to have to take a deep dive into this."

"Can I help?"

"That would be great." He took the journal and put

it in a plastic evidence bag. "This has to go to the station, but we can make a copy for you. And remember, this is evidence, and your work falls under the official clearance you received to be a consultant. So this is for your eyes only."

I hesitated too long.

"What?"

"Well, I'm just thinking I may need help deciphering some of this. Annie, Bitsy, and JJ may know people I don't."

Jack put up his hands. "I'm going to pretend I didn't hear that. This is evidence in an ongoing investigation. I'm entrusting you with it, and if anything goes awry, there will be hell to pay—for both of us."

"How about I look through it first, and if there is any sensitive information, I promise I won't talk about it. If it's just so-and-so was seen buying an armload of candy at the convenience store, it really doesn't matter, does it? Besides, they know not to discuss anything outside our circle."

Jack loomed over me. "What part of 'I'm going to pretend I didn't hear that' don't you understand?"

I scrunched down in my chair. "Okay, okay, I got it!"

He walked back to the desk. "You're a lot smaller than me. Would you squish down under here to unplug the computer? I need to take it back to the station. And look around while you're down there to make sure nothing slipped under or behind the desk."

"Sure." I knelt on the floor and contorted myself to reach the plug. I wondered if this was payback for annoying him just now, but I did as I was told and searched every possible nook and cranny. When I finished, I blew out a sigh, twisted around, and brought myself to my knees to make my exit. I happened to catch Jack watching me with a mischievous grin on his face.

"Anything else to do here before we go?" I asked, ignoring him.

"No, but I'm not releasing the house yet. When her sister comes, I'll advise her she will need to be accompanied by an officer to enter the house until we know we are done with it."

We made our way out, but before closing up, I looked back at the living room. What had initially seemed like a cozy cottage suddenly felt quite sinister. I could envision Winifred, sitting on her chintz sofa sipping a cup of tea while she neatly documented what she had seen that day. Even though it was warm outside, a chill ran through me.

Climbing back in the SUV, I said, "I'm famished. Can we stop for a burger?"

Jack looked at his watch. "I have time to do a drive-thru."

"Perfect! Let's go to Chuck-n-Cluck!"

Ten minutes later, we were parked with the windows down, laps full of napkins, and the only sound was the crinkle of the paper wrapped around our burgers.

"Want my pickles?" I asked.

"You know I do."

I plopped my pickles on his opened burger and then dove in. "Oh my gosh," I said, through a mouthful of bacon cheeseburger, "this is heaven." Once finished, I propped my boots on the dashboard and put the bag of fries in my lap. "Remember when we would go to the drive-in place at the edge of town? What was it called?"

"Fast Lane Burgers?"

"That's it!"

"Since we couldn't drive yet, we ordered at the call box and then sat on the curb."

"And Mr. Barnard would yell at us for kicking the soccer ball in the parking lot."

"You mean Mr. *Barnyard*," he said, drawing out the nickname he had come up with. Then he did an impression of him. "Hey, you kids stop playing out there! If you hit a window with that ball, I'll call your mom!"

I laughed so hard at his impression my stomach muscles hurt. "Oh man, those were the days."

"And who was the boy you were crushing on? He came with us a few times to the drive-in."

I immediately knew who he was talking about. "Marvin."

"That's right, Marvin. You were hilarious, trying to act all girly around him."

"I did not!"

"You totally did." Jack let out a big laugh. "But then he did something that made you mad, and you punched him."

I looked at Jack with wide eyes, nodding. "I did. He turned out to be a big bully, and he was giving one of the younger kids a hard time, so I punched him in the stomach."

Jack laughed again. "I can still see you, in a dress no less, turn around and punch him in the gut." Then he looked at me with smiling eyes. "You started early standing up for what was right."

"I guess I did. Whatever happened to him?"

"His family moved away the next year."

I grinned. "Ah. I guess the shame was too much."

We needed the release of some laughs, but the real world came crashing back when Jack threw his trash in the to-go bag and turned to look at me. "You still put up a good fight, and I'm not going to lie, that worries me a little. This murder is particularly vicious, cold, and calculated."

The smile left my face. "I know. And don't worry. This has unsettled me enough I'm not going to do anything stupid."

"I sincerely hope not," Jack said, starting the engine. "Time to drop you off and get back to the station. Come by later to pick up a copy of the journal."

****

I went straight to my apartment. I didn't want to talk to anyone until I had a chance to decompress from the shock of finding Winifred, not getting enough sleep, being interrogated, and then going with Jack to search Winifred's house. The burger tasted good, but it was not going to get me through the day.

I punched the button to brew a cup of coffee, and the homeyness of the aroma instantly made me feel comforted. I knew eventually I would have to go down to the garden, but for now, I avoided even looking at it through the kitchen window. Instead, I took my coffee to the couch, curled my legs under me, and stared, unseeing, at the whiteboard, which still had our scribbled notes from navigating the details of the skeleton.

How could so much happen in the span of six days? Either event would be enough to shock the system, but having both happen in rapid sequence was too much. No wonder my brain was overloading and my shoulders were hitched up to my ears.

I put my mug on the coffee table and slid myself

down to the floor. I lay flat and tapped into a few principles of a relaxation course I had taken back in college. Closing my eyes, I used my mind to control the weight of my muscles. Relaxed muscles are heavy and grounded, not by force, but by focusing on each one and its connection to the next, from the facial muscles down to the feet.

After about twenty minutes, I opened my eyes and felt refreshed. Or at least refreshed enough to get up off the floor. I brewed another cup of coffee—why not? I'd missed my usual allotment—and went back to the couch.

First, I grabbed my laptop and sent the email notifying the artists about the victim found in our garden, and the subsequent search of the Workshop. I advised them if they had any concerns about what took place in their studio to contact me. With that task done, I allowed my eyes to drift to the whiteboard, and this time, I looked at it a new way.

Instead of thinking about how overwhelming it was to have so many things happen at once, now I asked myself *why* this all happened at once. The sabotage, smear campaign, skeleton, plus Winifred murdered and staged at the Workshop, was too much of a coincidence. There had to be a connection, and I just needed to connect the dots to find the answer. It was time to rally the troops.

Chapter 14

The sun was low in the sky, and I was sitting on the floor surrounded by small stacks of pages from Winifred's journal. Jack had, as promised, let me take the photocopies, but reinforced the need for discretion, so I sifted through and divided the pages into stacks based on the degree of gossip and potential damage it could cause. There was some interesting reading here, and I was looking forward to hashing things over with the gang.

I had just finished and had a single criss-crossed stack when they arrived. Spencer had picked up sandwiches from the sub shop, and he stashed them in the fridge.

"Where's Maggie?" Annie asked.

"She's on duty downstairs until the last class finishes, then she'll be up."

Bitsy, JJ, Annie, and Spencer were trying to wait patiently while I acted like a hostess and asked who wanted what to drink, but finally, Bitsy couldn't stand it any longer. "Okay, enough. We can all get our own drinks. Start at the top and fill us in!"

I stopped what I was doing and looked at their anxious faces. "What has Annie told you?"

JJ answered, "Winifred was found dead in the garden, you were taken in for questioning, and then your email that there was a search here at the Workshop."

"Come sit down," I said, leading them to the living room. "There's a lot to go over. First, yes, Winifred is dead."

"How? What happened?" Spencer asked.

"From what Jack told me, it looks like she was hit on the back of the head. But here's the thing, there was no evidence it happened there, in the garden."

"You mean she was moved there?" Bitsy asked, incredulously.

"Yes." I could hear Jack's voice resonating in my ears, so I held up my hand indicating to wait. "This is a complex case and it was an atrocious murder, therefore, there are certain things Jack is not going to release to the public. Also, he was adamant that I not discuss it in detail."

Annie put her hands on her hips. "Well, I'll talk to him later about this, but as far as I'm concerned, this happened here, at the Workshop. We deserve to know what happened and have every right to try and figure out why."

"Ooo, I wouldn't want to get between you two when your hackles are up," Spencer joked.

"I'm serious! I think we can all promise we are not going to discuss things outside this room, and we can be trusted to honor our promise. But I'll be damned if I'm going to turn a blind eye to what happened right here in our garden, and just wait for something else to happen, possibly to one of us!"

"Okay," I said, putting my hands up. "I'll leave that to you and Jack to sort out."

JJ said, "So, continue. You said she was moved here after she was killed."

"Yes, and she was staged to look like a statue sitting

on a bench."

"How? You mean she was propped up on the bench?" Spencer asked.

Repeating what I had seen was not easy, and I hesitated before saying, "Um, she was spray-painted bronze and staged, sitting on the bench holding a rose."

"Oh my God," JJ gasped.

Bitsy put her hand to her mouth, Spencer just stared at me in disbelief, and Annie, who already knew the details, looked down at her clasped hands.

I decided the best tactic was to keep talking. "So since there was no sign of a struggle at the site, Jack had to search the grounds and the building in order to rule out that she was killed here."

Spencer found his voice. "But Annie said you were taken in for questioning."

"I was. They found notes on Winifred's computer outlining the social media smear campaign, which meant I became a person of interest. I had no alibi, so they had to question me, and then once the building and my apartment were cleared, I was cleared."

"A social media campaign is hardly a reason to kill someone. How could Jack let you be interrogated?" JJ snapped.

Annie now switched gears and came to his defense. "Listen, I was pretty hopping mad when Jack came to pick up Alex at the house. But in reality, he had no choice. They had to handle things the same way they would if this had happened somewhere else, and Alex understood that."

"But if you have no alibi, how have you been cleared?" Bitsy asked.

I relayed the whole story, and JJ said, "Damn, this is

intense."

Spencer stood up. "So, since they didn't find anything in the building, we know she wasn't killed here."

"Right," I said.

"And she was staged," Bitsy said, with a shiver.

"So what's next?" JJ asked.

"Okay, moving on, the next part happened after Jack cleared me from the investigation. He and I searched Winifred's house."

"What's her house like? I'm picturing fussy," Annie said.

"It's actually meticulously neat and tidy."

"Huh," she responded, as if trying to envision it.

"Anyway, Jack's thought was if she was targeting me, she might have been targeting others. Someone must have had a pretty serious motive to kill her, so it stands to reason she might have left a clue as to who. She might not have realized she was pushing the wrong person."

"That makes sense!" JJ said.

We all jumped when Maggie thrust open the door and rushed in. "So what did I miss?" she asked.

Spencer went to the fridge to pull out the sandwiches. "Come on, let's eat and we'll fill you in."

As we made our way to the table, Bitsy said, "We are just at the point where Alex and Jack searched Winifred's house."

"You actually know everything up to that point," I said to Maggie. "So your timing is perfect."

Once we were settled at the table and hunkered down over our sandwiches, Annie said, "Jack thinks if Winifred was targeting Alex, she was probably targeting other people, too."

"We don't know this for sure, but during the search, we found a hidden journal. She was keeping notes on people. Things she saw or heard."

"You are kidding me," Bitsy said, aghast.

"That's like something out of a movie," Spencer said.

I pointed to the stack of papers. "Jack let me take a copy of the journal, and this is when I have to reiterate if you speak outside this room about anything we discuss, I will be in deep trouble, and Jack could lose his job, because this is considered evidence."

They all nodded their understanding.

"Okay. So I've gone through this journal, and I've split it up into batches depending on the severity of the gossip."

JJ said, "I'm not sure if I'm comfortable hearing gossip about people."

"I know, it kind of creeps me out," Bitsy added.

I looked at them in turn. "I'm not going to give you any specifics. That would be inappropriate. But I can do this on my own if you don't feel right hashing over any of it."

Maggie cut in. "Look, you guys, I know this is awkward, but Winifred was murdered and left here, on our doorstep. This affects all of us, and I think we should do what we can to help. Besides, we don't have to know who Winifred wrote about, you're just talking the subject matter, right?"

"Absolutely," I concurred. "No names and no details."

"Maggie's right, we need to help," Annie said.

Bitsy sighed. "Okay, I'm in."

"Me too," JJ said.

I felt a swell of gratitude that I was lucky enough to have a circle of such good friends. "Thanks, you guys. Let's dive in. It seems like Winifred might have used information to sway things on the town council or with other civic groups."

"What would she want with them?" Annie asked.

From my life in politics, I knew even small towns were a hotbed for people wanting control over zoning and permissions. "It could be anything from speed bumps in a neighborhood to permit or zoning approval for a residence or commercial building."

Bitsy said, "She had a business on Main Street, and I'm sure everything from expansion or renovating a storefront to a sidewalk sale has to go through the council for approval."

"That's right," I said, thinking of Ben, from the hardware store, and his anger about the permit.

Maggie asked, "What did she write when referring to those things?"

I shuffled through the pages. "Here's one example: Someone was seen late at night visiting someone else's house. Then she writes she might get the needed vote at the next meeting. She used initials, not *someone*."

Bitsy said, "So she notated the incident for reference when approaching the councilperson down the road."

"Right. Except it doesn't have to be a councilperson. It could be someone to speak in favor of or against a proposition. Someone to provide additional support."

Annie said, "Does she think she can make mention of it to the person and then give a subtle hint about the upcoming vote?"

"Yes," I said. "But I know from my old life you don't actually have to spell things out. If someone is

189

presumed to be in a compromising situation, you don't have to say 'I saw you sneaking out of so-and-so's house.' Instead, you make a light mention of seeing them late at night in a specific neighborhood, and then later in the conversation you say something about hoping they will represent the wishes of the community and vote yes, or no, or speak up in favor of or against, depending on the situation."

Maggie said, "Oh, I get it. If the person is guilty, they will read between the lines, and then vote accordingly."

"Whoa, Alex." Spencer laughed. "It sounds like you know this from experience!"

I put my hands up and adamantly said, "Not me. I've just seen it done."

"But, you guys, would an indiscretion like this be enough motive for murder? Would anything in front of the town council be motive for murder?" Annie asked.

"I just don't see it," Bitsy said. "It's not like a larger city where it's a big development and millions of dollars are at stake."

"I agree. So what else did you find?" Spencer asked.

"There were a lot of stupid things. Someone letting their dog poo on the grass and not cleaning up. Listening in on someone filling a prescription and then wondering if they have a sensitive medical issue."

"Wow. That is crazy. How much of her time was spent spying on people?" Maggie questioned.

"She was an information gatherer," I answered. "And Aunt Claudia told me she's been a gossipy sort since she was a kid."

"Was there anything about any of us?" JJ asked.

"Well, I did come across something about you,

Bitsy!" I said, with a big grin and an eyebrow waggle.

"What?" she exclaimed, in horror.

"Don't worry, it's nothing bad." I flicked through to find the page I was looking for. "She says, 'Those bird hats aren't so silly now. The bird lady has become a celebrity. Can we convince her to move with us to Pine Brook? Butter her up and find an incentive.' " I put the page down and grinned at Bitsy.

Bitsy's mouth hung open in disbelief.

JJ chortled, "Hah! I honestly wasn't expecting we were interesting enough to be in her journal. Well, bird lady, you caught her attention."

Bitsy still looked horrified.

Spencer held up his hand. "Okay, we're getting off track here. We really need something that points to the investigation."

"I did find an answer to something we've been questioning. She wrote, 'Something odd happening. Social media campaign proving successful, but who is vandalizing the garden? Who else has something to gain from the downfall of the high and mighty Alex? Must find out.' "

Spencer blurted, "Talk about burying the lead! That's an important bit of information."

I defended myself. "Well, to me it wasn't all that earth shattering. It just proves what I've been thinking all along. Winifred was not responsible for what was happening in the garden. But it is important for Jack to know."

"Argh!" Annie groaned. "Now we have to figure out who the saboteur is!"

JJ said, ominously, "This is a tangled web, indeed."

I shuffled the pages back into a neat stack. "You

want to talk a tangled web—I also found some evidence of outright blackmail."

"What do you mean? Like blackmail for money?" Maggie asked.

"Well, I'm pretty sure one example is with a banker, maybe to push through a loan."

"Like for the new venture in Pine Brook?" Bitsy asked.

"Possibly. And nothing might have come from it. There are some numbers, but I'm not sure what they mean. Jack will have to look into it."

"I thought Eva had enough money to pull off the Pine Brook project without a loan," Annie said.

Spencer answered, "People don't normally put their own reserves into a business, because if it goes belly up, they lose their personal assets."

"So the company would go bankrupt, not the person," JJ said, for clarity.

"I think so. But don't quote me on that," he said.

"How many of the blackmail type entries do you see, Alex?" Maggie asked.

"A few in recent history, but it's not always clear who she's blackmailing," I answered. "But her final entry is possibly significant. It had three dollar signs and a single line, 'Time to pull out the big guns.' "

Chapter 15

JJ voiced what many of us were thinking. "Whoa, it's ominous to hear her words—Winifred thinks she's hit the jackpot, but instead, her big guns turned out to be her death knell."

"Well, there's your motive," Spencer said. "It's one thing to sway a vote on the council, but a whole different level when you are talking blackmail for money. Meaning, it was something worth paying for to keep silent."

"Maybe she crossed a person who believed Winifred would keep wanting payment, and murder was the only way out."

"Has Jack seen this yet?" Annie asked.

"No, I found it just before you guys arrived, so I'll call him when we're done."

Bitsy got up from the table and started collecting the sandwich wrappings to put in the trash. "Talking to Jack should be a priority, so we'll get out of your hair."

After everyone left, I got my phone and tapped Jack's number. "Hey, can you come over? I have some things to talk to you about."

"Sure. I'll be over shortly."

Thirty minutes later, Jack and I were sitting at the kitchen table.

"Has anything more come from the ME, like forensic evidence?" I asked.

"He's still working on it. Since she was spray-painted, some stuff stuck to the wet paint, and he has to determine what was environmental, like wind-blown, and then search for the tiniest thread, fiber, or foreign object that is actual evidence. Even a stray hair could have just blown onto her after she was placed."

I nodded. "A lot of people were in the garden yesterday."

"Plus, my crew and the ambulance guys were out there. I had them suit up, but it was tricky dealing with the body covered in wet paint. There could have been some cross-contamination."

"Oh geez, if everything has to be tested, it could take a while."

"Yup. So, what have you got for me?"

I separated the stack of journal pages. "Out the gate I'll show you this one. It proves my theory Winifred was not doing the sabotage."

"Right," he said, setting the critical page in front of him. "At least one question is answered, although it just opens up more questions. Go on."

"Okay, this stack contains innocuous things. Basic information gathering." I read him snippets about Bitsy and dog walking infractions. "All of these sections highlighted in green are similar in nature."

Jack chuckled at the reference to Bitsy, the bird lady.

"Although, there is a mention of 'the apple not falling far from the tree,' which reminded me of when Winifred was talking about Luke's father in an unflattering way. I think she's been keeping an eye on Luke, but I don't see anything noteworthy."

I patted the stack, then shoved it aside and pulled over the next one. "These will be worth looking into.

There are some references to council members or other business leaders."

Jack grew serious. "Okay, so there could be some zoning issues where votes went a certain way because of coercion."

"Right. Maggie and I actually witnessed an exchange between Ben, who owns the hardware store, and Winifred, about his permit being denied to have his smoker going in front of the hardware store during the sidewalk sale. He was pretty heated up. Worth murdering for? I hardly think so. But I'll let you take a look for yourself."

"I'll pull Ben aside for a little chat. If nothing else, he might know other people who had a bone to pick with her."

I paper-clipped the stack and put it aside, then said, "Now it gets complicated. These have some numbers and dates along with the initials. Have you looked at her bank accounts?"

"We have. There was nothing unusual. You're thinking blackmail?"

"Yeah. What about cash or a safe deposit box?" I asked.

"We didn't find any stashes of cash, but we may have to look deeper. The journal was hidden, so maybe she hid a safe deposit or lockbox key, too."

Jack pulled the third group of papers over and scanned them. "There's not enough information here, other than we know it's money because of the dollar signs. Did she threaten these people verbally? In writing? And did she keep tangible evidence, or just witness or overhear something she shouldn't have?"

"Your guess is as good as mine," I answered.

"It doesn't have to be something illegal. It could be an indiscretion or mishandling of something. I have a feeling there are some awkward conversations with a few folks in my future."

"Can you bring people into the station with this little to go on?"

"It's a murder case, so I can. But I can also have a chat on a more informal basis, which is a better way to start." Jack got out his notebook. "Let's take them one by one."

I retrieved the pile of papers. "Okay, first, I think Eva needs another chat. Was Winifred trying to wrangle a bank loan? Was she trying to coerce Eva into going into business?"

"I thought you said Eva indicated it wasn't a done deal," Jack said.

"She did, but maybe Winifred had something on Eva and was pressuring her."

He nodded. "I'll talk to her again. Who's next?"

"I think these initials are the bank manager Roger Pettigrew, unless there's another R.P. I'm not aware of. She doesn't note why he is in the journal."

"Someone like Winifred had her ear to the ground. Maybe there was some funny business with loans, meaning, who got them and who didn't. Maybe she caught him in a personal indiscretion and squirreled away the information for future use."

We continued through the short list of candidates, and I finished with the listing of the single letter T, and I asked, "Any ideas who T might be? There are three-dollar signs with an exclamation point after the initial."

"Well, I know a Theo and Tom. They're on my softball team. Of course there's my deputy, Travis, but none of these guys have significant money."

"And it could be an initial for a last name," I said, with frustration, then I had another thought. "Tucker starts with T, and he's been involved with the garden work which means he's been around Winifred. He's got money. He handles investments, so could there be something there?"

"Possibly. Maybe embezzlement?"

"But I really can't see him getting his hands dirty, literally, spray painting and staging Winifred. That kind of hate runs deeper than his personality indicates."

We both sat in silence, contemplating the complexities of the case. Then Jack pushed his chair back and said, "I'm going to take these home to work on. I'll also have Matt put his eyes on it while I have some conversations with the folks we unearthed from this tangle of trouble Winifred created."

"I don't envy you this one. What about people's finances? Can you look at them?"

"Not without a warrant, so there has to be concrete probable cause or the judge will laugh me out of the room." Jack walked toward the door.

"Do you want me to take a little peek? Off the record?" Jack knew I had some, let's call it, soft hacking skills.

"Absolutely not. You're working as a consultant, which means you have to do things by the book, too."

"Okay."

"Really," he emphasized.

"Okay!"

After Jack left, I flopped on the couch next to Baxter. "This is a tough one," I said to him. "How could one small town have so much intrigue?"

Baxter cocked his head, confused at not hearing words he readily understood, like *treat*, *walk*, and *hungry*.

I stared at the whiteboard, trying to make sense of everything. Something was nagging at me, but I couldn't put my finger on it. My head was foggy from the night before, the stress of the morning, and the nonstop day. I hoped a good night's sleep would bring some clarity.

****

Friday

I awoke to the sound of my phone ringing. My hand flopped around until it made contact, and with one eye open and the other deep in the pillow, I swiped to answer. "Hello," I said, in a groggy voice.

Maggie's voice sounded alarmed. "Alex? Were you still asleep? I'm so sorry, you're usually up hours before I am."

With bleary eyes, I looked at the time. It was after nine. "No, it's okay. I tossed and turned a lot last night, and I've overslept, so it's good you called. What's going on?"

"I'm at the front desk, and there's a man here to see you."

I propped myself up on my elbow. "Who is it?"

"I don't know. He's gone over to look in the gift shop windows. He just asked to see you." She lowered her voice to a whisper, and said, "He looks like he stepped out of a men's magazine."

"I'll be right down."

Who in the heck could that be? I got up and frantically pulled myself together. I managed to brew and drink a cup of coffee, brush my teeth, pull my hair back into a tight pony, and put on some clothes, all in a matter of minutes.

I was midway down the staircase when I stopped in my tracks. "Michael? What in the world are you doing here?"

Michael, my ex-husband, turned to face me and rewarded me with a big smile. "Good morning," he said. He was dressed impeccably, in gray slacks and a white button-down dress shirt. Coupled with his chiseled good looks, I could see how Maggie thought he looked like he was out of a magazine. Whereas to me, he was just Michael.

I approached him and grabbed his arm. "Why are you here?" I asked, quietly.

"Jack called."

I rolled my eyes. "You are kidding me." I couldn't help but notice Maggie was looking at us with undisguised interest, so I led Michael over to her. "Michael, this is Maggie, my assistant manager. She's an incredible photographer. Maggie, this is Michael, my ex-husband."

"Oh! It's nice to finally meet you! I've heard so much about you," Maggie gushed.

"And I've heard many wonderful things about you," Michael said, smoothly. "I'm happy to meet you."

He started to engage her in conversation, but I cut it short. "We need to talk." I turned toward the staircase, and he had no choice but to follow.

"We'll talk more later, Maggie," he said.

"Yes, I hope so." I could feel her eyes follow us up the stairs.

Once in the apartment, Michael squatted to pet Baxter after introductions had been made, and then I said, "Okay, spill it. Why did Jack call you, and why did you drop everything and come running?"

Michael straightened and gave me the stern look I had seen before. It usually annoyed me. "Jack called because a murdered woman was found on your property, you didn't have an alibi, your building was being searched, and it appears you had a motive. He has since let me know you were cleared, but along with the skeleton he told me about, the sabotage, and the social media campaign, I decided you might need a lawyer close by, and if you recall, I'm a good one."

I groaned. "Oh, for crying out loud." I went to the coffee machine and punched the button harder than I needed to. "Do you want coffee?"

Michael walked toward the kitchen. "Yes, please."

He was being nosy, a characteristic of his, and he opened and closed the cabinet doors and looked in the refrigerator before wandering back to the bedroom. I leaned against the kitchen counter and drank my coffee while his brewed, trying to ignore him.

Michael had intended to come for a visit in the spring, but his plans fell through, so this was his first time here. Was it odd my ex-husband had planned to come visit? Not really. We managed to end things before we hated each other, so he was still friends with my family, as I was with his, and he and I kept in touch fairly regularly. If I'm being honest, we fully trusted each other, which was invaluable, even if he aggravated me to no end.

I might have appeared nonchalant, but my eyes followed Michael's progress as he blithely crossed the living room to the other side of the apartment where the guest room, second bathroom with laundry, and my office were. The sound of closet doors and cabinet drawers opening and closing told me he was doing a deep snoop.

When he returned to the kitchen, he said, "Well, some things are the same, and some are different. Very interesting."

"What's that supposed to mean?" I asked, handing him his cup.

"You never cooked a lot, but at least you were eating out at proper restaurants. You don't have much real food here, and from what I saw driving in, my guess is you're dining mostly on take-out. I don't see any personal knickknacks or stacks of paperwork. Your guestroom is neat and tidy, and the closet is empty, if you get my drift."

"No, I don't," I said, even though I knew all too well he had been looking for signs Walter had left personal items here.

"Even your office is an organized chaos. I see lots of art, but only a few personal photos. And your wardrobe is a quarter the size and it consists of jeans and T-shirts. But your fancy coffee machine means you still have your priorities." His face broke into a grin.

"Very funny. And you know I was never into knickknacks." This was my way of not acknowledging the rest was fairly accurate.

He stood next to me, leaning against the counter. "I like your place. It's got style, but it's comfortable. Nice quality leather furniture, good rugs, but not fussy."

"That's me," I said off-handedly. Michael was standing close enough to me that his shoulder brushed mine, and I could smell his cologne. There was something comforting about the familiarity of his presence.

"Now, let's talk about how you are really doing. You look like hell, so I'm guessing this has been a strain."

Okay, now I remembered. Sensitivity was not his strong suit, and I reached up to straighten my ponytail before saying, "Thanks."

"I'm being serious."

"I know you are. I'm just a little groggy. It's been a long couple of days."

"Okay, let's sit down and talk it over."

"Let me go pull myself together, first. I literally jumped out of bed to go downstairs."

I closed the door from my bedroom wing to the living area and leaned against it to recover from the shock of Michael's arrival and the myriad of feelings his sudden presence had stirred up. I grabbed a quick shower, put my jeans back on but chose a different top—to disprove the T-shirt comment—and then, after drying my hair, I inexplicably took the time to apply my more comprehensive make-up routine: foundation to smooth out the blotchiness, finishing powder, eyebrow pencil, eyeshadow, mascara, and a touch of blush. I was not going to admit I was doing this for Michael, and instead, convinced myself I was doing this to refresh myself after a tough couple of days.

By the time I returned to the living room, Michael was fully absorbed in the whiteboard, and my attempts at a civilized appearance went unnoticed.

"This is comprehensive," he said, with admiration.

"Yeah, we put our heads together and made some good progress."

"Let's start at the beginning," he said, taking a seat in one of the leather armchairs.

"Okay. Some of this will be a bit jumbled in chronology because we've found out some stuff since we started."

Michael grabbed a pen and pad of paper off the coffee table to take his own notes.

"First, there was the social media campaign and the minor sabotage in the garden and the building. We have since found out Winifred, the murder victim, was responsible for the social media, but not the sabotage."

Michael was scribbling and asked, "Fact or surmisal?"

"Fact. It was in the notes we found in her journal. I'll get to that in a minute."

"What's next?

"Baxter and Poppy, who was here on a sleepover, uncovered the skeletal remains at the edge of my property, by the tree line."

"I'll have you show me where, later."

I nodded. "Then, on Wednesday night, Winifred was found in the garden. She had been murdered, spray-painted bronze, and staged to look like a statue."

Michael looked at me with intensity and then jotted more notes while asking questions. "Did it seem like she was painted in situ, where you found her, or was the craft work done elsewhere before she was moved?"

I shuddered at his reference to craft work, as if this was done like a craft or an intentional piece of art. But in truth, it did seem like a grotesque craft. "Um, I'm not sure."

"Well, if done here, there would likely be a lot of excess paint around the body, on the bench, and subsequently, on the perpetrator. If done elsewhere and moved, the site would be tidier, but there would be evidence elsewhere."

"Ah, I see. Based on what I recall, I think she was probably prepared elsewhere."

Michael nodded. "Okay, back to the sequence of events. What happened next?"

"During the preliminary search of her house, they found the evidence on her computer that she had written the social media posts, which gave me motive, and my prints were found on the wheelbarrow, which wasn't really significant because it's our wheelbarrow, but I didn't have an alibi."

"Which is why you were taken in for questioning, and they carried out the search of the property, building, and your apartment. I'm assuming the warrant was in order?"

"Yes, and yes. There was no evidence found of a struggle and no blood found, so it was determined she wasn't murdered here. Plus, the video footage shows someone jogging off the property."

"Jack told me you caught whoever it was just in time when turning on the surveillance cameras."

"Yeah, it's all my fault we didn't catch them in action."

"Doesn't matter. Sounds like they were well covered up, so it wouldn't have necessarily cleared you or anyone else connected to the Workshop."

"Except if they had been caught getting the wheelbarrow and wheeling Winifred to the garden."

"Maybe," he admitted. "But being well covered means that there should be clothing or coveralls with paint residue and potentially, DNA. Nothing's been found yet?"

"No. And I would imagine they were looking for

that kind of evidence during the search of the grounds, the building, and my apartment."

"You are lucky that the killer didn't tuck something away intending to frame you."

I shuddered at the thought and chose not to dwell on it. "Right. So once I was cleared, Jack and I searched Winifred's house, and we found a hidden journal where she kept notes on people. It appears she used information gathering to her benefit. In the journal, she inadvertently admitted responsibility for the social media campaign, but stated she was perplexed by the sabotage, and wondered who else might have an issue with me."

"Gee, Alex, how many people have you annoyed?" Michael asked.

I reared back. "I haven't annoyed anyone! Winifred was wanting to discredit us so she could open a competing gallery with artist studios!"

Michael chuckled. "Relax. I'm just winding you up." Then he returned to business. "So, the social media campaign question has been answered. Now you have to figure out the sabotage and how it relates to everything else. Any thoughts?"

I stood, staring at the whiteboard. "Both of these are big events. The skeleton is older history; the murder is new. Winifred's murder has sort of shoved the skeleton to the side, particularly because it's going to take a while for the forensic specialist to examine the bones."

"But should it be set aside? I think that's the question."

"You think we need to be asking if finding the skeleton is related to Winifred's murder?"

"Absolutely. I'm sure Jack is already thinking along those lines. He will know that it's too much of a coincidence for both of these events to happen so close to each other."

"Of course! That's what was nagging at me." I looked at him, and said, "Maybe it's good you came, after all."

"Aside from keeping you out of jail, I'm a fresh set of eyes. So let's talk about the skeleton."

I puffed up in pride. "We managed to narrow the timeline for her! With the information from the ME, and then doing some research, we arrived at the conclusions you see on the board."

"I see there were no missing persons in this area."

"Right. Now it could have been someone here on holiday or traveling through, which muddies the waters a bit," I acknowledged.

"If it had been a traveler, a report would have been filed from another state or county. The person would have not returned to work, or family would have been looking for them. From the description of the clothing and earrings, this was not a drifter, so someone would have noticed their absence."

"I hadn't thought about it like that."

"So what are you left with?"

I stroked my chin, deep in thought.

"Hello? Where'd you go?"

I sat on the edge of the couch. "Well, there's someone who comes to mind, but it really doesn't make sense."

"Who?"

"Over the last week, a name came up of a person who left town years ago. She was a friend of Aunt Claudia's, and her name is Eleanor."

"Okay, tell me what you know about her."

"She fits the age profile. I don't know about her height and size, but I can easily find out. She was married to Tucker, who lives behind the Workshop's property, and he's been volunteering in the garden."

"So what's the mystery surrounding her?"

"Not really a mystery, it's more of a conundrum. She walked out on Tucker and left town. But she did send Aunt Claudia a couple of postcards a few months after she left. Tucker told her she just left a note saying she was leaving him, and then he got some letters from her, but he never knew where she ended up settling."

"I'm assuming you've done some digging around to find her?"

"Yes."

"But it sounds like you didn't."

"No. I was going to ask Tucker some questions but had to contend with the reception, and then, of course, we found Winifred murdered."

"Jack knows about this?"

"Yes, but now he has his hands full with Winifred."

"Well, eliminating Eleanor as the skeletal remains would really help."

"It would, so I'm thinking maybe I can casually ask him some questions." I suddenly had an idea. "Or maybe I could get Bitsy to bring up something about looking for high school alumni. Yes! That's it. I'll talk to Bitsy, and then I'll go with her and we can hopefully get some answers."

"Uh, hold on there, Sherlock. Don't you think it'd be better if Jack did this?"

"Actually, no. He has no grounds to officially question Tucker. If he doesn't give us good enough answers, then Jack can go talk to him."

Before giving Michael time to respond, I grabbed my phone and stepped into my office to call Bitsy. It was a quick and fruitful call. She was already on site working in her studio, and after I explained the backstory, she was game.

I returned to the living room and said, "Okay, we have a plan." I started gathering my things and suddenly turned to Michael. "Oh, geez. Sorry. What are you going to do? Do you want to stay here? Or maybe Maggie can show you around the Workshop, or you can—"

Michael interrupted, "I'm a big boy. I can fend for myself. I think I'll stick close and explore the Workshop, and then you can fill me in when you get back. I'm not crazy about this idea, but I also know you know how to carry yourself in sticky situations, so I'll trust you won't say or do anything to bring on trouble."

I gave him a wry expression, and said, "At least you give me more credit than Jack does."

"Let's hope it's warranted."

I left Michael in Maggie's capable hands, and Bitsy and I met in the courtyard to go over our scheme.

I explained, "I know this is kind of a side tangent since Winifred's murder should be forefront in our minds, but Michael pointed out these two deaths could be related, so trying to track down Eleanor is a way to confirm or eliminate her as part of his hypothesis."

Bitsy said, "No, I get it. And this is a great idea, Alex. It's a low-key way to maybe get some answers, and it actually does coincide with something they've been working on in the high school office. They're wanting to update their alumni info, and I sat in on that committee when I was filling in at the end of the school year."

"So we can sound legit?" I asked.

"I think so. After you called, I printed off the alumni list and I even brought a clipboard from my studio, so I'll look like I know what I'm doing. Maybe we will not only find out where Eleanor is, but I'll get some helpful info for the alumni association, too. Sasha didn't grow up here, and she's a bit younger, anyway, but asking Tucker shouldn't arouse suspicion since they were in the same class."

Bitsy was looking at me earnestly, but she had on one of her elaborate pillbox hats showcasing a goldfinch with its wings spread, ready to take flight, and I had to choke back a chuckle.

"What?" she asked.

I quickly recovered. "Nothing."

We walked across the lawn and disappeared into the woods. When we emerged, we followed the path uphill, around the large stone patio and along the side of the house to the front door. While passing the patio, I noticed a workout area with an expensive-looking bike and treadmill, and a rack of dumbbell weights. This reminded me of what Maggie said about Sasha spending so much of her time working out. Even though I hated to work out, I admired the showroom quality of the gear and could imagine Sasha enjoying the beautiful view while sweating through her expensive workout clothing. For some reason, Tucker didn't seem like an intense exerciser to me, and my imagination pictured him on the bike with a gin and tonic in his hand.

The large house was made of stone, and it had a formidable front door with a heavy black door knocker, but I rang the bell instead. Sasha greeted us, and her sour expression told me she wasn't thrilled with having uninvited guests on her doorstep. Can't say I blamed her.

"Alex, what are you doing here?" she asked. "Did Tucker miss a garden meeting?"

I gave her my most radiant smile. "Hi, Sasha. No, nothing like that. I'm just along for the ride. My friend, Bitsy," I said, indicating with my hand, "is on an errand for the high school, and since she was at the Workshop this morning, I told her I would tag along."

"Hello, I'm Bitsy. I don't believe we've met." Bitsy held out her hand and received one of those limp, I-really-don't-want-to-touch-you handshakes in return. Bitsy kept smiling as she continued with our mission. "I've been working with Tucker on the garden. Is he here, by any chance?"

"Um, he's going to be leaving soon for the office. It might have been better to call first."

"Who is it, darling?" a voice called from another room in the house.

Sasha turned her head and replied, "Alex and Bitsy."

Tucker walked into the entry hall and said, "Well, hello, girls. What brings you here?" Then his smile faltered, and his face reflected the concern in his voice. "I heard about poor Winifred! Such a terrible thing. And so shocking for something like this to happen in our peaceful little town. Are there any new developments?"

I answered, "It's just awful, but no, no news on the investigation. But I do know the police have been working nonstop to find out what happened."

Sasha said, "It seems they have had to work a lot harder since you moved to town, Alex."

I cocked my head in a display of uncertainty about what she meant.

"Well, there was a murder last year at your retreat, two murders this winter, a skeleton was found, and now

Winifred has been murdered. Who knew art was such a dangerous business."

Chapter 16

"Sasha!" Tucker exclaimed. He anxiously looked at me. "She didn't mean for that to sound as bad as it did."

I couldn't help but let out an embarrassed laugh. "When you put it like that, it does sound like I'm a magnet for trouble. But believe me, I have not spent my entire life with disaster following in my wake, and I am finding this as unusual as you are."

"I'm sure this has been awful for you," she said, with what I chose to interpret as sincerity.

"Now, what can we do for you guys?" Tucker asked, wanting to close the topic of me being single-handedly responsible for the uptick in murders in Flat Rock Falls.

Bitsy answered, "We just want to ask you a couple of quick questions on behalf of the high school alumni association."

Tucker looked relieved. "Oh, are they wanting money again for the boosters? I already donated in the spring."

"Oh no. We're trying to fill in some missing information."

Tucker looked at his watch, and said, "I have a few minutes. Come on in."

We walked through the grand entryway to what would have been called a parlor in the old days. The loveseat and armchairs were clad in soft pastel colors, and the thick carpet muted the sound of our footsteps.

Tucker perched on the edge of the armchair and said, "So what can I do for you?"

Bitsy flipped through the sheets on her clipboard and said, "We are trying to track down alumni, and a few go back quite a ways. We have everything we need for you," she said, looking at Tucker, "but Eleanor Jenkins doesn't have any contact information and it was suggested that you might have it."

Tucker furrowed his brow. "Wow, this is the second time Eleanor has come up this week. That's going back a long time, you know. "

Sasha stood in the doorway with her arms folded, and the finely honed muscles in her arms flexed as she squeezed them with her tense fingers. She snapped, "This is fairly insensitive of you to come here asking Tucker about Eleanor. That silly woman left town years ago, and it was hard enough for Tucker back then, so to make him relive it again is just too much."

"Now, now, dear," Tucker appeased. "These young ladies don't know the history from so long ago. You see, Eleanor and I were married."

Bitsy's face registered concern, and she looked at me. "Oh, it appears this was a bad idea."

Tucker said, "No harm done. It was a sting to my ego back then when she up and left. That's all. But it was years ago. I should be over it now."

Bitsy said, kindly, "I don't think it's a case of getting over it. You just have to try and move on, which is what you've done. You two"—she nodded at Sasha—"have built a happy life and that's what matters."

"What a kind thing to say," Tucker said, and sighed. "Anyway, I already looked through my old correspondences for Jack but came up empty-handed. I received a few letters after she left, but if I recall, and please remember, this was a long time ago, she was moving around a bit, deciding where she wanted to live. After those first communications, we lost touch."

"You wouldn't happen to have a photo of her, would you? I might be able to use it for the alumni page," Bitsy said, earnestly.

Tucker shifted his eyes for a quick look at Sasha, then said, "No, after time, we felt it best to remove all reminders of Eleanor. Why keep mementos of someone who decided to walk away?"

Sasha stepped farther into the room. "Tucker, you don't have much time to get to your meeting. I think we should wrap this up."

Bitsy and I took this as our cue, and she said, "We won't take any more of your time."

Tucker walked us to the front door, and I couldn't help but ask, "Were you able to file divorce papers during the time you were in communication?"

Tucker looked forlorn. "No. For a long time I hoped she might come back. And then later, I couldn't locate her. I even hired a private detective. In the end I had to let it go. Besides, the experience soured me on the institution of marriage, so I never sought a divorce by other means."

Sasha entered the hall and hovered within earshot, so I said, "Well, marriage certificate or not, you and Sasha certainly have a deeply loyal relationship, which is what really counts."

Tucker smiled, but for some reason the smile didn't quite reach his eyes. Instead, there was a sadness there.

Bitsy lightened the mood with a cheery voice, saying, "Thanks again, Tucker. We'll see you guys at the sculpture garden grand opening, right?"

Tucker opened his arm as an invitation to Sasha to come stand with him. He put his arm around her and said, "Possibly. Sasha and I still want to get to the show in New York, so we'll see. Those tickets were hard to come by, so we don't want to miss out on the opportunity."

Bitsy and I were making our way back around the side of the house when we heard Sasha's voice call out to us in a loud whisper. We stopped and turned back as she approached us.

"Listen, I want to apologize for coming off as rude."

Bitsy chimed in, "Oh, there is nothing to apologize for. We should never have come without calling first."

Sasha flicked her hand. "No, that's not what I mean. Look, I worked for Tucker back when Eleanor left, and it really took a toll on him. He doesn't even realize how much of a wreck he was, and it took him a long time to get over it. I just don't want him to have to relive that pain all these years later."

"I totally understand," I said.

"Yes, and you've obviously been a godsend to him," Bitsy contributed. "Don't worry, we won't bother you again. I'll tell the alumni office there is no forwarding address."

"Thank you."

We waited until she turned back to the house, and then Bitsy and I retraced our steps and walked in silence until we reached the Workshop property. Even then, we spoke in hushed tones.

"Was that weird?" Bitsy asked.

"Definitely," I replied. "And I'm guessing that it was Jack who asked about Eleanor. Why didn't he tell me he went to question Tucker? How aggravating. Let's see who's around and have a chat."

Within ten minutes, Ryan, Maggie, Annie, Spencer, Bitsy, Michael, and I had congregated outside in the courtyard.

"I'm assuming you've all met Michael by now?" I asked.

"Yup, Maggie and Annie brought him around to all the studios," Spencer answered.

After we brought everyone up to speed on the plan and why we hatched it, Michael asked, "Okay, so how'd you fare?"

Bitsy answered, "Well, Sasha called out Alex and blamed her for the increased body count since she's moved here."

"What?" Spencer barked.

I shook my head. "Yeah, I don't think she meant it to be mean-spirited, but she just pointed out how much harder the police have had to work since I moved here."

"How awkward," Annie said.

"A little, but I have to admit, it has a ring of truth. Maybe I am a magnet for murder."

"Don't be ridiculous," Maggie chided. "We're not even going to dignify such a comment with any further discussion. So, did it end there or were you able to follow through with your plan?"

"Bitsy did a great job as the emissary from the high school," I said.

Annie grinned. "I'm not surprised. She could make me believe anything."

"Well, it helped that I had a legit reason for being there. Although, I never would have gone if not for this ruse," Bitsy said, with a twist of her mouth.

"So…what happened?" Maggie asked, impatiently.

"I wouldn't say we came away with any firm conclusions, but I found the exchange a little odd," I said.

"Me too," Bitsy agreed. "I think it was more the difference in dynamic between Tucker and Sasha than anything Tucker said. It's almost like Sasha manages him. But of course, she worked for him before they got together, and she probably managed his schedule and office back then."

"I agree. By the way, Tucker does not have a current address or phone number for Eleanor. But he seemed to have a good explanation. Of course, unbeknownst to me, I think Jack already talked to him, so he's had time to come up with a good story."

"What did he say?" Spencer asked.

"He said they communicated some through letters after she left, then he lost touch with her."

"Lost touch?" Michael asked. "If she left him, wouldn't he want a divorce?"

"He said he was hoping she might come back," I answered, "and I believed him. He seemed almost wistful."

"Sasha, on the other hand," Bitsy said, "seemed territorial and clearly didn't appreciate our intrusion."

"Hunh," Maggie uttered. "From my standpoint as a single person, I can well imagine not having a ring on her finger might make her a little protective of the life she's built with Tucker."

Bitsy added, "Absolutely. And Eleanor has been frozen in time. She represents Tucker's past, a love lost, and she's still young and beautiful in his mind. Living in her shadow could be intimidating, no matter how long they've been together."

I contemplated this. "You may be right. I could be

judging her too harshly, but my spidey sense is nagging me that there is more to this. What do you think, Michael?"

Michael had been quiet during most of the exchange of ideas, but now he leaned forward with his elbows on his knees and said, "Well, Scooby Doo, I can see how you and your gang work through your mysteries, and I'm impressed. But as an attorney, this is one case I would not take."

"What do you mean?" Annie asked.

"It's flimsy, at best. There's just no evidence of foul play here. Sasha's possessive, and Tucker's conflicted between remorse for a bad marriage and being happy in his life with Sasha. There's no physical evidence; there's barely any circumstantial evidence."

"Don't you think it's enough for Jack to talk to him again?" I asked.

"Uh, you've kind of meddled to the extent where he can't just casually keep asking Tucker questions 'for the purposes of elimination,' " he said, with air quotes.

My cheeks flushed at his comment. "Hey, that's harsh."

He put his palms up and shrugged. "You went in under the guise of looking for alumni. Then what, the same day Jack stops by again to push for more about Eleanor's whereabouts as part of his investigation into the skeleton? First of all, what more would he gain? Tucker already told him he doesn't know where she is and he doesn't have the old letters from her."

"You can't prove a negative," Ryan said, shaking his head slowly.

Michael continued, "And if Tucker *did* receive letters from her, then she was alive and well and left town of her own accord, which is what he claims."

I put my hands to my face. "Awwgh," I groaned.

Michael patted my knee. "Look, all is not lost. Jack will continue to look at concrete evidence as it comes in."

"Right," I said. "The test results from evidence found on Winifred's body and clothing should be completed soon, plus the dental records search on the skeleton, but that might take more time."

Maggie added in encouragement, "Eventually, the actual crime scene from Winifred's murder will be found, and hopefully it'll reveal more clues. And Jack's team is poring over Winifred's journal."

"They have a lot of work to do," Spencer said.

"They do," Michael responded.

Ryan raised his hand. "I think we need to broaden our scope. Who wanted Winifred dead?"

We all looked at each other in turn, then I said, "I think it's hard for any of us to fathom killing Winifred just because she was a busybody."

"I agree," Annie said, "but we are talking about someone willing to murder, which is not normal behavior. So it's hard for us to think like a killer."

"What would you kill for?" Michael asked us.

"Whoa, that's a heavy question," I said.

Spencer became practical. "Look, we all know the reasons people commit murder; revenge, love, money, and greed top the list. So let's think like the killer. What would push us to kill?"

Ryan answered first. "For me, I don't know what I would do if someone threatened my family. But that's like something out of an espionage or mafia movie, not Flat Rock Falls."

Annie spoke up next. "Right. And on a more practical note, I don't see a financial gain from killing Winifred."

Maggie added, "And revenge? I don't think so. This is small-town stuff. There just isn't cause for revenge in sidewalk sales and art galleries."

"The risk to the Workshop certainly isn't worth killing for, and that's my own business," I said.

Bitsy concluded, "Which leaves us with love. And boy, love is more complicated than any of the others. Did she threaten someone's marriage and family life? As Ryan said, people will kill to protect those they love."

Annie whined, "We're not going to figure this out before the opening tomorrow, are we?"

I let out a sigh. "I doubt it. And we have a few things to do before tomorrow, so I guess after I talk to Jack, this will need to be put aside, at least for the time being."

Maggie got up, and said, "Speaking of things to do, Ryan brought the tables down, so why don't we get those set up now, and then you can go talk to Jack and I'll hold down the fort."

"Sounds good. Thanks, you guys, you are the best at brainstorming, even if we haven't had any major breakthroughs yet."

Annie was lingering, chatting with Michael, and I asked him, "So what are your plans?"

"Since I'm here, I thought I'd at least stay through the opening tomorrow. I'm assuming you don't mind."

"Of course not."

Annie cheerfully said, "That's great, Michael. I know Jack would love to spend a little time with you. Maybe you could even stay over through Sunday. I know he's talked to you about hanging out to watch a baseball game, so since you're here, you might as well make a little holiday of it."

"I might be able to swing an extra day or two," he said, with a smile.

"Where are you staying?" I asked.

"I packed a bag just in case, but I hadn't really thought through the lodging part. What hotel do you recommend?"

Okay, this was getting a tad uncomfortable. I had a guest room, but Walter was supposed to arrive later today. I could offer the guest suite downstairs, but before I had the opportunity, Annie came to the rescue.

"Why don't you stay with me and Jack?" she suggested. "We have a guest room, and I put fresh linens on this morning."

"I don't want to put you out. Jack has so much on his plate, and he may just want to come home to a quiet house."

"Hold on, I'll call him." She pulled out her phone and moved off to the side to talk to Jack.

Michael and I avoided looking at each other until he said, "If you'd rather I go, I understand. Is Walter coming this weekend?" Michael was aware I had recently started seeing Walter.

"He's supposed to. And honestly, it's okay. I'm kind of glad for you to meet everyone and see what we do here."

"Okay. I brought some work to do, so I shouldn't be underfoot too much." He scrutinized my face, then said, "This is a helluva mess going on here, isn't it?"

"Yeah, and I kind of feel like I'm holding on by a thread. But as long as I keep moving, I don't think I'll fall apart."

Michael walked over and enveloped me in a hug. "It's going to be okay."

Even if I didn't fully believe it, I needed to hear it.

Annie cleared her throat. "Eh-hem, Jack says it'd be great if you stayed with us. You can follow me over and drop your stuff, and I'll give you a key. And then you can easily walk back here or into town if you don't want to drive."

Michael released me from his grasp, and said, "Sounds perfect, thank you!"

"Alex, I'll see you later, and we'll do a text chain for dinner, okay?" Annie asked.

"Sounds good."

****

With Ryan's help, Maggie and I got the tables set up under each canopy, and when we finished, the three of us went over the checklist.

Maggie said, "So the only thing left to do in the arts and crafts area is for each artist to set up their displays, right?"

"Yup," I answered. "Since the festivities start at two p.m., they have plenty of time tomorrow morning."

"With everything going on, we really don't want things left unattended for too long, anyway," Ryan said.

"You got that right. We don't need any more problems. So just to be on the safe side, Diego and Spencer have volunteered to be our watchdogs starting late morning so the artists can come and go while setting up and someone will always be out here."

"Good thinking," Maggie said.

"Two of Aunt Claudia's staff will bring the fruit, drinks, and desserts, and they are going to handle the setup and serving so we're free to roam around with the visitors. The food trucks will arrive at about noon, and then we're off and running!"

Maggie looked frantically at Ryan, and in a rushed voice, said, "What about Movie on the Green? With everything going on, I totally forgot!"

Ryan laughed. "Don't worry! It's under control. Elliott and I are setting up the movie screen tomorrow morning, and then it's a matter of playing the movie. It doesn't get much easier."

Maggie said, "I just hope people will come with the intention of having fun and not be ghoulish about wanting to see where Winifred was found."

"Me too," Ryan said. "But then again, the general public doesn't know as many details as we do."

I said, "Listen, there's nothing we can do about what has happened and how people will respond, but my goal is to make this the best event possible. I think with the arts and crafts tents, the incredible sculptures and garden, the food, the bustle of people, and the movie, there will be no resemblance to a murder scene."

Maggie took a big breath. "Right, we shall carry on in the best manner possible."

My phone rang. "This is Walter. I'll catch up with you guys later." As I walked toward the courtyard, I answered, "Hey, you, are you en route?" I sat at one of the tables with my feet propped on the chair next to me.

"I was, but my flight was cancelled due to bad weather. It looks like I'll be getting to Flat Rock around the time of the opening."

My stomach dropped in disappointment, but I didn't let it affect my voice. "It's okay. There's nothing you can do about it. You think you'll make it tomorrow, though?"

"Based on the forecast, yes, and if not, I'll swim."

I laughed. "I'm glad you're so motivated, but I think it's fine to wait for a seat on an airplane."

"So tell me how you're doing."

"I'm hanging in there, but it takes a village, as they say." I filled him in on what had happened since we last talked, and finished with, "So luckily I've got supportive friends who are helping me get through this."

"And how long is Michael staying?" Walter asked, nonchalantly.

"Probably through the weekend."

"Good, I look forward to meeting him."

After we hung up, I sat for a moment. An ex meeting a current could be nerve-wracking. I knew Walter was mature enough to handle it, but Michael's courtroom tactics of throwing people off kilter could sometimes spill over into real life. It was like a game for him. So would he pull some stunt to make Walter question our relationship? Well, I had way more important things to worry about, and I would have to take this one step at a time. And if need be, I'd go toe-to-toe with Michael. I'd done it before, and I could do it again.

On my way back to the front desk I stopped by the gift shop. "How are things going here?" I asked, cheerily.

When Daisy turned around, her usual porcelain skin was splotchy, and she swiped at a tear.

"What's going on?" I asked, with concern.

She sniffed and answered, "Luke has been taken in for questioning in connection to Winifred's murder."

"What? Why?"

"I don't know. I'm so worried. He would never do anything like that, and I don't understand why they think he would."

"Were you with him? Try and remember exactly

what was said," I instructed, attempting to keep her from falling apart in front of my eyes.

"I was with him, and they said he was seen in the vicinity around the time of the murder."

I pulled Daisy in for a hug. "Try not to worry yet. This may be a matter of ruling people out or asking Luke if he saw something." I pulled back and looked her in the eyes. "You hold tight, and I'll see what I can find out."

I spoke with more confidence than I felt. If Luke was mentioned in Winifred's journals and he was seen nearby at the time of the murder, was there reason to be concerned?

I needed to go see Jack, but first I wanted to stop by the library and look at old yearbooks to see if I could find a photo of Eleanor. I grabbed my keys and within short order I was back in the library.

"Yearbooks are over there in the town archives," the woman at the front desk said, pointing to the far corner.

I had to do some mental calculations to figure out what year to look for. I started with 1970, when Eleanor would have been seventeen. I grabbed the yearbook and took a seat in one of the study carrels. Thumbing through the pages was like looking at a time capsule of fashion trends and hairstyles. First, I looked at the class photos, and luck was on my side when I found Eleanor's face, smiling back at me in her senior class picture. She looked petite, but it's not really possible to tell that from a headshot, so I looked at the various after-school clubs, scanning the names listed under photographs.

Eventually I found her. The drama club had a number of photos, and she was in the one of the crew working on the stage sets. From the image, I could tell that, indeed, she was petite, because the boy standing next to her and her fellow classmates were quite a bit taller. Her dark hair was tucked behind her ear, and she smiled at the camera with a long paint pole clasped in her hand like a royal staff. The good-looking boy next to her had his arm draped around her shoulder. Was that Tucker? I read the fine print of the caption. No, the boy's name was Cecil Thompson. Hunh, that was Luke's last name. Could this be a relative of his?

I used my phone to snap a pic of the image, then sat staring at the page. Teenagers, full of hope and promise, feeling invincible. I remembered what it was like at that age. It was the age before most of us learned life was often hard, or that we would occasionally feel the weight of the world on our shoulders. Later, we would realize the moments of beauty and happiness were a gift, not a given.

Chapter 17

When I got in the car, I called the Café, hoping Aunt Claudia might have a minute. When she answered the phone, I said, "Hi, it's me. I have a quick question. Did you know a Cecil Thompson back in the day?"

"Wow, you certainly are going down memory lane these days, but you're going down my lane, not yours. That's a name I haven't thought about in years."

"So you know him?"

"Well, I knew him. I don't think he's with us any longer. He was a really nice boy who grew up here and then his family moved to Pine Brook. Actually, you know his grandson, Luke."

"I wondered if he might be a relation."

"What's this about, Alex?"

"Oh, nothing really. I just saw a picture, and I got curious."

"I can't believe how you've brought back all these memories for me. He was totally smitten with Eleanor, and they dated for a year or so in high school."

"What happened?"

"Her parents wanted better for her. Which I thought was a pile of crap. Cecil was a true gentleman."

"Interesting."

"Yeah, they broke up before she went to college. Look, I've got customers lining up at the cash register, so I better run."

"Okay, talk to ya later."

I arrived at the station, and Matt waved me through, saying, "Jack's in his office."

I found Jack hunched over his desk, sifting through his notepad. "Hey," I said, taking a seat, uninvited, on the chair next to his desk.

"How's it going?" he asked.

"I've got a few bones to pick with you. First, I can't believe you called Michael and told him to come here."

"Look, Winifred's murder put you in some hot water. I did what I thought was best to protect you. And I did let him know you had been cleared. So his showing up was of his own accord."

I reverted back to a teenager and pursed my lips and squinted my eyes. "Whatever."

"What else?" he asked, with a touch of humor.

"Well, it appears you questioned Tucker about Eleanor. It would have been nice to know that *before* Bitsy and I went over there to pump him for information."

"You what?" he said, with wide eyes.

I back-pedaled. "Pump isn't the right word. We went under the guise of Bitsy trying to track down alumni for the high school. Oh, and here is a photograph I found of Eleanor in a yearbook at the library." I texted him the image.

"For crying out loud, Alex. I can't believe you guys went over there. You really should have talked to me first."

"Why? I had no idea Eleanor was even on your radar!"

"Of course she is." He began to tick off his fingers. "One, the general details of the skeleton match her age.

Two, I talked to Mom, and she is fairly sure she recognizes the earrings as ones Eleanor had. Three, you weren't able to track Eleanor down. Four, Winifred was an information gatherer and had a recent entry with dollar signs. Five, the skeleton was found near Tucker's house. I would have to be an idiot not to try and find her."

"Oh."

"Yeah, oh. This is my job, you know."

I became defensive. "I know it is! But you know I can't just sit around and do nothing. I figured Bitsy and I could gather some information for you. And, by the way, now you know her body type fits the skeleton," I said, with satisfaction, holding up my phone with the image I had texted him.

He ignored me and continued his lecture. "This case is different. You were targeted. Someone was trying to keep you away from the woods. Winifred was left on your property. So if you start digging around, whoever it is may feel threatened and strike. I've intentionally left you out of this, hoping you would just stick to Workshop business and the grand opening. You would have had to pull off a really good acting job if you knew I was focusing on Tucker."

As hard as I tried, I couldn't stop my eyes from welling up.

"Are you crying?"

"No," I said—unfortunately at the same time I sniffled.

"Yes, you are," Jack said, stunned.

A tear toppled onto my cheek, and I harshly swiped at it. "I'm mad. I thought we were a team."

Now Jack's eyes crinkled in humor. "Oh my gosh, this is like when we were young, and you were left out of the older kids' kickball game." Then he leaned over and grabbed my knee. "We are, and will always be, a team. I trust you more than anyone."

"Really? It doesn't feel like it."

"Yes! But I'm serious. You're in a different situation than in the past, and I'm not willing to put you at any risk. Now, if I have to keep you informed of every little thing so you don't go off half-cocked, then I will. But frankly, I've been a little busy trying to solve two cases."

I stared at his serious face, then caved. "Oh man, I'm being such a jerk."

"Of course you are, and just know, when you least expect it, my revenge will be sweet."

I couldn't help but let out a laugh. This was true to form for our relationship. We could argue like cats and dogs and then flip a switch and be over it.

Jack tilted his chair straight and picked up his notepad. "Thank you for the photo. It does help."

"You're welcome. So can you tell me what you thought after talking to Tucker?"

"Frankly, I think he's off the list. He told me Eleanor left without any warning, and initially, he said he no longer had the letters she sent. But then later, he came here to the station and handed me a few of Eleanor's letters. He told me Sasha thought he had gotten rid of them and he didn't want to admit in front of her that he had held on to them."

"Really! Did he have the envelopes with postmarks?"

"He did. This is simply a case of a marriage that went off the rails. Sasha wanted him to move on, and he pretended he got rid of all trace of her, but he secretly held back a few things. He told me he later attempted to find her, and when he couldn't, he hired a private investigator."

"Did he give you the name of the investigator?" I asked.

"Yes, but he died over ten years ago and unfortunately his business died with him."

"Great," I said, with sarcasm. "What did Tucker think?"

"The investigator told him sometimes people don't want to be found. She had communicated with him, so technically she wasn't missing. And yes, he could have filed for abandonment in order to remarry, but he just wasn't interested in going down that road a second time."

"I wonder how Sasha feels about that? It must sting a little."

"She was fairly tight-lipped on the topic of Eleanor, which is understandable, but she's living a good life, and after all these years, I don't think she has to worry about her long-term relationship with Tucker. He seems fairly dependent on her. But I told him I would keep the letters in confidence. No need for Sasha to know about them. He told me that he didn't really know Sasha on a personal level when Eleanor left, but later, Sasha sometimes felt like she was competing with her even though she wasn't there."

"Oh, I have seen that before in relationships my friends have had. That has to be hard on Sasha. So, what do you think now?" I asked. "What about the earrings?"

"I actually showed him a photo of the earrings, but Tucker was of no use. He said he'd just buy something the jeweler recommended and didn't pay much attention."

I grimaced. "I know that type. They don't give a lot of thought to make gift giving personal. They just buy stuff to make themselves feel good about the gifting."

"That's kind of harsh. Some men just stink at buying gifts women would like and need someone to help pick things out."

"I guess."

"And he said she often donated items after a period of time so that others could have nice things to enjoy."

"So they could have been passed to someone else. Argh!" Now the field was wide open again.

"Regardless, it was a long time ago, so maybe Mom is remembering earrings that were similar to the ones we found, or someone else had them, but because Eleanor came up recently, she associated them with her. That would not be out of the realm of possibility. And at the same time, we do have other avenues to investigate. So we keep an open mind."

"Is one of those other avenues Luke? Daisy was super upset because Luke was taken in for questioning. What was that about?"

"A witness came forward who saw him near the Workshop during the timeframe of the murder."

"He seems like a genuinely good kid. Although, I did just find out that his grandfather dated Eleanor back in high school and was totally smitten with her, but her parents wanted better for her."

"Should I even ask how you found that out?"

"When I was looking at the yearbook photos, she was standing with this handsome boy and I checked the caption to see if it was Tucker. It wasn't, it was Cecil Thompson. A quick call to Aunt Claudia confirmed that was Luke's grandfather, who I think has since passed away."

Jack jotted some notes. "I'll talk to Luke and his father and see if this amounts to anything. As you pointed out yourself, it would seem that Winifred was watching Luke. Something bothered her enough to have made note of him in her journal."

"Well, based on what I read in that journal, that's not really a reason to condemn someone."

"No, but the people Luke gave us as his alibi are not willing to corroborate his story."

"What? Why not?"

"They don't want to become involved."

"Well, that's the lamest excuse I've ever heard. Who are these people?"

Jack opened his notebook. "He was playing basketball at the community center, and then he went to some sort of underground video game den that's in the basement of the hardware store. Bert lets his kid and his friends use the space."

"That's near Winifred's shop. I wonder if she saw him coming and going and was trying to find something on him?"

"Who knows. We asked around and no one would talk, not even to help their friend."

"Unbelievable." This was indeed alarming. Were his friends not wanting to lie for him? Could Luke have been involved in her murder? I wanted to talk to these friends.

As if he could read my mind, Jack said, "This is another case of someone in your orbit who is a potential person of interest. So keep out of this. Right?"

"Right," I answered, absent-mindedly as I thought about how I could scope out the game den. "Who else have you looked at?" I asked.

"Another avenue is Eva Beaumont. I interviewed her again."

"Oh, what'd she say?"

Jack flipped through his notes. "She confirmed what she told you. She hadn't yet decided about the direction of the gallery in Pine Brook. She did admit Winifred was trying to pressure her, though."

"How? Was she being blackmailed?"

"Not blackmail, but sort of hinting she could get her business loan turned down."

I leaned forward with my elbow on the side of Jack's desk. "Ah, so another reference to the bank officer."

"Right. Eva was disconcerted by this, but not overly concerned. If someone in the banking world spread it around that she was a risk, it could affect her, but she had other means to move forward. She told me she had been planning to cut ties with Winifred."

"Does she have an alibi for the time of death?" I asked.

"No, she was home alone, so I'm still digging around about her. But quite honestly, I just don't see her as a murderer, or at the least, not in the manner Winifred was murdered."

"Who else have you talked to?"

"Ben, from the hardware store," Jack said. "He's a straight shooter. He was mad as a hornet at Winifred but said he was just spouting off. He had no reason to kill her. Plus, he has an alibi for the window of time Winifred was murdered."

"What about Roger Pettigrew, at the bank?"

Jack grinned. "He put on quite a show."

"Really?"

"Yeah. He first expressed deep sadness that a pillar of our community had been murdered. Then when I told him she had made notes on him, which was a slight bluff, since I didn't know for sure it was him, he crumbled."

"Did she have something on him?" I asked, anxiously.

"He asked if what he told me would be kept out of any public statements, and I told him as long as there was nothing illegal or pertaining to Winifred's murder, I would do what I could to keep it in confidence."

"Got it. So, what was it?"

"Winifred had gotten wind he had a fling with a dancer in Pine Brook, and she was using that information to pressure him to sign a loan for her project with Eva. She said she'd tell his wife and tarnish his reputation as a church deacon."

I suppressed a giggle.

"He was sweating bullets when he told me. But he also has an alibi for the time of death, believe it or not, with the dancer. So he's in the clear, and his secret will remain within these walls."

"What a hypocrite," I snapped but couldn't help myself from chuckling at the absurdity.

"That's certainly nothing new," Jack said. "But thus far, he hasn't compromised himself professionally, so it's between him and his conscience."

I leaned back in my chair. "Whew. Man, the more you know, the more you don't want to know."

"Generally, yes. Although I have to say, sometimes you're pleasantly surprised by how decent people are."

"Hopefully the scales tip in the decent direction."

Jack flipped his leather notepad closed. "So that's where we are."

"Is there nothing I can do to help? Things are under control for the opening, and I have some free time this afternoon."

Jack stared at the wall as he mulled this over. "There is one thing you can do. Winifred's sister is arriving in about an hour, and she wants to go to the house to make a to-do list for when the estate has been settled. It would be a big help if you would escort her there."

"Sure, I'd be happy to."

"You'll have to wait with her and actually follow her around. The house hasn't been released yet, and we have to keep a watchful eye."

"No problem. I'll be back in a bit." I was being overly helpful because I was guilty of a sin of omission for not telling Jack I was heading off to see if I could find Luke's group of gamers.

****

I drove over to Main Street and parked behind the block where the Emporium and hardware store were. The back entrances were labeled with the shop names, and there were a few with no markings at all. While I wavered about which door to try, I mulled over the prospect that Luke might actually have played a part in Winfred's murder. Maybe his friends didn't want to get into hot water themselves by giving him a false alibi. Nah, I wasn't convinced.

I didn't know Luke very well, so why was I championing him? Well, for one thing, Daisy liked him, so if I could help get him ruled out as a person of interest, then I would. And if he was responsible, then these boys needed to set the record straight that he had lied about where he was when Winfred was murdered.

A teenager emerged from one of the doors. He had

a slight build and wore a beanie cap. This had to be the place, and on impulse, I walked with authority to the door and entered as if I belonged there.

I was caught off guard by the dark room with high end monitors and fancy gaming chairs. Those present were so engrossed in their games that no one even gave me a second glance.

"Excuse me," I said, politely.

There was no response.

"Excuse me," I said, a little more forcefully.

No response.

I went to the door and felt along the wall until my hand reached the light switch. Suddenly the room was bathed in a harsh fluorescent light. Now I had their attention.

"What are you doing, lady?" one asked, with annoyance.

Lady? Well, at least he hadn't called me ma'am. "You gave me no choice, and don't worry, I'll only take up a minute of your time."

Someone called out, "We're busy here. Turn out the lights on your way out."

I walked to the front of the room. "Those of you who consider Luke to be a friend need to man up. Was he here with you on Wednesday night around midnight, or not? He's told the police he was."

"So what?" a voice in the back of the room asked. "Maybe he was, maybe he wasn't."

I had no patience with truculent teens. "From the look, and quite frankly, the smell, of things, you guys must rarely leave this room, so if he was here and you saw him here, you need to tell the police."

"We don't want to get involved with the police,"

said another beanie-capped youth.

"Yeah," drawled another voice.

"Look, Luke could be in real trouble if you don't. There are no video games in jail, folks. This is real life— your friend's life. Do the right thing." I started toward the door, but I couldn't help myself and added, "And for crying out loud, get outside and breathe some fresh air. And maybe get some exercise to get your blood moving. Seriously, you shouldn't need a wool hat in the summer."

I didn't wait for a response and simply flipped the light switch off on my way out the door.

****

I returned to the station and found Jack in the lobby introducing himself to Winifred's sister, Millie.

Jack indicated toward me, and said, "And this is Alex Montgomery, our consultant. She will be escorting you to your sister's house. She is also the director of the Creative Workshop, our art center here in Flat Rock, and she was an acquaintance of your sister."

"I'm so sorry for your loss," I said.

Millie shook my hand. "Thank you. I appreciate you taking the time to let me check on some things at the house." She turned back to Jack, "Have there been any developments since we last spoke?"

Jack ushered her to the pew and took a seat next to her. "I'm afraid we don't have any definitive answers yet, but please be assured, this is getting one hundred percent of our attention, and I am doing everything I can to find who murdered your sister."

I didn't often get a chance to see Jack in this role, and I was impressed at his ability to be gentle and kind, but forthright. He was encouraging, without delivering overly dramatic promises. He was also giving her his full attention, which let her know he cared.

"Have you thought of anything else that might help with our inquiries?" Jack asked.

Millie looked down at her hands. "I haven't. Winifred and I were so different. We were as close as we could be, but Winifred was a take-charge woman, and we didn't share confidences like so many sisters do. She never really showed her inner self." She looked up at Jack. "Do you know what I mean?"

"I think I do." He guided her up by her elbow. "I will keep you apprised of any new developments." He turned to me, and said, "I'll be right back with the key, and then you guys can head over to the house."

Millie followed me to Winifred's in her own car, and as we walked to the front door, I commented on the front garden.

She stood for a moment looking at the flowerpots. "Winifred always did have a green thumb and loved tending to her flowers. She could nurture her plants in a way she couldn't quite do in her relationships with people."

I turned the key in the lock, and as we entered, I said, "Please don't mind me. I'm just here to document anything you might take with you. And take your time. I have nowhere I need to be right now."

"Thank you, Alex. I shouldn't be too long."

As Millie moved from room to room, I engaged her in casual conversation, and then once the initial awkwardness had past, I left her with her own thoughts and was essentially a fly on the wall.

Our last stop was the kitchen and office expansion, and I said, "This is such a pretty room."

"It is. It's a happy space," she replied, looking

through the cabinets. She jotted down inventory notes in her notepad, and then we moved to the office.

"Have you seen her artwork?" I asked. "Some of these are quite good."

Millie looked at the stacks of paintings. "Yes, she loved her art projects. However, she was also prolific. I have a number of her pieces already. But I will sort through those once the house has been cleared and decide what else to take or offer to the rest of the family. Chief Maddox mentioned your connection to the art community, so maybe you can help me with whatever is left over?"

"Of course, I am happy to help."

While Millie looked over the office, I flipped through and looked more closely at some of Winifred's collage paintings. I then turned to the one on the easel. I stood for a few minutes staring at the images and suddenly the hair stood up on the back of my neck. Clues emerged from what initially just looked like commentary on a chaotic world.

I didn't have any more time to analyze it because Millie said, "I think I'm done here." She made her way back through the kitchen toward the living room.

I took out my phone and snapped five photos of the painting, and then followed her out the front door.

On the front stoop she said, "Thank you for letting me make some notes. I will come back once everything is settled to make arrangements for the contents and get the house listed with a Realtor."

"You are welcome," I replied. "If you need anything, just let us know. I'm going to go back in to turn off lights and make sure everything is locked up. Do you need to follow me back out to Main Street?"

"No, I'm good. Thank you, again."

Once she started her car, I dashed back into the house. I went to the linen closet to grab a sheet to wrap the painting in. In my haste, the stack toppled over, and as I put things back in order my fingers grazed something hard. I shifted the sheets and uncovered a key. It was small, like a safe deposit key size. I tucked it in my pocket and finished the task at hand.

****

With the painting under my arm, I rushed through reception to the precinct room. Jack was in his office, talking to Travis, and I called out to them, "Hey, you guys, I have something for you. But first," I said, digging in my pocket for the key, "I found this amongst the stack of sheets."

"Looks like a safe deposit box key. Travis, call the bank and find out if she had a box there."

While he made the call, I found an empty spot on one of the evidence tables and set down the painting.

A minute later, Travis returned, and said, "Yup. She's got a box there. We can go over, and the manager will meet us to open it up."

"Great," Jack said. "Now what's this?" he asked me.

I folded back the sheet and said, "This was on her easel."

Travis stood over the partially finished painting and grimaced. "Don't tell me it's something valuable."

"No, not monetarily. But look closely at what she's done so far."

When both of them stood mute, I said, "First, look at this area. From a distance, it looks like abstract moodiness. But if you lean in, you can just see the outline of the words love, hate, deception, destruction, earth to earth, ashes to ashes."

"Whoa, that's pretty dark," Jack said, looking more closely.

"Compared to her floral collages, yeah, I'd say so. Granted, her stuff was becoming more brooding or emotionally complex, but this is a bit over the top. Now, look here," I said, pointing to what could be interpreted as an abstract grove of trees under an ominous sky. Dark and uninviting, but with enough definition to be interpreted as tree trunks.

Jack leaned on the table and looked at the incomplete area. "There are pencil marks here."

"Artists often sketch prior to painting—plotting out what will go where. It helps with scale and continuity," I explained.

"This looks like it could be the start of the Workshop building."

I nodded in encouragement. "And if you look closely, this is a muted cross sign."

The image I pointed to was also dark brown, but one tick lighter than the trees. At first glance, it would all blend together.

"A grave marker," Jack said.

I was excited now. "So, what we have here, boys, is Winifred's abstract interpretation of the crime scene for the skeleton. I believe she put two and two together, and she had an inkling of who buried a body in the woods."

"There's your motive," Jack said, with satisfaction.

"Granted, it could just be a flight of fancy. But we know Winifred was here when Eleanor was here. We know she gathered information. Maybe she was just guessing, at first, but then she said something to the person she believed responsible, thinking if she was wrong, no harm, but if she was right, it was a homerun payday."

"And in the end, they killed her to keep her quiet," Travis said.

Jack turned to me. "Good catch, Alex."

I was excited, hopping back and forth from one foot to the other. "So what can we do with this?"

Jack sighed, and said, "Nothing."

I was crestfallen. "Nothing?"

"The judge would toss me out of her office if I brought this in as grounds for a warrant."

"But—"

"This has value for us. It means we put aside the petty information from her journal, and we only concentrate on the more serious entries. And I know you're not going to like this, but the painting doesn't point a definitive finger at anyone's identity—neither the victim nor the person responsible."

"But it could be Eva, Tucker, or Luke, or even Luke's father!" I insisted.

"Look, I made a call this morning to have the dentist's office do a records search for Eleanor. If they are able to find old X-rays and they are a match for the remains, then I've got grounds for a warrant, and I can bring all of them in for official questioning. And if there's no match, then we'll be able to close out that line of inquiry."

"So you're going to tell me to be patient," I said.

"Yes. And now you have to keep your cool when you see any of these people and not tip your hand that you are aware of any of this. Can you do that?" He asked.

"It will be the performance of my life," I said theatrically.

"I hope so, because if not, it could cost you your life."

Chapter 18

Friday Night

The gang assembled at the Lodge for dinner. There was a jovial atmosphere as plates of food were passed around, and everyone was enjoying Michael's company as he regaled them with stories.

"You should have seen this one," he said, nodding toward me. "You wouldn't recognize who she was back then."

"Do tell," Spencer said. "We know she was a high-flying politico, but she doesn't talk much about those days."

"She was more than ready to leave that life behind."

Maggie said, "So come on, tell us some good dirt on our Alex."

"Eh-hem. You better watch it," I said ominously to Michael.

He looked at me with mischief in his eyes. "Can you envision that she used to budget over ten thousand dollars a year just for her wardrobe and hair styling?"

JJ was incredulous. "You are kidding me."

"Hey, I had to dress the part!" I said, in defense. "But I will gladly never put on another pair of designer heels again. This is more who I am," I said, pointing to my jeans and work boots.

"Man, I wish I had been there when you were getting rid of stuff," Maggie lamented.

"I happily shed all of it, including having to act interested in some blowhard just to raise money for a candidate."

Michael laughed. "You should have heard her rants after political dinners. She would use language that even made me blush."

"And I will again if you don't stop talking about me like I'm not here," I said, with a laugh.

"So you are exactly where you are supposed to be," Spencer said, raising his glass. "Cheers to you."

Shortly, the focus shifted off me, thank goodness, and I excused myself to go to the restroom. I had chosen a cubicle in the alcove part of the bathroom, so when two women entered, it appeared the rest of the stalls were empty, and they didn't realize I was there.

"I'm so glad we're out celebrating. Thankfully, that woman will no longer be a thorn in my side," one of them said.

"I know," the other agreed. "We needed the money more than the booster club, and they just filed insurance on it. No one was hurt. But boy, she held that over my head for years."

I hadn't begun my business yet, so I silently brought my feet up and squatted on the toilet seat just in case they checked for legs under my door.

"I gave her so many tidbits about bank clients, and she acted like I was her good friend, but she never let me forget I owed her for keeping our secret."

"You bore the brunt of it, and it was time something was done about her."

"Well, what's done is done, and now we can relax. So how's my hair look?"

"Fabulous. Do I have lipstick on my teeth?"

"Nope. Come on, the boys are waiting for us."

When the door closed, I crept off the toilet, and after emerging from the stall, I quietly pushed the door open to catch a glimpse of who had been talking. Even from a distance, I could tell it was Fran and her sister walking toward the two men waiting for them in the lobby. Winifred had told me herself that the gossip about Luke's dad came from Fran at the bank, and clearly, Fran had been an information pipeline for a long time. Maybe she'd had enough. I went back into the bathroom, did my business, and rushed back to the table.

I leaned forward so I didn't have to talk too loudly, and said, "I think we may have a new suspect or two!"

"You were only gone a few minutes, what could possibly have happened?" Ryan asked.

Instead of answering, I asked, "Were any of you here when money went missing from the booster club?"

Bitsy answered, "I was. They had raised money to send the marching band to a big competition down in Florida. They had to put in an insurance claim and barely got the funds in time to go. Why?"

"I think I just overheard the culprits talking about the theft and about Winifred!" I hoarsely whispered.

"You need to call Jack," Michael said.

I pulled out my phone and stepped to the corner of the room to talk to Jack. After I filled him in, I said, "So I think maybe I was off base about all of it. It looks like Fran and her sister are now prime suspects."

"I'll pull them in for a chat." And then I could hear the joke in his voice as he said, "I want to officially thank you for holding your pee long enough to listen in on their conversation."

"All in the line of duty," I returned.

When I got back to the table, JJ asked, "So, what did he think?"

"He's going to bring them in for a chat. Boy, you guys, I feel like a weight has lifted. It would be such a relief if her murder had nothing to do with the skeleton."

****

Saturday

It was grand opening day, and I hit the ground running. Armed with coffee, I went outside to help the artists with their displays. The morning revealed clear blue skies and just enough breeze to knock out the humidity. We could not have asked for a better day, and it was thrilling to see the arts and crafts tents coming to life.

Ethan and Hannah, our two professional potters, were setting up their tables, and I stepped in to offer help.

"Mornin'! What can I do?" I asked.

"Hi, Alex, we have some large flowerpots on the dolly if you want to help place them," Hannah said.

"Sure!" There was an array of gorgeous pots with carved designs, glazed in greens, browns, and blues. "These are spectacular! I hope you have more, because they will be big sellers today."

"We have plenty. We've been building our stock since the winter festival," Ethan said.

"And check out these smaller ones," Hannah added. "We have three different sizes. And then some vases. We figured for a garden show it would be better to put the focus on plants instead of just bowls and mugs."

"So smart!"

While we were working on the displays, Hannah asked, "So it's been quite a week, but you seem pretty well-balanced."

I let out a laugh. "It's all smoke and mirrors! Truthfully, it's been hellacious, but I'm giving myself today to try and enjoy what we've accomplished."

"Is there any news?" Ethan asked. "We've kind of assumed when you had something to tell us, you would." Ethan and Hannah were, by nature, the types not to get involved in drama.

"No news. Jack and his team are working the investigation around the clock, but there isn't a lot to go on yet."

Hannah set a pot on the table and said, "I don't mean to sound callous, but I don't think the community is mourning Winifred in the same way they might for anyone else."

"Hannah, that's pretty harsh," Ethan chided.

She brushed her long straight hair off her shoulder and said, "Don't get me wrong. It's absolutely horrific what happened to her. But she just didn't create warm relationships. That's all I'm saying."

"So you're saying it's about the horror of what happened to her, not the loss of her," I suggested.

Hannah scrunched her face. "Oh, gosh, that sounds awful, too. I wouldn't have ever wished her any harm. No one would. But I'm not feeling her loss, personally."

Ethan just shook his head and mimed shoveling a hole, as in she was digging a deeper one every time she spoke.

"I get what you're saying. I don't think Winifred had deep personal relationships. She was a fixture in town, but I don't know anyone who felt close to her."

Hannah looked relieved. "That's what I'm trying to say, and it makes it easier to carry on with what we're doing today."

This conversation made me realize I had something I needed to do, so I finished the current batch of pot placing, then made my excuses and left to find Bitsy and JJ.

Their booths were across the way, and I found them both prepping their displays. JJ had portable easels for some of her paintings, and her table was full of jewelry and her hand-designed watercolor cards. Bitsy's had lots of hat stands alongside her jewelry and hair accessories. Their color schemes were vibrant and happy.

"Hi, you guys," I said, cheerily.

"Hey," they choroused.

I stepped into Bitsy's booth and called JJ over to join us. "So, things have been so crazy it just dawned on me we should do something to appropriately acknowledge Winifred's death. We don't want something morbid, and we don't want to draw attention to the fact a murdered woman was found in the garden just a few days ago. So what should we do?"

Bitsy furrowed her brow. "Oh, you are right! We can't just have people walking around and sitting on the bench where she was found. Talk about morbid."

"Yeah," I said, with some urgency.

Bitsy became decisive. "Okay, first, I think the bench has to be moved. Just get it out of there."

"Of course, good idea," I said.

Now JJ chimed in. "Then, I think we take one of the large flower pots and move it to the spot where the bench was, and I will run home and get some incense."

I wrinkled my nose. "Incense?"

"Nothing too heady. I have a gentle sandalwood and sweet orange combo."

I looked at Bitsy. "What do you think?"

"I know the one she's talking about. It's really nice."

"And when people are walking by, the murder won't register, but they will get a soothing sensation."

I dropped my shoulders. "You guys are brilliant. I'll go get Ryan to help me move the bench. Thank you!" I said, turning to leave.

"Anytime," JJ said.

I found Ryan, and we moved the bench next to the lounge doors in the courtyard. Frankly, because it would be a constant reminder, I didn't think we'd ever be able to use it, but I'd sort that out later. Then we found the perfect garden pot, which was full of double begonias, and moved it to where the bench had been. Problem solved.

The rest of the morning was easy. By eleven thirty all of the arts and crafts tents were done. I took a leisurely stroll past each one. Next to Hannah and Ethan's pottery, Shelby had two tents, one with needlework crafts and the other with the quilts. Diego's tent was next, with his intricate textiles, which included exquisite wall hangings and rugs. The variety of textures and colors made each a unique piece of art.

Across from him, Spencer had displayed a collection of his trompe-l'oeil and floral paintings, and Annie had her colorful photorealism paintings. Both had giclées and prints to make things more affordable for the general public.

I walked past Bitsy and JJ's tents and came to Maggie's, which was brimming with her photography. Some were framed, but she also had bins with matted photographs. Next to her, out in the open, there was a table set up where Ari would do face painting for the kids.

On the grassy area in the middle, Ryan and Elliott had placed some of their sculptures and birdbaths, and another of our artists had made beautiful wind chimes and wind catchers. The entire picture was one of abundant creativity and beauty.

Before I could go any farther, my phone rang and it was Jack, so I stepped to the side to answer.

"Hey, did you talk to Fran?"

"I did, and she crumbled under my steely gaze."

"She confessed to murdering Winifred?" I asked, gobsmacked.

"No. She confessed she stole the booster money. She said Winifred had been blackmailing her for gossip on bank clients for all these years. But she didn't kill Winifred. She and her sister also have an alibi."

"Dang it."

"All is not lost. She's been charged with theft, although it will likely be reduced to community service and probation with a promise to reimburse the money."

"I was so hoping they were responsible for Winifred's murder."

"Sorry, it's back to collecting evidence," Jack said, and hung up without as much as a see ya later.

The news deflated my mood a tad, and I stopped in to see Maggie for a pick-me-up and said, "I think we might actually have some free time. Do you want to take a walk with me?"

"Sure! I'm all set up."

I checked to make sure Diego or Spencer, our watchdogs, were visible, and then we took off across the lawns.

"I'm going to have a long day out in the sun, so let's walk through the woods."

She chuckled, then said, "Okay. I know you are one of those strange creatures who doesn't like too many sunny days."

"Well, today, I'm super glad it's going to be a pretty day." It was true, though. A couple of sunny days were great, but then I needed some clouds or rain to quench my soul.

Before heading into the woods, we turned back to assess the entire scene. "Look how good it looks," Maggie gushed.

"I am so fricking proud of us," I said, with conviction. "It's even better than I had imagined."

As we walked through the woods, I enjoyed the sudden drop in temperature. Our chatting was interspersed with moments of quiet, just listening to the birds and the occasional crack of a stick under foot.

Maggie stopped and leaned against a tree. "So, do you want to talk about Walter? Did Michael's arrival stir up any old feelings?"

I looked up at the treetops as I thought about her question, then answered, "I don't know. Well, I know Michael and I are done as a couple, but I've found comfort in his coming here because we know each other so well, and I feel safe with him. But it's a friendship. I just can't get a read on my relationship with Walter."

"In what way?" she asked.

"We seem to have plateaued. It was so good to talk to him about everything we've been dealing with this week. It felt, what's the word I want—right," I said, for lack of a better word. "But I don't know where this relationship is going."

"Are you wanting to get married?"

I reared back. "No way, not at all."

"So then what do you want? You've got a great companion situation, and it's not tapping too much of your personal space. He's mature, and a silver fox, to boot. Stop overthinking it."

"You're probably right."

"And it still stands—" She interrupted herself. "What is that?" She was looking to the left of my shoulder.

I jumped. "What? Is there a bug on me?" I quickly brushed my shoulder and arm.

"No." She stepped closer and pointed to the tree. "What does this look like to you?"

I pulled my glasses down from my head to look. "Uh, looks like paint. Bronze paint," I said, softly.

She and I looked at each other, mouths agape.

I scanned the woods. "Could the killer have come through here?"

The woods were fairly thick, and Maggie asked, "How far have we come? Are we on Workshop property?"

I spun around, trying to get my bearings. "Our property doesn't go this deep."

"So, the person you saw jogging out of sight cut back through the woods to, where?" she asked, looking all directions.

My wheels were spinning. "You're not going to park on the street behind our block, go get the wheelbarrow and then wheel a dead body through other people's properties, and then run back to your car, all dressed in black, like a ninja."

"No. But this also means they probably didn't drive her to the Workshop."

"But where is the crime scene? I know Jack and his

team checked the grounds of the Workshop, but how much of the woods did they search?"

"Well, that's a big undertaking. These are old growth trees and the woods span all the way to Bennet Park."

"That's true. I'll have to ask Jack. There's also the houses behind here with their big lots."

"He'd have to get permission to search private property, right?"

"I have no idea, I'll ask. Oh, and speaking of Jack, he called earlier and told me Fran and her sister have an alibi for when Winifred was murdered. So the field is, once again, wide open."

I pulled out my phone to take a picture of the paint-stained tree, and then a few to try and pinpoint where we were. I then filled her in on the latest news about Luke and the connection to Eleanor.

"Oh man, I thought it might be over," Maggie said, with disappointment.

"Okay, I got enough pics to hopefully remember where we are. Now it's time to call Jack."

"Yeah, come on, let's go."

Maggie and I cut a straight line through the woods and emerged about a third of the way down the Workshop property.

****

Twenty minutes later, Jack and I were tromping through the woods. I kept looking at the pics I took as we tried to find the tree, and eventually, we stumbled across it.

"See, it's bronze paint," I said.

"Sure is. Okay, you go on back to the Workshop and carry on like normal. I'm going to walk through here and see if there's any more evidence pointing to what path they took."

I nodded and turned to leave.

"Alex," he called.

"Yeah?"

"Proceed with caution, right? Play your role."

I gave him the thumbs-up sign and wound my way out of the woods and back to the garden.

The food trucks had arrived, and they were putting out their menu signs. The smell in the air was intoxicating, and even though I was anxious to see if Jack had learned anything, my stomach told me I better eat now before the public arrived. Chick-on-a-Stick, one of my favorites, was here, but I was drawn to the aroma of Up in Smoke's barbecue, and I sidled up to see if they had any ready to go.

"Hi guys," I said, in greeting. "Do you have anything ready to come off the grill?"

"We sure do, how about some baby back ribs with potato salad?"

"Oh my gosh, yes!"

I grabbed some napkins and took my plate of food over to the courtyard, where Annie and Spencer were hanging out.

"Look what I got!" I sang out.

"Oooo, the food trucks smell amazing," Annie said.

Spencer rubbed his hands together. "I'm going over in a few minutes, but first, tell us what you and Maggie were doing in the woods. We saw you come out and make a beeline back here."

I filled them in on what we found, then said, "Jack's in there now, trying to find more evidence."

"Oh man, everything is converging at once. What if

all this untangles during the opening festivities?" Annie asked.

I bit my lip at the prospect. "I doubt it will happen so quickly, and in truth, I hope it doesn't. We don't need a cluster of police activity right there in the woods while the opening is going on."

Spencer nodded. "I have to agree. We want this resolved, but maybe not when hundreds of people are here. We've done our part to help the investigation, and now we need to be able to enjoy the fruits of our labor with the sculpture garden."

"True. We are artists, not detectives. So come on, Spence, let's get back to the art," Annie said succinctly.

I was licking the last of the sauce off my fingers when Jack approached. "Did you find anything?" I asked.

"No, but it's a big area. I'm going to need the whole team out here, and I've had to give them some time off this afternoon because I've been pushing them hard with a lot of overtime. So we'll tackle it tomorrow."

"The trials of being a small-town cop shop," I said.

"Yup."

"What happened with the safe deposit box key? Did she have one, and was there anything in it?"

"Yes, and she had cash, and a lot of it. Over ten thousand."

"Really! Do you think from blackmailing people?" I asked, incredulously.

"I don't know. Some people keep cash in the event of an emergency. It's going to take a deeper dive into her finances to see."

"Whew. I thought keeping a twenty in my kitchen drawer was good. Anything else?"

"Believe it or not, older journals. It would appear she'd been gathering information for a long time."

"That's just creepy. What are you going to do with those? They really should be destroyed."

"Once the case is over, if none are considered evidence, I'll ask her sister if she would like us to destroy them."

"Good."

We sat for a moment in companiable silence, then I asked, "Is Michael still at your house?"

"He was when I left. He wanted to get some work done and is coming in a little bit. Wasn't Walter supposed to be here already?"

"His flight was canceled. He should hopefully get here before the opening is over."

"Good," Jack said. "I'm going to the station to cover things while Gabe gets lunch. I'll be back at some point."

"Okey doke. I'll be here, being the hostess-with-the-mostess," I said, with more wit than I felt. I wasn't really sure I would be able to play hostess all afternoon when there was evidence to search for.

Chapter 19

The grand opening was in full swing, and it was proving to be a success. Along with the familiar faces from the Flat Rock community, a good number of folks had come from neighboring towns. As I walked through the garden to visit with the patrons, I was thrilled there was such appreciation for Ryan and Elliot's sculptures, and I came across a few more people who wanted to be added to the volunteer list for the garden.

The food trucks were doing big business, and Aunt Claudia's table full of goodies was a hit. The courtyard tables were in constant use with a steady rotation of diners, and I was happy to see many people had our signature gift bags by their chairs, which meant they had been shopping at the craft tents.

Even better, Hank and Twila had arrived, and after big bear hugs all around, I was able to show them how their glass pieces added another level of beauty to the garden. It was such a relief to tend to normal things, like walking through the garden with these dear friends.

Later, after making the rounds, I stopped in Maggie's tent. When she finished with a customer, she turned toward me with bright eyes.

"I just sold one of my large landscapes!" she gushed.

"Congrats! While it's calm, do you want me to cover your booth while you go take some candid shots for our social media?"

"Great idea." She gave me the lowdown on pricing, then grabbed her camera and took off for the garden.

I visited with customers and had even made a few sales when Michael sauntered in.

"You're not Maggie," he said.

I laughed. "She's out getting some photos. Since you've stopped in, what can I sell you?"

"That's not exactly smooth salesmanship," he quipped.

"I don't have to be smooth with you," I countered.

He took his time looking at her framed photos, then said, "I do like these."

I stepped over to stand next to him. He had homed in on one of her creative landscapes done in black and white except for one pop of color. "Mmm, you have a good eye. This series is one of my favorites. They've been big sellers, and she only has these few originals left."

He looked at me and grinned. "Now that's smooth salesmanship. I'll take this one."

I laughed. "Good! Now, do you want us to ship it, or are you going to take it with you today?"

"I'll take it with me."

I ran his card and had just put a sold sign on the large print when Maggie returned.

"You've made a sale!" she cheered.

"More than one, and this gentleman is a discerning customer."

When Michael turned around, Maggie grew shy. "I'm so honored you want one of my pieces."

"You are very talented," he said, in return.

I rolled my eyes. "Talk about a mutual admiration society."

Michael winked at Maggie, then turned to me and said, "I'm going to wander around. Can I pick up the photograph later?"

"Sure."

After he left, Maggie said, "So I just saw Tucker and Sasha. I thought you said they might be going out of town."

I craned my neck to scan the area but didn't see them. "Maybe they decided to leave after the opening. I'll go find out."

I found Tucker and Sasha in the garden. "Hi! I'm glad you could make it," I said, cheerily.

Tucker said, "It just didn't feel right to leave before coming to the grand opening. After all, we've been working on it for weeks."

"Well, I hope you take the time to soak it all in."

"It really is a masterpiece, don't you think, Sasha?" he asked.

"It's lovely. But we do need to keep an eye on the time, dear," she said, smoothing down the front of her pleated sundress.

I think Tucker was enjoying the accolades from the guests, because he said firmly, "Oh, we've got plenty of time."

I didn't think the food trucks were Sasha's style, so I suggested, "Be sure to help yourself to the table of goodies from the Café. And you can lose yourself in the arts and crafts booths. There are some beautiful chimes and garden pots which would look great on your patio."

Sasha perked up at the thought of shopping. "I will check them out."

My phone dinged with a text. "Oh, please excuse me, I need to tend to this." I stepped aside to read a text update from Jack.

—Accident at the junction, don't know when I'll be done. Hope all is going well at the opening.—

It looked like it would be a while before Jack and I could hash over how the woods played into the crime scene, so I continued with my duties as host and talked with the visitors. Later, I ran into Maggie, who was taking a break.

"Who's manning your booth?" I asked.

"Daisy. What are you up to now?"

"I've just been making the rounds, but the event seems to be running itself, so I was thinking about doing a little more exploring in the woods. Want to come?"

"Sure," she answered, hesitantly, "as long as you think it's okay. What would Jack think?"

"Jack is tied up with an accident out at the junction, so he won't get here for a while, and I don't want to bother him. We'll just wander around a little and see if we can find any more evidence. I can't really be gone very long anyway, so it'll be quick."

"Okay, but let's go in on the far end past the lounge parking lot. I don't want people's curiosity to be piqued seeing us go into the woods."

"Good idea."

We meandered through the garden to the parking lot and then cut into the woods. As we walked, I updated her on what Jack had relayed about his earlier chat with Tucker. "I just find it odd he never worked things out so he and Sasha could get married."

"There could be a perfectly innocent reason," she said. "Maybe he simply didn't want to get married again. You haven't either, if you don't mind me mentioning."

I ignored her comparison. "Maybe, but things keep

coming back to him. I believe in my gut the skeletal remains are Eleanor."

"Yes, that's possible, and you told me earlier about Luke's family connection to Eleanor. Are you forgetting that now? Or is it that you like Luke and don't want him to be involved?"

"No, you're right. There could be a connection there. Jack's going to talk to Luke and his dad. But I saw Winifred and Tucker in an intense conversation before she was murdered."

"You did?"

"Yes. It was during the patron event. She was close-talking, all in his personal space, and he looked none too pleased and sort of stalked off. At the time, I thought it was just her usual issues with boundaries, but now I'm thinking maybe she was letting him know she believed the skeleton was Eleanor."

We were walking with purpose as I talked, and Maggie suddenly stopped. "I don't know, Alex. This feels like grasping at straws. Winifred got in everyone's personal space. You are all over the map. First the focus shifts to Eva, then Luke and his grandfather. Now it's back to Tucker. You're not around Luke or Eva very much, but you have been around Tucker."

"So?"

"How could Tucker possibly act as normal as he has if he not only knew those were Eleanor's remains, but he had also murdered Winifred? It would take a special kind of sociopath, and I just don't see Tucker pulling it off. Do you? Surely Sasha would have an inkling, and do you think she would sit idly by, knowing he was a killer?"

"Maybe she's involved," I surmised.

"Now you're really reaching. I put forth the same

theory. If Sasha was involved, Tucker would have to know, and he would not be able to pull off pretending he didn't. And they are not acting like a killing team. They are actually behaving quite normally, under the circumstances. So this is just getting ridiculous. These are people's lives you're messing with."

I had walked farther ahead, continuing my search.

"Alex, stop," she implored. "You are too close to this, and you have got to step back and let Jack handle things."

I turned back and suddenly felt stupid when I saw the look on her face. "Argh. What am I doing?"

"You're desperately trying to find answers. And I get it, but this just doesn't add up, and it's not helping."

"Maybe you're right, but we found the smear of paint, which tells me something happened in these woods."

Maggie came up to me and spoke quietly, but firmly. "Something probably did happen in these woods, but should you be traipsing around out here while the event we've been planning for almost three years is happening back there?" she asked, pointing toward the Workshop.

"Okay, I can admit I'm kind of going off the rails here. Why don't you go on back? I'm going to clear my head, and I'll be there shortly."

"Are you sure? Do you want me to stay with you?"

"No, no. I'm fine, really. You go on, and I'll be along soon."

"All right." Maggie retraced her steps but turned back to look at me with her brow pinched in concern before continuing on.

Once Maggie was out of sight, I walked on at a slower pace, relishing the silence. It felt like it hadn't been quiet since Baxter and Poppy dug up the skeleton. When I reached a small clearing, I took the opportunity to sit down and think. Was I starting to lose my mind? It had been a helluva week, so it would be natural to jump to conclusions and lose my ability to think logically.

Now I lay flat on the ground, and after staring through the treetops for a few minutes, I closed my eyes. I don't know how much time had passed when I heard my name.

It was Ryan, and he asked, "Alex, what are you doing?"

I pushed myself up to a sitting position and instead of answering, asked, "What are you doing here?"

"Looking for you!" Ryan said. "Maggie came and got me and told me you were wandering in the woods."

"Oh, sorry, I didn't realize I had been gone so long." But when I looked at my watch, not much time had passed since we left the garden. "I haven't been out here more than a few minutes. Maggie is just a little concerned about me."

Ryan plopped down on the ground next to me. "I kind of see why. So what are you doing taking a nap in the woods while we have a crowd of people back there for the grand opening?"

I laughed, and said, "Trying to clear my head."

Ryan just nodded in understanding. "Did it work?"

"Not really," I replied, with humor in my voice. "How'd you find me, anyway?"

"You're not very far in from the tree line, and actually, you're fairly close to where the skeleton was found."

"Seriously?"

"Yeah. Only took me two minutes to see you."

I got up and swiped at the forest detritus that had attached itself to my jeans and shirt. I suddenly felt a sharp prick, right where my leg met my rear end. "Ooo, something is sticking me. Turn around, I may have to drop my jeans to get this thorn out."

Ryan obliged, but said over his shoulder, "I can probably get it without you going to such an extreme."

"I'll just go over here behind this tree." Dang, whatever it was stung like crazy. "Maybe something bit me, and I'm not going to have you examine my backside."

"Good call."

A minute later, I called out, "Got it! I think it's some kind of cocklebur."

"Oh man, it's going to hurt later."

I emerged from behind the tree, fully clothed, rubbing my hind end, and said, "Yeah. It stings. Will you check my hair?"

Ryan took a quick look. "Good thing you're rockin' the ponytail today. You're all clear."

"Thanks."

We continued walking for a few minutes before Ryan said, "We better start heading back, right?"

"Yeah, I guess so."

"Uh, wait. Alex, what's that?" Ryan pointed at the ground behind me.

We walked the few feet to where he had pointed and examined the ground. The ground cover had been disturbed, and upon further scrutiny, a cluster of leaves looked like they were matted and stained—with blood.

"Did we just stumble onto the crime scene?" I asked, incredulously.

Ryan knelt down to look more closely. "Could be."

I tried to orient myself. "Okay, we are currently farther down than when Bitsy and I walked through to go to Tucker's house. But we're not far from where the skeleton was found, based on what you said when you got here."

"Right. But don't forget, we did continue walking for a bit."

I could hear Maggie's voice chastising me, but I asked anyway. "Were Tucker and Sasha still at the opening when you came to find me?"

"Yeah. They were sitting in the courtyard talking with some people when Maggie came to get me."

"Are you up for a little sleuthing?"

Ryan grinned. "Of course! Do you think we can?"

"I do, if we're quick about it. Jack is tied up at a car accident scene, so I'm not going to bother him. But let's follow this route up and see if we find more evidence."

Ryan and I walked slowly and managed to follow a path of crushed vegetation. "Something happened here," he said.

"I agree, let's see where we come out."

When we emerged from the woods, we weren't far from the open grass of Tucker's lawn. "I knew it!" I exclaimed, shaking my fist.

"So what now?"

"Let's go explore a little while they are over at the Workshop."

"Okay. But what's our excuse if they come back?"

That one had me stumped. "I don't know. I'll think of something. But if we get a move on, they'll never know we were here." I looked at my watch again and marked the time. "Ten minutes, and then we'll hightail it back."

We trudged up the hill and went around the side of the house to the front door. I peered through the sidelight windows and saw two pieces of luggage neatly lined up.

"They're ready to leave town. We need to find something so Jack can keep them here."

Ryan looked around. "Where do we start?"

"Well, spray paint was used. Who has one random can of spray paint? There must be more, somewhere. Either in the garage or basement, right?"

"I guess. I'm just along for the ride. You lead the way."

We followed the circular driveway around to the opposite side of the house to the garage. It had expensive-looking solid wood doors with carriage lights on each side.

"Maybe there's a window around here," Ryan said, making his way around the back. "Yeah, over here," he called to me.

"It's too tall for either of us. Can I get on your shoulders?"

He looked at me skeptically, and I snapped, "I'm not that heavy."

"I know you're not. I just don't want to get caught in that position. We'll look ridiculous."

"Come on, we'll be quick."

Ryan squatted and I swung one leg over his shoulder, then grabbed onto his head to leverage myself to swing my other leg over.

"Okay, ready?" he asked.

"Yup."

He slowly stood, and I was able to grab the stone windowsill.

"Can you see anything?" he asked.

"I can see the cars. Shift to the right so I can see the shelves on the wall."

Ryan did a slow shuffle until I said, "Stop. Okay, hold on." I used my hands to cup my eyes. "Yes! There are paint cans and a few spray paint cans."

"Okay, can I put you down now?"

"Yeah."

Ryan did a slow squat, and I climbed off.

"Well, that was fun! What now? How much time do we have?" he asked.

I looked at the time. We really needed to go, but I wanted to check one other thing. "We have a few minutes. Can you hoist me up so I can see over the patio wall?" The house was built into the hill, and the stone patio was above ground with a retaining wall.

"There aren't steps down to the lawn?"

"No. I noticed there weren't any when Bitsy and I were here."

"Okay, let's do it over here. I think it's the shortest height off the ground."

We went toward the corner, and once again Ryan raised me up on his shoulders. "I can't get a good enough look. I'm going to go over the wall."

"You're going to do what?" he said in a muffled voice.

"Yeah, shift farther over to the corner, and I'm going to get a foothold and go over the wall. Don't worry. It's not too far up."

"Don't worry," he muttered to himself. "Jack is going to kill me, you know."

"I can handle Jack. Let's just get a move on. There's a reason I want to do this."

We maneuvered over to the corner to where I could

grab the top of the patio wall and then I used my foot to gain the leverage needed to hoist myself up. I got into a position where I could swing my leg over the wall, but then I tumbled in the most ungraceful manner onto the patio.

"Oomph," I expelled.

"You okay?" Ryan called up to me.

"I'm fine." I peered over the edge and said, "If you hear anyone coming, you take off and get out of here. Go through their yard," I said, pointing to the neighbor's property, "and you won't be seen."

"What? I'm not going to leave you here."

"I'll be fine. You cannot get caught here. I'm serious. No argument. But it's not going to happen, anyway. I'll be quick," I assured him.

I scrunched down and duck-walked across the patio. I noted a generous seating area and an outdoor fireplace. Wait, it looked like there was ash in the fireplace. It'd been too warm for a fire, even at night, and they were not the types to leave old ash in the fireplace. I waddled over to look. Definitely, something had recently been burned. I used my phone to snap a photo. Could this be where the clothing and any other evidence from Winifred's murder had been disposed of?

I moved on to the exercise area, and the rack of dumbbells intrigued me. One of these could definitely inflict some damage. I started to create the scene in my head. Winifred had suspicions that the skeleton was Eleanor. She let this tidbit drop to Tucker. Then she tries to blackmail him. Maybe he paid her once, but then she came back for more. He sets up a meeting with her, but instead of negotiating a payoff, he threatens her. She runs, he grabs a dumbbell and gives chase. They end up in the woods, where he kills her.

Or the meeting place is the woods, and he takes the dumbbell along with the intent of killing her. Then he has to go back to his house to change, gets the idea to stage her at the workshop, and the rest we know about. Even to my own imagination this all was sounding a bit farfetched, but I was in too deep to give up.

I moved closer to the rack, took my glasses down from my head and looked closely at the dumbbells, searching for any sign of blood. I couldn't see any, but it didn't mean there weren't trace amounts still left on the metal surface. I did notice that one was a lot cleaner than the rest, which was telling. I snapped another photo.

"Alex," Ryan said, in a hoarse whisper. "Someone is coming."

"Go! Get out of here now!" I ordered with a hiss.

Chapter 20

I heard the voices now, and I knew there wasn't time for me to climb back over the wall. I would have to hide and hope I wasn't visible and then slip out later. I scrunched down on the other side of the array of exercise equipment and made myself as small as possible with my knees tucked up to my chin.

The sound of the heavy patio doors gliding on their tracks, followed by high heels click-clacking on the stone patio made me inwardly groan. Every nerve ending prickled in fear of getting caught.

Tucker said, "I don't know why you are in such a hurry. We could have stayed longer, and it was a little rude to leave so abruptly."

Sasha's tone was clipped. "I know you love that precious garden, but I need to get away." Now, her voice became kittenish. "And I just want to spend time with you. I don't want to share you."

They moved to the edge of the patio, and I could see them from my vantage point. Tucker walked up to Sasha and put his arms around her from behind.

"You know I'm all yours, sweetheart. Maybe we could just wait and go tomorrow. We could go to the movie tonight and snuggle on a blanket like teenagers."

Sasha whipped around and out of his embrace. "Oh, Tucker, you are so thick sometimes."

"What do you mean?" His voice sounded hurt.

"You've seemed really tense lately, and I don't know why."

"Don't you realize we are being watched? We're under scrutiny, and we need to leave town. Now."

"What are you talking about?"

I reached into my back pocket and silently pulled out my phone. I found the memo app, hit the record button, and rested it on my knee.

"You don't realize what the questions about Eleanor signify, do you?"

Tucker looked perplexed and didn't answer.

"First Chief Maddox, and then Alex and her little friend come here on some ruse about the alumni? Don't you get it?" Sasha's voice rose when she said, "They think the skeleton is Eleanor!"

"Well, that's ridiculous. Eleanor left town! I got letters from her. So how could Eleanor have been in the grave?"

Sasha didn't answer right away and just stared at him.

Tucker sat heavily on the wall of the patio. "Sasha, what are you saying? What do you know?" When she didn't answer, he looked at her and said, "What did you do?"

"I did what I had to do. Now pull yourself together. We've got to go."

Tucker didn't move.

I didn't move a muscle, either. Fear gripped me. We did have a sociopath on our hands. It just wasn't who I thought it might be.

"Tucker, what's done is done. I did what I had to do to save you—us."

He looked at her in shock. "This can't be. Are you

actually telling me you killed Eleanor?"

"Oh, Tucker, it was so long ago—a lifetime ago."

Tucker blanched. "Tell me what you did. Now," he said, in an angry voice.

She knelt in front of him and took his hand. "It was an accident. I tried to reason with her. I knew neither of you were happy, and I couldn't stand to see you unhappy. So I talked to her and told her you would both be better off if she left you."

"And what did she say?"

"She said she didn't want to leave, she just wanted to figure out how to make the marriage work better. She dug in out of spite."

"So you killed her?"

"No! You aren't listening. I already said it was an accident. She became aggressive and told me to leave. We shoved each other, and then she went over the wall and hit her head on one of the rocks below."

Tucker was in a state of shock and looked over the wall to the large stones placed to help with water drainage, then he looked back at her. "Why were you even here? Where was I when all this happened?"

"At work. I called in sick and met her in the morning. It all happened so fast. I knew the police would never believe it was an accident, so I found a spot to bury her, then came back to the house and wiped everything down, packed a bag, and wrote the note for you to find."

"That's why you were so adamant about the benches at the Workshop's garden not being too close to the tree line! You had me push back on their plans!" Tucker's hands flew to his mouth, and he got up and spun in circles. "Now I know why Winifred was speculating about Eleanor. I thought she was just being a gossip. She probably thought I had killed her!"

"Winifred had it coming. Believe me."

Now Tucker looked at her in horror. "Oh my God, Sasha, tell me you didn't murder Winifred." He started pacing. "What have you done? We have to go to the police! You can explain everything."

"We are not going to the police, Tucker."

"But if you explain that it was an accident. You can tell them Winifred was blackmailing you and then maybe say it was self-defense. We can't run away from this, Sasha. We must go to the police."

Sasha now started to pace, and I cringed, hoping she wouldn't see me. Thankfully, she stopped and turned back to him.

"Oh, Tucker, I really hoped you would be able to play along."

"Play along?" he asked, incredulously.

"I have spent all these years protecting the life I've built. I hoped if it came to this, you would choose me over anyone else, but I have recently had to prepare myself that you might not."

"What do you mean? I don't understand."

"I mean I'm not going to lose it all now, not after everything I've invested. Disposing of you in New York would have been easier, but I'll figure out a way, just as I've always done." Her tone became mocking. "Poor Tucker, so despondent over what he did to both Eleanor and Winifred, he took his own life."

I stopped the recording and sent it to Jack along with a text SOS to get here now. Then I crawled out from my hiding place. "Sasha, it's over," I said boldly.

She whipped around. "What are you doing here? Where did you come from?"

I tried to remain calm and replied, "It doesn't matter. What matters is I heard everything, and I doubt you can handle disposing of both me and Tucker."

Sasha moved jerkily around the patio as if trying to come up with her next move. Tucker was in a state of shock and could only drop into one of the patio chairs, so I was on my own. I feared she might run, so I decided to try and stall her.

"I would like to know why you staged Winifred the way you did, and on my property."

"I don't have to tell you anything," she snapped.

"Come on, it was incredibly creative to dispose of her in such a way. What did she do, try and get more money out of you?" I was sounding more confident than I felt, but I was angry now. Angry at how she deceived Tucker all these years, angry at what she did to poor Eleanor, and angry she had murdered Winifred and left her in such a hideous way.

"When Tucker told me she was probing about Eleanor, I set up a meeting with her. I took money out of one of our investment accounts and gave it to her. But then she hinted it was just the down payment. She had a new business venture, and she expected us to be silent benefactors. The nerve of that woman."

I needed to keep her talking to give Jack time to get here, so I said, "You decided to set up another meeting."

"Right. Tucker had a rotary meeting and came home and went straight to bed. I snuck out and met her in the woods. She wanted to meet near Eleanor's grave, as if doing so would have special symbolism. Gawd, she was always so theatrical."

"So you took one of those dumbbells and went down there with the intention of killing her."

Sasha slowly clapped her hands. "Bravo. You are smart, aren't you?"

"But why stage her in my garden?"

Sasha tilted her head, and said, "I had a feeling Winifred was behind the social media campaign against the Workshop. That kind of thing would be right up her alley. So I thought putting her there might shift the focus onto you. And listen, if you had just stopped the garden work long enough for me to move Eleanor, this would never have happened. It's just as much your fault as mine. Initially, you had no plans to do anything anywhere near the damned tree line," she scolded me. "Everything would have been fine if you hadn't strayed from the original plan."

I ignored the lunacy of her last statement and said, matter-of-factly, "So you were behind the sabotage, too."

She pursed her lips. "I knew I couldn't stop you from expanding the damn garden, but if I could delay it, I could move her. When it didn't work, it made me mad, so planting Winifred in your garden seemed—poetic."

Where was Jack? I had to keep her talking, so even though I was totally creeped out, I continued in a conversational tone, "So you killed Winifred, then came back here to get a can of spray paint, then over to the Workshop to get the wheelbarrow."

She nodded. "I'm strong, but I couldn't carry her such a far distance."

"You wheeled her to the bench. Did you spray paint her first or once she was in place?"

Sasha looked pleased with herself. "I spray painted her first, then let it dry a little while I planned out the scene. When I was in the garage, I found the straw hat with the flowers on it. I thought it would add a nice

277

touch. Anyway, then I got the wheelbarrow. I had grabbed a canvas tarp from the garage so I could transport her and do touch-ups once she was on the bench, without getting paint everywhere."

Tucker groaned.

"And then you burned everything," I said, pointing to the fireplace. "You need to turn yourself in, Sasha," I advised.

"I don't think so. And I'm sure as hell not going to lose everything because of you." She lunged at me.

I tried to slip past her, but she was quick. She grabbed my arm, bending it awkwardly behind my back, and lurched me over toward the wall. "There will be an awful accident. We came home and found you on our patio, trying to break in. In your haste to get away, you fell over the wall."

"It's too late, Sasha, I recorded what you said earlier and I've sent it to Jack," I gasped.

"You what?"

The fury in her voice made a chill run down my spine. "He'll be here any minute."

"I think you're bluffing." Her eyes were wild as she tried to shove me off the wall.

I used every muscle in my body to hold myself back from plunging over the side, while flashing thoughts ran through my head. If she killed me, who would take care of Baxter? Would Walter know how important he was to me? What about Maggie? And Ryan? They were young, they needed me. And boy, Jack was going to be mad, and Aunt Claudia would be so disappointed in me for crossing the line.

Those last two thoughts gave me a surge of adrenaline, and I held on to the wall so hard I could feel the stone cut into my hands. But I was getting tired, and Sasha wasn't. If anything, she grew stronger the more I resisted.

Her breathing was almost normal. "This is how it will play out, Alex. You will die. Then I will have to help Tucker understand why this has all been for the best. But if he's not on board to go away with me, his death will be a suicide from the remorse of killing Eleanor, Winifred, and you. It's more work than I wanted to do, but this is what I've been training for. I'm ready for anything."

I twisted sideways in the hopes of getting my foot raised enough to shove her away from me, but the next thing I knew, her grasp loosened and she crumpled with a little yelp and landed half on the ground and half on top of me. Behind her was Tucker, with a fireplace poker in his hands.

Chapter 21

Tucker dropped the poker and rushed to pull me out from under Sasha. "Are you okay?" he asked, urgently.

I was shaking, and said, "I'm all right. Is she—?"

"I don't know."

I cautiously returned to Sasha and felt her neck for a pulse. There wasn't one. I turned to Tucker and quietly said, "She's gone."

Tucker fell back into the patio chair, and I dropped to the ground. I could feel the cool tile through my jeans; I think it was the only thing keeping me from passing out. Tucker was visibly shaken. His brow was furrowed and he shook his head slowly as if in disbelief, and his lips parted, but no words came out.

"I'm so sorry, Tucker," I said.

He raised his eyes to mine. "I couldn't let her kill again." He sighed deeply, and added, "I should call the police."

"No need. I really did text Jack with the recording. He'll be here soon." I pushed myself up to my knees, then stood. "Let's go inside."

I led Tucker through the patio doors to the den and lowered him onto the sofa. I then went to the bar and poured him a stiff scotch, then poured one for myself and took it to a chair nearby. I was reeling, so it was fine with me if we sat in silence, but Tucker eventually spoke.

"I just can't believe it," he said, taking a deep pull

on the scotch.

"So you had no inkling?"

"No. But how could I not know? She killed Eleanor and covered it up. All these years living with her, and I never knew."

"Were you seeing each other back then?" I asked, gently.

"We actually weren't. We got together a few months later, after I had gotten the letters from Eleanor. She comforted me during a difficult time."

I looked down at my hands. "So Sasha set it all up. She must have traveled to those places and mailed the letters to you and the cards to Aunt Claudia. How did she know her handwriting?"

"She was my secretary, so she would have seen it at one time or another. She was very smart, which drew me to her," he said, shaking his head. "And oh my God, Winifred. How could she have done something so cruel?"

"She built a life with you, and she would have done anything to protect what she had."

I remembered when the gang talked about the reasons for murder, and love was the one we landed on. I just had it wrong. I thought it was Tucker protecting his life with Sasha, not the other way around. But this wasn't love. This was dark.

Tucker continued. "I knew she had been acting a little tense lately, and maybe on some level, after the skeleton was found, I had some nagging doubts, but I didn't want to face it. I had never questioned anything, and because of my own cowardice Winifred is dead. I just can't believe she would do something so brutal."

"Cut yourself some slack. You and Sasha weren't

even together when she killed Eleanor. And all this business with Winifred happened this week. There wasn't time for you to question things."

"I should have known something was wrong when she started interfering in the garden plans, and then she became so adamant about going to New York. She wasn't usually so pushy about things." Tucker put his head in his hands.

"Going to New York wouldn't have changed anything. She would have had to come back."

"I guess she hoped the suspicion would shift to someone else."

"Tucker, do you not realize what she said to you? I know this is hard to face, but the truth is, she had a plan to make you the scapegoat for both deaths if the need arose. Jack was already homing in on the remains being Eleanor, and if all else failed, Sasha was going to emerge from this intact, even if it meant killing and framing you."

Tucker looked like his brain was overloading, and he was only able to focus on one part of what I had said. "He really believes the remains are Eleanor?"

I was out of my depth with this kind of shock. Tucker was going to need more help than I could give him, so I simply said, "Yes. I'll let him explain it all to you."

His face crumpled in agony. "Can you just tell me if Eleanor suffered?"

I thought for a moment about how I should handle this. I didn't know the answer with any certainty, but I definitely knew what I would want to hear if I were in his shoes.

"I honestly don't think she did. Whether Sasha hit

her, shoved her over the edge, or if it was an accidental fall, like Sasha wanted you to believe, I think it was over instantly."

He shook his head. "Thank goodness."

After this brief exchange, we sat in silence until I heard a car pull into the driveway.

When I opened the door, Jack said, "I listened to the recording. Travis and the paramedics are on their way. Where is Sasha?"

I took Jack outside to the patio, and after he checked to make sure there was no pulse, we stood looking down on Sasha's lifeless body.

I said, "Tucker had no part in any of it. And he saved my life."

Jack looked at me for a beat and then walked back inside to talk to Tucker.

They talked for a good fifteen minutes. Their voices were quiet, and Jack was handling the situation like a pro, getting the information he needed from Tucker while providing some emotional support. I had moved to the kitchen and was dealing with my own shock. My arms and legs were shaky and growing stiff from holding off Sasha, and I gently massaged them to loosen them up. I looked at my watch and couldn't believe I hadn't even been gone an hour. It felt like an eternity.

The calm was shattered by the sound of an ambulance and Travis's police car arriving. Travis took my statement, and then he got Jack's permission to take me back to the Workshop.

When we pulled into the parking lot, it felt like I was in a time warp. There was still a good crowd for the grand opening. Curls of wood smoke came from the food trucks, the banners blew in the breeze, kids were running around, and loads of people milled through the craft tents and the garden. It was like time had stopped while I was in a life and death situation.

When I hadn't gotten out of the car yet, Travis asked, "Do you want me to take you to the front so you don't have to go through all the people?"

"Hunh? Oh, no, thank you. I'm just grappling with the juxtaposition of all this going on while everything unfolded up at Tucker's house."

"Take your time. We can sit for as long as you want."

I noticed he pulled out his cell phone and figured he was taking care of some business while he let me get my bearings. I was incredibly grateful and said, "Thanks. I just need a minute."

Shortly, I noticed a line of people walking toward us. "What in the world?" I asked myself. I saw Maggie, Ryan, Annie, Spencer, Bitsy, JJ, Michael, and yes, Walter, all walking side by side. It was like a scene in a movie as they emerged from the craft tents, in what felt like slow motion, coming toward the parking lot.

Travis said, "I texted Ryan you might need some backup to face the crowds."

I reached over and squeezed his arm. "Thank you, Travis."

I opened the door, and Walter reached in to help me out of the car. He enveloped me in a hug, and I hopped up to wrap my legs around his waist. Holding on tight, I said, "I am so happy to see you." In that moment, I knew exactly how I felt about Walter. Maggie was right, my gut did tell me.

He put me down, and the gang huddled around.

"I was so worried when you didn't follow me out,"

Ryan said. "What happened?"

When I saw the questions in everyone's eyes, I explained what Ryan and I had been doing, and then what happened after he took off.

"Holy cow!" JJ exclaimed. "It was Sasha all along?"

With wide eyes, Annie said, "She never even made our whiteboard!"

"Well, she and Tucker weren't together when Eleanor supposedly left. So she wasn't on my radar, either," I said. "And Tucker was the one being pushy about the tree line."

"Are you okay?" Bitsy asked, looking at me with concern as I rubbed my arms.

"I'm going to be sore tomorrow, but I'm all right."

"Your hands are all scraped up," Walter said, turning them face up.

"Oh yeah, I scraped them when I was holding on to keep her from tipping me over the wall."

"What?" Annie shouted, then lowered her voice. "You said you recorded her confession. You neglected to say you had to fight her off."

"Well, Tucker actually saved me. I'm not sure how much longer I could have fought her."

"So she's in custody," Spencer said.

"Uh, no. Tucker struck her hard with the fireplace poker to stop her, and she did not survive."

Everyone was silent for a beat, then JJ said, "Poor Tucker. How will he get through this?"

Walter said, "As Alex said to me recently, 'It takes a village.' She got through this week with the help of her friends, and you all will now help him through it."

It really was too much of a pendulum swing to go from the nightmare with Sasha to the happy-go-lucky garden festivities, so after assuring everyone I was fine, Walter and I went to my apartment. He kept an eye on me but knew I wouldn't want him to hover, so he put a ballgame on the TV while I took a little time to decompress and acknowledge what I had just been through. This involved a few tears, lots of hugs with Baxter, back-to-back cups of coffee, and a quick shower and change of clothes. Now I was ready to resume my duties.

****

The evening was perfect, all things considered, and there was a good crowd for Movie on the Green. The smell of popcorn hung in the air, and the food trucks stayed long enough for people to get a picnic dinner. I couldn't really focus on the movie, but I could see everyone else was having a great time.

After making the rounds to make sure the artists had cleared their craft tents and a walkthrough of the garden to pick up any stray trash, I stood at the back, where Ryan was manning the projector. Diego and Lena were sharing a blanket, which made me smile. And then my smile slipped when I noticed Michael and Walter standing off to the side with their heads together, deep in conversation. Just what I needed, partners in crime.

Jack pulled into the parking lot, and I walked over to meet him.

With reluctance, I said, "Hey, I know we haven't had a chance to talk yet, but I'm really sorry I got in the middle of things."

He looked at me sternly, then his face melted and he pulled me in for a hug. "Believe me, I'll lecture you at some point. But for now, I'm just relieved you're okay. And even though I in no way condone you going off half-cocked with some hairbrained scheme to look for evidence, had you not been there and recorded her confession, they would have left town, and we would have been focusing on Tucker, and she might have pulled off framing him for everything. It's likely that you saved his life."

"Yeah, it actually worked out to be an ironclad confession. How is Tucker doing?" I asked.

"As you might expect, devastated. He killed the woman he loved and thought he knew. And he's mourning Eleanor at the same time."

Feelings of remorse overwhelmed me. "I do feel horrible. If I hadn't been there, Sasha would still be alive. She's dead because of me."

"She's dead because she tried to kill you, after already killing two other people. So no, it is not your fault. As I said, I'll lecture you later about putting yourself in such a dangerous situation. But for now, there's only one person responsible for what transpired, and that's Sasha."

"I know you're right." And I genuinely knew he was right. Sasha very well might have gone on to kill again had I not been there. "It will take some time, though, to get over the shock of it."

"You're tough, and you'll get through it." Jack opened his car door. "Oh, I almost forgot. A most interesting thing happened earlier."

"What?"

"Two guys came to talk to me and corroborated Luke's story. They were gaming and had all the stats to show me. I guess this stuff is recorded because they are trying to get to a national competition."

"There's a national competition for video games?"

"Oh yeah. It's big business."

"I had no idea."

Jack grinned at me. "You wouldn't happen to be, quote, *some weird lady who came in and harassed them into coming forward,* would you?"

"Hah! Maybe."

"Well, whatever you did, it worked."

"I'm glad. I like Luke, and I'm happy his friends came through for him."

"Yeah, they did. Okay, I need to go give Mom the news about Eleanor. I want her to hear it from me. And then I'll be at the station pretty late tonight wrapping up these two cases. Even though there won't be a trial, we have mounds of paperwork ahead of us. We know the skeleton is Eleanor based on what Sasha said, but we have to prove it with evidence. Hopefully the dental records will come in since Tucker doesn't have anything of hers to provide a DNA match."

"I have no doubt you'll get there in the end. Tell Aunt Claudia I'll talk to her tomorrow. And, um, please don't tell her my involvement in this. She'd be furious."

Jack chuckled. "Yeah, I think I'll leave your part out of it."

After Jack drove off, I walked around the edge of the parking lot to the tree line. Fireflies were dancing amongst the trees, and I experienced a swell of emotion thinking about Eleanor. She had spent over thirty years in these woods, alone and anonymous, and now she had a name and would be properly mourned.

Walter approached. "Everything okay?"

"Yes," I said, turning to him with a small smile. "I think it is."

"How were things with Jack?"

288

"Well, I'm not looking forward to when he has the time to ream me out for meddling, but otherwise, we're good."

Walter grinned. "I hope I'm here for that. Come on, let's take a walk. There's another hour left of the movie, and Ryan has things well under control."

I looked back at the movie scene and said, "Yeah, I think I can slip out for a bit."

We walked out to Main Street, and then took a right on Maple. Walter stopped at the corner and, "Remember how I said I had a surprise for you?"

"Yeah, what is it? Did you bring me something from London?"

"I did." He pulled a small cloth bag out of his pocket and handed it to me.

I dug around in the bag and pulled out a key ring. I was baffled and looked at him with a head tilt. "A key ring?" Not exactly what I would classify as a surprise, but I laughed when I looked at the iconic British phrase *Keep Calm and Carry On* stamped on the key ring. "I think I may need to wear this around my neck!"

"It sure has become your motto," he said, with a chuckle.

We continued on and were talking about his upcoming schedule, when he said, "I think I need to put down some roots. I know I'm still going to be on the road a good bit of time, but I want to have a more permanent home base. What do you think?"

I was a little nervous he was getting ready to let me down easy and tell me he was moving on. "Do you know where you want to be?"

"Oh, I have a pretty good idea."

We stopped when we reached the cottage with the

sold sign that Maggie and I had walked past earlier in the week, and I said, "Remember how we admired this place last time you were here? Well, it looks like there will be some new owners. It sold last week."

Walter said, "What a lucky buyer. It sure is a beauty. Come on, let's go peek in the windows."

"We can't do that!"

"Sure we can, it's empty."

He grabbed my hand and pulled me down the cobblestone path to the front porch. We peered in the sidelight windows and could just make out the vintage original woodwork and built-in bookshelves in what looked like a library.

"Check the mailbox," he suggested. "Maybe we know the new owners."

"Oh, this is so invasive," I said, but I flipped the top of the mailbox next to the door and pulled out a thick envelope. My mouth dropped open, and I looked at Walter. "What the heck?" The name on the envelope was Walter Sarnov.

"Surprise!" Walter sang.

"Shut the front door!" I said, slapping him on the arm. "You bought this house?"

"I did. It came on the market around the time I decided to put down some roots here. I took care of everything when I was in London. It's bought and paid for, so I hope you're okay with me being around a little more."

"Are you kidding me? I'm thrilled!"

Now Walter pulled out a key and gave it to me. "This is the spare key, and it can go on your new key ring."

I wasn't sure what this meant. "You're not wanting

me to move in with you, are you?"

"No, of course not. I know you need and want your own space. Neither of us are ready for a move like that. Right?" He looked a little worried he had made the wrong call.

"Right!" I said, relieved. "But I sure am happy you're making Flat Rock your home base and that you got this house!" My hands shook as I attached the key to the ring, and I said, "I can't wait to see inside!"

"Well, let's go."

Epilogue

Jack successfully wrapped up both cases. After the memorial service for Eleanor, her remains were buried in the town cemetery. Sasha was cremated, and Tucker scattered her ashes at a destination unknown. I would assume, since it was within a week of what transpired, he actually scattered them and didn't flush them. With the help of all of us, he was slowly coming to terms with what had happened, and chose to throw himself into community activities to keep busy, including tending the Workshop's garden.

The Workshop was moving through the summer schedule with a full docket of classes and regular visitors to the garden. Ms. Bunkle came frequently to sit on the bench named in honor of her husband, Henry, and she would talk things over with him. And often, after a respectful amount of time, I would go out and sit with her. I needed someone to keep me on my toes, and she fit the bill perfectly.

My gang was busy creating beautiful art, and I even found time to start a new stained-glass project. Diego and Lena were officially an item. Daisy and Luke broke up but were back together again. I had a feeling both couples might make it for the long haul.

Jack never told Aunt Claudia about my role in the case, but she found out anyway, and properly dressed me down for it, but then brought me a piece of pie, so we were good.

Walter furnished his new house and had already been spending more time here. As a housewarming present, I bought him a coffee system like mine. He guessed it was as much for me as it was for him.

Eva Beaumont decided to move forward with a gallery, but thankfully, not the artist studios, and we were working together on ideas for joint art shows.

And I've received a request to bring a group of artists to do the art exhibits, lectures, and classes on a cruise later this year. I'm not sure how I feel about a cruise, but the pay seems pretty good and it would provide a working holiday for some of my artists. After ironing out some details, I suspect it's going to happen. And maybe, fingers crossed, there won't be a murder!

A word about the author...

Sydney Abrams' arts and crafts cozy mystery series is steeped in a life's experience in the arts coupled with a love for mystery books. She was immersed in both these worlds from childhood, and that influence stayed with her as an adult. Sydney has created artwork for auctions and commissions, and has been part of an art group of professional and amateur artists for twenty years. Literature and the arts go hand in hand, but these worlds collided when Sydney realized that her art group offered up the perfect cast of characters for a cozy mystery.

An Artless Murder is the third book in Sydney's Arts and Crafts Mystery series. Other books in this series include *Still Life, Still Dead* and *A Deadly Craft*.

To learn more about Sydney, please visit https://www.sydneyabrams.com/

Thank you for purchasing
this publication of The Wild Rose Press, Inc.

For questions or more information
contact us at
info@thewildrosepress.com.

The Wild Rose Press, Inc.
www.thewildrosepress.com